I0642703

SUBAQUEOUS

A FABULOUS UNDERWATER ADVENTURE
IN SEARCH OF A LOST CIVILIZATION

BY GARY GENTILE

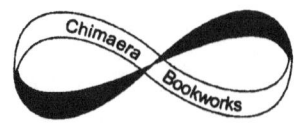

Chimaera Bookworks
3 Lehigh Gorge Drive
Jim Thorpe, PA 18229

Additional copies of this book may be purchased from the same address by sending a check or money order in the amount of $20 U.S. for each copy (plus $4 postage per order, not per book, in the U.S. Inquire for shipping cost to foreign countries). Alternatively, copies may be ordered from the author's website, and paid by credit card:

http://www.ggentile.com

The front cover photograph was taken by the author.

Dedicated to the works of Immanuel Velikovsky.

International Standard Book Number (ISBN)
1-883056-41-1
978-1-883056-41-4

First Edition

Printed in the U.S.A.

Part One

All the fountains of the great deep were broken up, and
the windows of heaven were opened.
And the rain was upon the earth forty days and forty
nights. . . .
And the flood was forty days upon the earth; and the
waters increased . . .
And the waters prevailed, and were increased greatly
upon the earth; and all the high hills, that were
under the whole heavens, were covered.
Fifteen cubits upward did the waters prevail; and the
mountains were covered.

The *Bible*, Genesis, Chapter 7

Chapter 1

Tod dropped slowly through the clear icy water, like a plastic statue in a vial of mercury. Below him yawned an inky darkness that was blacker than any night he had ever seen or could possibly imagine. It appeared to his unadjusted eyes that he was gazing into a bottomless pit which had absorbed all vestige of light, and even the possibility of admitting any. He basked in the feeling of sensory deprivation with uncommon delight. He could have been in a rocket zooming through the vast reaches of outer space instead of inside an armored subsuit falling down the maw of an unexplored Blue Hole.

The stereophonic microphones embedded in the subsuit's helmet broke his reverie of voluntary solitude. "Hunk! Hunk! This is *Reef Cruiser*. Come in, please." The shrill voice was clear and undistorted by static. "*Reef Cruiser* calling Hunk. Come in this instant!"

Tod tapped the chest communication pad with his finger. "Aw, Squirt. I was just enjoying the absence of sight and sound. Why did you have to go and ruin it for me?"

"Because you're supposed to stay in constant contact, that's why. And you know it." If anything, Lisa's voice was even more shrill, and the volume a few decibels higher. "And according to the telemetry links you're approaching the study depth."

Tod flipped the switch on the helmet's heads-up display panel and scanned the readouts that surrounded the acrylic faceplate. "That ledge has got to be another fifty feet . . . " It was closer than he anticipated.

"It's twenty-three feet and coming up fast. If you'd been paying closer attention instead of daydreaming like always, you'd have known that."

"So what if I miss it by a couple of – "

"Because you took so much time taking observations on the shallow ledge that slack is nearly over. If the tide turns before you get the data that the professor wants on this mission, we'll have to wait another twelve hours for the next cycle. And we've got to turn in the saucer by oh-eight-hundred tomorrow or Denny will be furious. We'll be traveling all night as it is."

Tod could care less about Denny Harker's peace of mind. He had never gotten along with the base marshal and vessel dispatcher, and would be happy to return the reconnaissance sub late just to irk him.

"And you know he can hatchlock our next mission if we don't keep on schedule."

Tod did not dislike Harker so much because of his authority, but because he was always using that authority to intimidate trainees. "Okay, Squirt. I'm sorry." He knew when to argue and when to comply with formality. Now was the time for compliance. With practiced ease he manipulated the vernier attitude controls on the chest panel inside the subsuit, so that the side propellers spun enough to rotate the subsuit until the front faced upward. From his position deep within the Blue Hole, he felt like a bug looking up the tube of a microscope.

The fading circle of light above appeared geometrically perfect except for the curve of the disklike submersible that protruded past the rim. It was from the instrument package in the overhanging sponson that Lisa monitored real-time events with line-of-sight telemetry equipment.

He switched on the waist lamps. Twin cones of light shot toward the faraway surface like a pair of glowing rapiers.

"What're you trying to do?" Lisa screamed over the headphones. "Blind me?" The submersible boasted no acrylic ports, but external video pickups had finer receptors than the human eye.

"Sorry." Tod rotated the subsuit on its longitudinal axis until it became vertical and upright, and was facing the rock wall that appeared to be slowly rising in front of him. It took a moment to re-orient his mode of thinking, and to accept the reality that the smooth granite wall was not ascending but that he was descending. From a distance of twenty feet the rock appeared smooth, although Tod knew that a closer inspection would show its true coarseness.

The earphones called out, "You're passing 330 feet. Target depth is 345."

"I *know* that, Squirt." Tod took in the readouts at a glance, then hit the attitude propellers again and rotated the subsuit until it had a slight forward tilt. In the artificial light he could see the ledge rising to meet him. Electric motors whirred as he actuated the back-mounted counter-rotating propellers in reverse, and slowed his descent to a crawl. He confessed to himself that if Lisa had not gotten his attention, he might very well have missed the ledge; but he would never admit that to her. Besides, what did it matter if he had to ascend a few feet after going too deep?

Tod stuck one arm through an articulated sleeve and wrapped his fingers around the manipulator controls. He spun the subsuit's rotating wrist and actuated the gripclaw hydraulically. With the hand extensor he detached the portable transcriber from the subsuit's tool belt. The power cord kept him from losing the transcriber if he accidentally dropped it.

"Switch on the recorder, Hunk."

Tod bit his tongue. Lisa could be such a nuisance at times. "Switching on." The resignation in his voice was real.

The transcriber – a combination digicam recorder and interface device – was a sophisticated scientific instrument that took all the work out of note keeping. Everything in view of its lens was automatically saved to chip at the same time that it was telemetered to the mainframe in the reconnaissance sub. No data escaped its peripheral pickup feeds. Images were indexed by subject matter for instantaneous recall.

At the moment, nothing but the naked rock wall stood in the transcriber's field of view. Across the rectangular backscreen facing him were generic, specific, and scientific words and explanations: Rock – Granite

– Igneous – Quartz – Mica. Underneath "Quartz" was written "Orthoclase" and "Microcline."

"This is not a geology field trip, Hunk. We're here for biology samples."

"I know, Squirt. I haven't gotten there yet."

Tod powered the subsuit closer to the wall. The ledge was less then ten feet below his footpads. He took on ballast instead of firing the hoverprops because the downwash would disturb the biota that he was there to study. Water trickled into the legtanks – enough to add a couple of pounds of negative buoyancy to the subsuit, so he could walk on the ledge if the need arose. He touched down lightly on the rocky shelf.

The water ballast lowered the subsuit's metacentric height by depressing the center of gravity so that the subsuit remained upright without the activation of attitude propellers – much like an inflatable punching doll with a packet of sand in its base. The subsuit was shaped like the human body, with articulated arms and legs, and a globular domeport that looked like an upside-down goldfish bowl. Although the subsuit resembled a robot from mid-twentieth-century science fiction films, it was actually a one-person submersible.

"I see something." Tod swiveled the subsuit so that the lights illuminated the biota at the back of the ledge. The platform measured less than five feet in width, but extended sideways for more than twenty yards. The rear corner appeared to be painted in multiple colors. He swung the transcriber . . .

"I can't see anything, Hunk. Aim the transcriber . . . Oh, that's better." After a pause, "What is it?"

Tod made the subsuit do a deep knee bend. At the same time, he activated the transcriber's zoom control and locked on the steadycam function. The transcriber reduced the picture area and focused on a group of brightly colored sponges, some of which were variegated. The undersea world was populated by hundreds of species of filter-feeding sponges (phylum Porifera), some sessile and some not. The transcriber's integrated computer chip contained a databank that identified every class, order, family, genus, species, variety, and type that was known to science, as well as the same for every other marine invertebrate in the animal kingdom.

As the videocam's center focal point passed over an individual sponge, the heads-up display posted a list of genera and species. The highlighter scrolled through the list, toggled between closely related species, then homed in on the individual in question with the proper identification.

"*Haliclona viscosa,*" Tod announced.

"I can read." Lisa's monitor in the *Reef Cruiser* displayed everything that the mobile transcriber saw, including the heads-up display of taxonomic identifiers. Binomial nomenclature was used exclusively because no common name equivalents existed.

Tod triggered high-resolution digital stillshots for storage in the computer's picture database for comparison with previously recorded images. A miniature strobe provided light for automatic exposure. He panned the transcriber to the left of the main group. The animal kingdom was well represented as bryozoans and tunicates came into view, as well as a couple of orange worms. The primary study concentrated on sponges, but he photographed the other phyla for future reference.

"There's a *Tentorium semisuberites,*" Lisa called out.

Now it was Tod's turn for rebuttal. "I can read."

Lisa stated the obvious. "Take a stillshot."

Tod grimaced. He had already triggered the stillshot button on the armgrip of the transcriber. The back of the transcriber head was fitted with a screen that showed the image as it was taken, while the heads-up display that floated in front of his eyes provided species identification. The transcriber was the "eye" of the computer chip. In case of a malfunction in the heads-up display, the transcriber screen could be used to display information. The screen also served as a touchpad with information links.

"Hey!" shouted Lisa. "What's that?"

Sometimes Lisa could be annoying, but Tod loved

her anyway. "If the transcriber doesn't know, Squirt, I certainly don't." It wasn't impossible to memorize the names and to identify the species of every Antarctic invertebrate, but considering the diversity of south polar organisms and expanding speciation, Tod had a long way to go in his biological studies. It was often said that a transcriber made people lazy; why memorize information that could be recalled with a fingertip?

The display flickered quickly as the highlighter attempted to identify the species or find a close approximation of the individual in the focal point. It flickered so fast that he could not read the possibilities before a different name was highlighted in yellow. The highlighter finally selected a species, but added a notation: "Subspecies unknown."

Tod was excited. "Looks like we found a new one. Prof will be – "

"Stop moving around!"

Tod was having difficulty in holding his depth. "The tide must be changing. I can't maintain vertical control." He realized his mistake as soon as he said it.

"That's because you lollygagged too long on the shallow ledge."

Both tides were strongest at midpoint. The maximum water flow of this Blue Hole – dubbed BH-14 – was better than five knots: a knot or two faster than the subsuit's propulsion unit could generate.

During an incoming tide, the downward flow would be so strong that it would overpower the subsuit's electrically-driven propellers. In that case, the subsuit would be sucked down into the Blue Hole and trapped in cavernous depths until the tide slackened – perhaps taking time that exceeded the subsuit's endurance.

Blue Holes were entered only during slack before an outgoing tide, when the water wasn't moving. Then, as the tide began to turn, the water would move upward and out of the cylindrical shaft. In case of power failure or total battery drain, the outgoing tide would propel the subsuit out of the opening into open water, much like a dryland farmer spitting a watermelon seed into the air.

After a moment's contemplation, Tod knew that Lisa was right. The tide had turned. "Squirt, I – "

"According to the flow meters, the water is accelerating faster than normal. That's impossible."

That's what I just said to myself, thought Tod. But he didn't speak into the microphone because he was too busy altering the subsuit's attitude and adjusting the speed control of the propellers. *Something weird is happening.*

"I'm getting a sonar alert." Lisa's voice was ominously calm. She might yell at Tod under normal circumstances, but when an emergency arose, she lapsed into the professional calm of the experienced submersible pilot that she was. "Something big."

"A whale?"

Whales were known to sound to deeper than half a mile. The entrance to the Blue Hole lay at 180 feet, a depth at which whales could easily cruise.

"Too dense for a whale, I think. Something solid."

"Look around on visual."

Water clarity in the Antarctic Ocean exceeded two hundred feet in ambient light.

"It's coming – up."

Tod imagined that he could hear her gulp. "Up? You mean from below?"

Instinctively, Tod looked down. Where he looked inside the close confines of the subsuit didn't help. In order to see what lay beneath him, he had to change the attitude of the one-person one-atmosphere armored suit, direct the twin light beams toward the bottom of the Blue Hole, and peer through the faceplate.

Blue Hole was a strange name for the geological feature that Tod was exploring. The name originated from deep submerged caverns that were found in the Bahamas, in the Caribbean Sea, where the warm water was tinted pale aquamarine. Here along the edge of the Antarctic continent, the water in the rock-lined cylinder appeared ebony. The blackest of black. The absolute absence of light. Pure nothingness. In his imagination,

Tod understood what Alice must have felt as she followed the White Rabbit into its hole to enter Wonderland.

Lisa was far too calm to suit him. "It's big. It's really big."

The calmer she sounded, the more dangerous the situation.

The upwelling water pushed Tod upward and away from the ledge. All thoughts of scientific research for the fulfillment of his basic marine biology degree were forced to the back of his mind as he shifted active mental gears to confront this out-of-the-ordinary phenomenon. The subsuit's light beams reflected off something dark against the darker background.

"I can't see anything . . . "

"Sonar is showing the shape of a cigar."

The image of a whale returned to Tod's imagination. Could a whale have entered the Blue Hole in its search for food on the seabed? Had it been sucked into the hole during the previous tidal phase, and drowned when it was unable to escape against the strength of inrushing water?

Tod turned the light beams to full intensity. Twin spears stabbed downward into the gulf of darkness. He squinted behind the clear plastic faceplate. He thought he detected movement in the inkiness. Before his penetration into the Blue Hole, Lisa had measured the distance to the bottom as 560 feet. This was not beyond the depth rating of the subsuit, but there was no reason for Tod to contemplate such a descent for his project to study coldwater Porifera.

Could a thick cloud of detritus be emerging from a side tunnel, propelled perhaps by the upwelling water? Or a swarm of closely packed macro-organisms? Dense schools of krill or benthic baitfish often reflected a sonar beam to give the appearance of a single hard target. Yet little if no life was found in dead-end tunnels beyond the light zone, where the water was stagnant and largely deoxygenated. Or perhaps it was some kind of viscous fluid, like molten lava erupting from a hydrothermal vent . . .

Tod could not control the anxiety in his voice. "Did you check the heat sensors?"

"Uh . . . Temp is steady at 28 degrees Fahrenheit. No fluctuation."

Tod breathed easier despite his limited air supply. At least he wouldn't be poached like an egg yolk inside the subsuit. Only a few seconds had passed since Lisa's first observation of his slow ascent, yet he felt as if several hours had gone by. His upward movement was increasing, as if the object below was pushing a wall of water ahead of it.

"I'm getting a metallic ping on sonar."

Tod was rising quickly as the column of water above the invisible object accelerated beneath him. Now he could barely distinguish what his eyes interpreted as a dark shade of purple-black from the pure black water beneath the object. It looked like a giant finger stretching nearly from side to side of the Blue Hole, which was more than two hundred feet in diameter. Suddenly he heard a raucous grating or scraping, as sound was transmitted through the liquid medium and the titanium shell of the subsuit.

"Did you hear that?"

"Sensors detected low frequency modulation within a short range."

Either Tod's ascent was decelerating or the object was rising quicker than he was, for it was coming closer and was now nearly in view. The blank heads-up display started flashing lines of text where before it had registered the Latin names of sponges. He was momentarily distracted by the object. When he shifted his attention he saw the textual read-out on the phantom screen.

"Submarine! It's a submarine! Coming up from the bottom of the Blue Hole."

Chapter 2

The transcriber that Tod still held in the subsuit's mechanical hand was transmitting information through its coaxial cable to the subsuit's onboard heads-up display. The databank was routinely searched until approximating matches were found. Subheadings scrolled for a moment, then selected nations that possessed submarines whose silhouettes conformed to the one that the transcriber pictured: the USAC (United States of America and Canada, excluding Quebec), Britain, Eastern China, Indistan, the Scandinavian Bloc, the United Provinces of Africa, the South American Conglomerate . . .

"Persian! The submarine is Persian."

The United Persian Republic had no business operating in the American Exploitation Zone. The UPR – pronounced "Yuper" as a disparaging acronym – was less interested in scientific research than it was in preventing competing nations from discovering new natural resources: by fair means if possible, by foul means otherwise. The Persian Oil Cartel (POC, pronounced "pock") did everything in its power to keep the global economy destabilized in its favor.

"They're not supposed to be here," Lisa singsonged.

"Tell it to the pilot!" Tod actuated the appropriate propellers and backed away from the vast bulk of the rising Persian submarine.

"I don't know their wavelength."

Now the submarine was close enough for Tod to distinguish hull characteristics with the naked eye. The transcriber flashed appropriate make and model features on the heads-up display. The Persian submarine was a warship that was armed with six nuclear-tipped long-range missiles and nine high-explosive torpedoes. Torpedoes could be launched from three tubes: two forward and one aft. Each torpedo compartment contained two reloads for each tube. Naval personnel were furnished with handheld low-voltage high-amperage electrostim devices, called stunguns, ostensibly to combat boarding parties or suppress insubordination, but in actuality for assault against non-Persian vessels. Persian piracy was only one mode of economic warfare.

"Sonar is showing some scatter."

Tod could not afford to be as calm as Lisa. Any second now the submarine was going to collide with him. If the hull ruptured a seal . . .

Tod was as skilled at piloting a subsuit as Lisa was at piloting a submersible – which was why they were working in their respective roles. With deft manipulations of the propeller controls, he spun the subsuit out of the path of the enemy submarine and ascended toward the shallow ledge at 270 feet. In his haste to avoid collision, he slightly overpowered the forward propellers, but banked and rotated at the last second and touched the back wall with a barely noticeable bump.

The ledge blocked the upwelling current that he utilized for lift. The sudden loss of support caused the subsuit to drop before he could eject the ballast water from the leg tanks. He cringed as the subsuit footpads came to rest on the rock platform – and crushed some of the sponges that he had only recently been examining. He returned the transcriber to its holder on the belt.

A few seconds later the submarine rose past eye level. Tod clung to the back wall like a limpet, because the ledge was narrower than the deep one.

He managed to keep the excitement out of his voice. "I see large bubbles escaping from numerous places along the hull."

"That accounts for the scatter."

"Some of the hull plates are dented and missing paint, and most of the external sensor heads are snapped off, but I don't see any gross structural damage."

"Too bad. I may have to fight."

The *Reef Cruiser* was equipped with the standard package of scientific instruments. It didn't carry weapons.

"With what? Your attitude?"

"I'm backing away from the lip. You're on your own if I have to flee. What's your scrubber status?"

Tod checked the digital readout on the oxygen recycling apparatus. Granular soda lime absorbed, or scrubbed, carbon dioxide from exhaled air, and forced the reclaimed gas into the subsuit's breathing loop. Solenoids operated injectors that added bottled oxygen to the breathing mix, in order to replace the oxygen that the body consumed as part of the metabolic process.

"Eighty percent. And I have two replacement canisters."

Lisa could no longer hear him. When she backed the submersible away from the lip of the Blue Hole, the telemetry links were broken because they operated on line-of-sight.

In his haste to avoid contact with the submarine, Tod had failed to notice if the torpedo bay doors were open. He replayed the recording on the transcriber. The bow doors were closed; the stern door could not be seen from his angle.

Sunlight from overhead was blotted out by the bulk of the submarine. Tod stepped off the ledge into the upwelling current, and allowed himself to be pushed along under the sub. He watched as the hull cleared the mouth to the Blue Hole. Its flight pattern then described a vector as the crosscurrent in the open sea dragged the hull away from the cavernous opening.

Tod gunned the propellers in order to increase his upward speed. He scooted across the shaft and emerged from the mouth of the Blue Hole, closely following the Persian submarine. His mind processed information with lightninglike speed. The *Reef Cruiser* was still backing away. The enemy submarine was now describing a trajectory. Free from the upwelling column of water and caught in the crosscurrent, there was no outflow to support the submarine: it was slowly flooding and becoming heavier with the additional weight of water in its breached compartments.

Tod had expected to see water being ejected from the submarine's bilge valves. Instead, the sub reached the apex of its trajectory, then started settling in a gradual arc. It was operating under no motive power of its own.

Line-of-sight was re-established. "This doesn't look good." The calmness in Lisa's voice belied the seriousness of the situation. She twisted the saucer-shaped submersible on its axis in an attempt to get out from under the Persian submarine.

"Squirt, the sub is coming down on top of you."

"I see that."

The submarine was rotating with the vagaries of the current. Bubbles continued to escape from punctures in the pressure hull. The submarine dropped faster than the *Reef Cruiser* could spin away. Tod gasped as he saw the bottom of the Persian submarine's hull graze the top of the *Reef Cruiser*. The submersible's aft propellers created mad swirls in the water as Lisa applied emergency power.

The transcriber was still switched on. It recorded what Tod saw. The heads-up display flashed recognition signals as the subsuit's chip interpreted propeller cavitation, and properly identified the *Reef Cruiser* from information that was stored in its databank.

"I know that," he mumbled.

As the Persian submarine continued to flood, it settled hard on the *Reef Cruiser's* stern and pinned it to the sandy seabed. He heard the crunch of metal on metal. The *Reef Cruiser's* propeller wash kicked up clouds of sand and other particulates, partially obscuring the point of contact.

"Got a breach in compartment AS-2." For all the emphasis that was in her voice, Lisa could have been reading a recipe from a cookbook.

Tod tried to think. The second compartment in the after stern was for stowage, so it was not critical to the operation of the submersible. "Activate the pumps."

"Activating now."

Tod plunged into the swirling cloud to examine the

point of contact. "Cut the props so I can inspect the damage."

"Disengaging propulsion unit." She sounded like a mechanical voice.

Tod drove the subsuit cautiously so as not to crash into the Persian submarine's horizontal diving plane. The sharp edge could crack his acrylic faceplate.

The horrible crunching sound increased in volume as the submarine continued to gain weight by means of flooding.

"Breach in AS-3."

Stirred-up sand and silt settled too slowly to suit Tod's frame of mind. "I can't see anything."

"I've lost the starboard aft sensor cluster."

Tod could imagine Lisa sitting calmly in the pilot seat, scanning the instrument panels. "I can see you on visual from the starboard forward video feed. The hull of that Persian sub is so riddled with holes that it looks like Swiss cheese."

Tod was still blind in the middle of the cloud. "Any radio contact?"

"I found their frequency but they're not responding. Hunk, I think that sub is dead."

The thought had already occurred to him. The submarine didn't act at all as if it were under any kind of control. Its movements had been directed strictly by the upwelling tide and ocean current. The crew must be either unconscious or dead. Tod and Lisa could not expect any help from that quarter, even if the enemy were to act in a humanitarian fashion.

Persia was not technically at war with the rest of the world. That is, war had never been officially declared by any nation or multinational union. But open hostility was expressed through threats, intimidation, and economic sanctions. Persia was entering a stage of disadvantage as the industrial countries decreased their reliance on fossil fuels by increasing their production of nuclear energy. The majority of Persia's oil was sold to so-called backwash countries: those that lacked either the incentive or the technology to pursue alternative energy sources.

Exacerbating the tension of a world that lay on the brink of global conflict were unexplained disappearances of vessels in all seven seas. Granted that land-locked Western China and Indistan (the confederacy of India and Pakistan) were at odds with each other, and often exchanged fire across their Himalayan borders, no other countries were militarily active – except Persia. Yet although everyone knew – or suspected with conviction – that Persia was responsible for most terrorist activity, nothing could be proven. Vessels that disappeared with all hands left no evidence of piracy or physical attack.

Tod made an executive decision. He still couldn't see the damaged area of the *Reef Cruiser*, but it didn't matter. He could not effect repairs to broken welds or ruptured hull plates. What he had to do was to lift the Persian submarine off the saucer's hull before the *Reef Cruiser* was crushed like the pancake that it so closely resembled. To do that, he had to work the controls of the submarine. And to do *that*, he had to enter the submarine through the emergency escape hatch.

"Hold tight, Squirt. I'm going in."

Chapter 3

"Going in? In *where*?" There was a hint of inflection in Lisa's voice.

"Inside the submarine. I have to activate the bilge pumps in order to lighten the load."

"You – you – you can't go inside a Persian submarine."

"Sure I can. It's equipped with an OVA chamber."

Even if the transcriber hadn't informed him of that fact, all submarines and submersibles were fitted with a chamber to enable outside vessel activity.

Lisa sputtered. "But – but there are Persians in there."

"So logic would dictate. I figure they must be incapacitated in some way, or else they would have made an effort to control their vessel, instead of letting it scrape along the walls of the Blue Hole. Maybe their oxygen apparatus malfunctioned. Or their scrubber system got water in it."

Oxygen generators were standard equipment on all underwater craft. One type operated on the principle of electrolysis; it used electricity to crack water molecules: breaking them into their constituent gases, then separating the oxygen from the hydrogen by utilizing the difference in molecular weight. The unit would supply oxygen as long as the atomic pile generated electricity to power the cracking mechanism.

Another type was a chemical plant that was known as a sponge, or lung, or artificial gill. It used synthetic hemoglobin and artificial polymers to absorb free oxygen that was dissolved in seawater.

While these systems replenished the oxygen supply, a scrubber was necessary to remove exhaled carbon dioxide. Too high a concentration of carbon dioxide in a breathing medium had a soporific affect that eventually led to death without premonition that it was near. Death from asphyxiation occurred unannounced shortly after the scrubber ceased to function.

When soda lime got wet, it formed a caustic gas that burned the lungs and the lining of the throat, and that destroyed the hemoglobin that transported oxygen throughout the body.

Lisa's normal volubility lapsed into silence. She had not quite regained her composure when she cautioned, "It might be dangerous."

Tod deigned not to comment. He was already scooting to the top of the submarine in search of the OVA hatch. Bubbles trickled upward all around him as he vaulted over the sievelike side of the hull. The upper skin of the submarine was flat and hydrodynamic. Missile silo caps and withdrawn sensor heads were inset flush with the metal sheathing to allow for the smooth passage of water. The only protuberance above the hull was the battered conning tower. This early twenty-first-century model had escape hatches for each and every compartment, but only one of them was retrofitted with a chamber from which the water could be expelled. The other hatches led to trunks which had direct access to the compartment underneath. They could be used only when the submarine plowed along the surface, or when it was put into an airdock: a submerged, air-filled hangar.

Tod passed over two hatch covers from which the transcriber drew a blank. Although the onboard chip was loaded with basic information relating to the offensive armament of obsolete Persian submarines, intelligence reports about design and construction were severely lacking. Tod would have to operate this submarine without much help from the databank.

For subconscious reasons that Tod could not comprehend, the third hatch cover seemed right. It was larger in diameter than the others – wide enough to accommodate a standard issue subsuit. It was also beefier in construction. The subsuit's knees were not articulated well enough to enable Tod to bend down and reach the hatch's handwheel. He had to lie in a horizontal attitude, and stretch the mechanical arms in front of him.

"I'm watching you, Hunk." Lisa's voice had regained its even pitch.

"How's the flooding?"

"Minimized. The pumps are ejecting nearly as much water as the sub is taking on." That was a euphemistic way of saying that the sea was gaining – the submersible was losing ground, in a manner of speaking, and replacing air with natural saline solution. "All three compartments are sealed from the rest of the interior."

"Three! I thought only two compartments had been breached."

"Apparently one of the separating bulkheads collapsed. Or else the Persian sub landed right on a watertight bulkhead and caused flooding in both adjacent compartments."

"What's the third compartment?"

"AC-1."

The center compartment aft held the main propulsion machinery. Fortunately, the reactor was safely ensconced in an armored compartment that occupied the middle of the saucer with all-around protection.

Tod used the subsuit's manipulators to grab and turn the inset handwheel. At first it failed to yield to the hydraulics, and he feared that the frame had been distorted sufficiently enough to jam the hatch in place, but not enough to break the seal. He applied more torque. The handwheel snapped free, then spun easily on a well-greased wormgear. The hatch cover screwed upward on a threaded shaft until the ingress ports were exposed. Then air escaped madly from four points of the circular hatch at the same time that seawater strove to pour inside.

Several minutes passed before the gurgling stopped. When the chamber was fully flooded, and the external pressure was equalized, he spun the handwheel the rest of the way and swung the hatch cover open on two massive hinges. He inspected the interior. He saw that the annunciator lights on the watertight control panel were brightly illuminated. This established that there was still electrical power in the vessel and that the OVA chamber was operational.

He rotated the subsuit to vertical orientation.

"Please be careful." It was the first time that Tod had ever heard Lisa use the word "please."

"Thanks, Squirt." He tapped the propeller controls and positioned himself directly above the opening. "Down the hatch."

He pumped ballast water into the leg tanks. Slowly the subsuit lowered itself vertically into the water-filled chamber. During the short descent, Tod oriented the subsuit so that it faced the control panel when the foot-pads settled on the platform. Tod's first obstacle was to pull the hatch cover down and seal it in place. He was barely able to do this with the limited articulation of the mechanical arms and manipulators.

The chamber was dark except for the lighted touch-pad and annunciator lights on the control panel. The next obstacle was to decipher the Persian writing on the keys of the touchpad. Tod knew nothing about the language except for its history.

In a fervent civilian movement to overthrow wide-spread oppression, a massive and all-consuming jihad engulfed the Middle East nations in the first half of the twenty-first century. Local leaders who opposed free elections were either ousted or assassinated. Provisional governments were created until officials could be elected by the populace. Political borders were obliterated practically overnight. Hundreds of sovereign states were formed during the biggest national reorganization since the fall of the Soviet Union.

Each sovereign state was fiercely independent, bounded not so much by physical terrain or ethnic group or cultural conformity as by religious faction. In an unprecedented movement for the Middle East, each state pledged to tolerate the mores and religions of its neighboring states as long as they could practice their own. This collection of miniature sovereign states satisfied the spiritual needs of the people, but caused economic disaster.

Through a series of alliances, the sovereign states formed a consortium whose sole purpose was to mediate economic affairs among the subscribing states. Each state became an autonomous economic enclave within the greater whole. This instrument of financial management came to be known as the United Persian Republic (although it was anything but a republic).

While the individual states retained their own languages and dialects, the UPR needed to unify its means of communication in order to negotiate effectively with the rest of the world. And even though Arabic script, or Farsi, was used by most of the consortium's members, the language disfavored those states whose citizens harbored ill feelings against it. As a way of conciliation, the UPR reverted to the language that dominated the Middle East a thousand years earlier: Old Persian.

"Squirt, can you hear me?"

"Loud and clear."

"Do we have any language modules on board?"

"I've already checked."

Tod should have known that Lisa was not sitting idle in a flooding submersible with death only a bulkhead away, but was anticipating his every move.

"We have a basic Old Persian dictionary with recognition software. For words only; no grammar or syntax."

"That's all I need."

"Transmitting now." A few seconds later, she said, "Done. Now you can read the instrument panel."

"Thanks, Squirt. You're a charm."

Tod held the transcriber in front of the keyboard and zoomed in on the script that was printed on individual keys. The transcriber provided the equivalent English word. He was gratified to learn that the keyboard had function keys and not letter and numeral keys, like on a computer keyboard. He pressed the Automatic Cycle key. He heard the soft whirring of pumps in operation.

"That was easy."

OVA chambers on U.S. submarines and submersibles were password protected. Onboard personnel had override options that could either cycle the chamber or expel the occupant. Not so for retrofitted Persian submarines, which lacked many security features that more advanced technological nations installed against piratical invaders. As far as Tod could remember, no one had ever boarded a Persian submarine unannounced.

"It means the Persians didn't configure a lockout protocol during retrofit."

"Lucky for us."

"Maybe. Don't forget that when the interior hatch opens, you may find the compartment filled with water or lethal gas."

Tod fingered the emergency oxygen mask and detachable cylinder. "I hope not."

"Or armed Persian sailors."

Water drained out of the flooded chamber. Streaks and droplets remained on the subsuit's acrylic faceplate. When the chamber was completely empty, a hissing sound indicated that the interior hatch was unsealing automatically. The hatch swung open to reveal a dry compartment and soft illumination.

"Looks like emergency lighting."

Platform motors actuated a treadmill that drew the subsuit into the staging area. Tod could not walk the subsuit in a non-water environment because it weighed more than a ton. The staging area consisted of lockers in which subsuits were stowed when not in use.

He donned the oxygen mask as a safety precaution before actuating the breakseal circuit. The subsuit separated at the midpoint of the chest, above the instrument panel. The top portion swung up and back on hinges. Tod closed the subsuit's breathing loop, and switched the gas monitors to external mode. The digital monitor registered 20.9% oxygen, 78% nitrogen, .9% argon, and the balance trace gases such as carbon dioxide. Deadly carbon monoxide registered zero. There was no need for the oxygen mask.

"Are you reading this, Squirt?"

"Sure am. It's atmospheric air, not processed. This sub has been on the surface in the not too distant past. Did you check for radioactivity?"

"Checking now." Tod flipped the switch for the Geiger counter. "Looks normal."

"I hate to be a pest, Hunk, but AS-1 is now flooding."

Tod stuck a short-range audiotab in his left ear. The miniature transmitter/receiver was linked to the subsuit's telemetry equipment, enabling him to communicate with Lisa on board the *Reef Cruiser*. "On my way."

Tod climbed out of the subsuit as if it were a pickle barrel. The air felt cold on his face and hands. The rest of his body was insulted by gray syntactic foam: the standard garment worn by all subaqueous inhabitants. The waterproofed booties had extra padding and a thickened sole that made no sound on the metal deck grating.

Tod detached the transcriber from the belt of the subsuit. He unplugged the watertight fitting that connected the handheld unit to the cable, then activated the wireless transmission switch.

He ducked through the hatchway into the adjacent compartment forward, in the direction of the control room. Bunks lined both sides of the crew's berthing compartment. His whole body shivered when he noticed a person lying on one of the port bunks. Tod stood stock still. From close quarters he observed the partially uncovered face and scraggly beard. The man didn't move. Tod glanced around the compartment and saw that it was otherwise unoccupied.

Tod stepped cautiously toward the unmoving body. He studied his bare neck for several seconds. There was no telltale throbbing of the jugular vein. Slowly he reached out to press his fingertips against the carotid artery, but before he touched the man he saw that the uniform was stained red on opposite sides of the body.

"Are you seeing this?"

"Transmission is clear."

Tod checked for a pulse. "He's dead."

He didn't waste any more time on the man. He had more important things to do. He vacated the berthing space and proceeded forward into the control room. The bulkheads were a maze of pipes, valves, and gauges. Like sideways rain, water spurted into the compartment from a number of places in the pressure hull. The water did not accumulate in puddles on the deck, but passed through holes in the grating and into the bilges.

Two men were slumped over their controls in the command center, one on each side of a longitudinal bulkhead that stood even with the top of the seatbacks. In front and on both sides of the men stood a triptych array of instrument panels that appeared to be undamaged. Flip switches and round push buttons were everywhere.

Tod saw a circle of blood on one man's back. The other man had multiple head wounds.

He ignored the dead men, and the jetting steams of water that shot across the compartment under the force of high pressure.

Tod focused the transcriber lens on the script that adorned the instrument tags. Quickly he panned across the panels until the words "Bilge Pumps" showed on the transcriber's backscreen. Each one of a cluster of ten buttons controlled the pumps in a different bilge. All the buttons were illuminated, indicating that the bilge pumps had been activated automatically by float switches.

"I've got to blow the ballast tanks."

Lisa's voice was clear and composed. "Understood."

"How's the flooding?"

"Holding."

Tod suspected that she was being less than frank. He resumed focusing the transcriber lens on the instrument panel tags. The transcriber instantaneously translated Old Persian script but offered multiple choices. As in English, some words had more than one meaning. Without knowing the context, the computer was unable to determine which definition suited best. It was up to Tod to choose the appropriate English equivalent.

"What was that?" The audiotab was detecting background sounds in addition to Lisa's voice.

"Another compartment has been breached under the weight of the submarine."

Tod searched frantically for the ballast tank switches. He ducked under a stream of water that was bouncing off a gauge cluster. Water was spritzing everywhere across the control room. One by one he focused the lens on the instrument tags, until he found one that read "Emergency Ballast Dump."

"Got it!"

He lifted the protective cap and pressed the red button underneath. His heart sank when nothing happened immediately. Then the first of a series of annunciator lights illuminated dimly. According to the translation, each illuminated annunciator indicated that water was being ejected from one of the submarine's ballast tanks.

"Good work, Hunk."

Gradually the submarine commenced to lift. Grinding sounds ceased to reach Tod's ears through the audiotab. A grin broke out on his face. He breathed a deep sigh of relief.

"Squirt, I think we're the first people in history to capture a Persian submarine."

Chapter 4

"Before you start gloating, remember that we've got two badly damaged vessels on our hands."

"That's what patch kits are for."

There was a long silence on the audiotab. "I think we should pop an acoustical beacon and send an SOS to base."

"And give our position to the enemy? You know that's a last ditch – Hey, what's your condition?"

"Still holding." Pause. "Actually, improving." Pause. "Water level is going down in all breached compartments."

Tod was still aglow with the fact of a great achievement. "Okay, so I'll go outside and start patching the leaks."

"If you want to take back that captured sub, you had better start thinking about stabilizing the depth control, too."

"Take back? . . . I never thought . . . I figured we'd send a towsub after it."

"If that sub surfaces and goes adrift, the Persians might have time to reclaim it before a towsub can get here from base."

Tod's and Lisa's thoughts and schemes were leapfrogging each other.

"Okay. Okay. I'll go along with that. Uh, you get the *Reef Cruiser* out from under this submarine, then I'll stop blowing ballast and let the hull settle back on the bottom. After I get both subs patched, I'll work on obtaining neutral buoyancy in this antique tub."

"Sounds like a workable plan."

What sounded like a good plan in conversation was difficult in execution. All thoughts of scientific research went out the porthole as the duo commenced to salvage not one but two underwater vessels that were in dire straits.

Tod went OVA. Lisa placed a patch kit in the auxiliary transfer chamber: a miniature airlock that was used to exchange tools and sample bottles. The patch kit consisted of a twin-nozzle squeeze tube that was subdivided internally to hold two thermoplastic resins that self-heated upon contact with each other to produce a strong polymerized bonding agent that solidified within seconds.

The stern starboard quarter of the *Reef Cruiser* was badly bent and crushed, and some of the welded seams were sprung. Permanent repairs could be made only in an airdock. Tod squeezed synthetic resin over cracks in the pressure hull. Inrushing water pulled the viscous material into the compartment. The resin expanded as it hardened, creating a bulge both inside and outside the crack. When the resin solidified, the expansion bulge would not extrude in either direction except under extreme pressure.

The single-hull design of the *Reef Cruiser* made it easy to repair. The antiquated Persian submarine was another matter entirely. The pressure hull was surrounded by an outer hull or skin whose purpose was to present a hydrodynamic surface to the water. Between the two skins were large watertight pumps, huge pipes that connected external ballast tanks, tacked-on accessory modules, and so on. Air that escaped from the pressure hull rose to the overhead, then traveled along the inside of the outer skin until it found a way to escape. This made it difficult for Tod to locate the leakage points, and to reach those points in order to apply the bonding agent. He had to open access panels on the outer skin, then look for the origin of escaping bubbles. What took minutes on the saucer took hours on the Persian submarine.

"There are some holes that I can't reach," Tod announced.

"How big are they?"

"The same as the others – about a quarter inch in diameter. They look like bore holes except for the irregular periphery. I've never seen anything like it."

"Maybe they discovered some unknown species of

starfish. One that uses stomach acid that is strong enough to eat through steel in addition to clam shells."

Tod knew that Lisa was being less than serious. "They must have encountered a whole bed of them. I've filled in at least a couple dozen holes."

"Thirty-eight."

"And that's not counting the corresponding holes that I didn't repair on the outer hull. They're like pinpricks that traveled in a straight line through both hulls. Starfish don't do that."

"Hunk, forget about the inaccessible holes. The bilge pumps will eject the little amount of water that enters through them. Go ahead and secure the towline. Then get inside and work on buoyancy control.

"Aye, aye, Skipper."

Lisa positioned the *Reef Cruiser* forward of the submarine's bow. Even with the subsuit's heavy-duty hydraulic systems, it was a great deal of effort to remove the thick towing hawser from the locker in the saucer's bow, haul it aft, secure one end to the sled-towing bridle, and attach the other end to the Persian submarine's forward bitt.

When Tod re-entered the submarine, he took some time to examine the various compartments. The interior was in a state of general disarray. Stowage lockers were open, articles and paraphernalia lay strewn on the deck, half-eaten comestibles decayed on dishes in the galley, stungun charging ports were locked and loaded, old-fashioned projectile guns filled only half the available racks, ammunition canisters were open and bullets were scattered across the arming platform, and several crates were filled with items that neither he nor the transcriber recognized.

"Are you viewing this, Squirt?"

"I am, but I don't know any more than the transcriber knows."

"Not only that, but did you notice that there are two berthing spaces for the crew?"

By counting the bunks and cabins, Tod ascertained that the normal complement was six officers and thirty-two crewmembers. Yet only three bodies were on board.

Tod could picture Lisa nodding affirmatively. "Old as it is, they should be able to run this sub with half that number. Are you thinking marine detachment?"

"Exactly. But where are the marines? And the rest of the crew?"

"Two posers among many. Like why is this sub here in the first place? The Persians aren't supposed to be anywhere within a thousand-mile radius of here. That's why we need to bring this sub back to base. Grand Intelligence will want to go over it with a fine-toothed comb."

"I agree. I just don't like the idea . . . "

"Take it easy, Hunk. I know it's gross, but dead men can't hurt you."

"I realize that, but you don't have to move them."

"You can do it, Hunk. Think of them as dead weights. Oops, I didn't mean it that way."

At six-foot-three and two-hundred-forty pounds, Tod would have no physical difficulty in lifting the bloody victims out of their command seats and dragging them out of the control room. His qualms were purely emotional. He could do what was necessary but was not happy about doing it. He kept telling himself that he should be overjoyed that the Persians had perished in such a painful manner.

Although it had never been proven, it was pretty much a forgone conclusion that Persians had been responsible for the death of his parents. He should hate Persians for that. Part of him did. But the greater part existed on a more merciful plane.

"I know you didn't."

He set about the gruesome task in silence. He placed the bodies on the deck in the berthing space near the first victim he had encountered.

Back in the control room, Tod ignored the propulsion instruments and concentrated on obtaining neutral buoyancy. He blew water ballast out of the tanks until the depth meter readout indicated that the sub was rising. He switched off the ballast pumps and actuated the trim controls. All this took time because he had to use the transcriber to read the Persian script on the tags. He finally achieved a balance point between positive and negative buoyancy. The sub hovered ten feet above the seabed on a close-to-even keel.

"That's about as good as I can get it," Tod exclaimed.

"Okay. Let's head for the barn."

Lisa slowly took up the slack on the towing hawser. After the cable was pulled taut and the submersible saucer was straining at the bit, she applied more power to the propellers. There was a soft jerk as the catenary straightened. Gradually she increased propeller revolutions until the motors reached full throttle. Sub and tow proceeded smoothly at one-third speed – the best the *Reef Cruiser* could make with the drag of a submarine that was better than five times the saucer's tonnage.

By this time the sun had long since set. Tod and Lisa were expected to return to base by 0800: less than eight hours away. In addition to the late start that was caused by the advent of the Persian submarine, the reduction in speed was going to make the return passage three times longer than planned. They would be traveling for the rest of the night, all the next day, and all the following night.

Tod groaned inwardly – not because Harker would be apoplectic at their overdue arrival; his anger would be more than offset by the ecstasy the Grand Intelligence people would evince – but because he was already exhausted from the intensity of the outside vessel activity.

Lisa was in no better condition. Although she had put the controls on automatic pilot, she had to stay alert despite her suffering from sleep deprivation. Proximity alerts would warn her of obstacles in the submersible's path, and of approaching shoal water, but autopilot could not change anything: it merely maintained course, depth, and speed. Only she could implement avoidance maneuvers. And she had to ensure that the engines did not overheat under the additional load. Coffee helped her to stay awake.

Tod must have dozed. The sharp scraping of the submarine's keel across the bottom brought him to full alertness in an instant. There were viewscreens for every quadrant, including above and below. External light beams illuminated an extensive field of coral. Lisa had flown the saucer high over the reef, but the towing hawser did not lift the Persian submarine shallower than its preset depth.

"Only underwater weeds," Lisa quipped.

Tod saw that the coral was bleached white and dead, else Lisa would not have treated the grounding incident so lightly. Living coral was greatly depleted along the Antarctic shelf. In truth, living coral was a rarity throughout most of the subaqueous world except in tropical seas: it clung tenaciously where it used to thrive. Dead and dying coral was a chronic global issue in environmental circles.

"I wasn't paying attention," Tod admitted.

"Neither was I, or I would have alerted you. Sorry."

Tod drew some water from the scuttlebutt and splashed it on his face. He took some processed food out of the freezer. He didn't bother to translate the packaging literature. The microwave oven worked the same as any other unit: they were all manufactured in Eastern China. After nuking the unfamiliar meal, he returned to the control room and chewed in silence while sitting in the starboard command seat and staring vacantly at the viewscreens.

Dawn arrived slowly under water. Most of the sun's light reflected off the air/water interface until grand old Sol rose high enough for its yellow beams to pierce the waves. Surface turbulence and particulate matter in the water column conspired to reduce the amount of light that was able to reach the bottom. Twilight conditions prevailed.

"Hunk, the drift is getting worse. I'm changing our vector by five degrees east."

"Probably a storm."

Benthic storms were not uncommon. Adverse weather in the atmosphere reached down hundreds of feet, affecting current speed and direction, and sometimes scouring the seabed and altering the bottom topography over broad areas. Under extreme conditions, sediment could be lifted into whorls that obscured visibility much like dense fog in air.

"I think we're skirting the perimeter." Lisa sighed deeply. "Hunk, my eyelids feel like lead. How about if we take a thirty-minute power nap?"

"Okay by me. I can use some shuteye."

Lisa took on ballast water and set the *Reef Cruiser* down on a patch of white sand next to a bed of manganese nodules. The nap turned into a deep slumber from which neither one awoke until three hours later. They both felt immensely refreshed and eager to complete the voyage. Lisa created a waypoint for the manganese nodules, so the bed could be relocated and examined at a later date.

The storm did not worsen as the day droned on, but strong currents prevented Lisa from following the outbound route that was plotted on the tracknav unit. Because of the limited speed and maneuverability of the tandem subs, they were deflected westward of the route.

Once they had to maneuver around a hydrothermal vent. Because Lisa was busy piloting, Tod used the transcriber link to the *Reef Cruiser* to record the position for future study and evaluation.

Hot water and gas that erupted from the Earth's crust often originated deep in the mantle. The vents transported heavy elements such as iron, zinc, copper, and gold, and deposited them on the seafloor in the form of fine dust. Oxide and sulfide ores were precipitated as well. All these elements and minerals were valuable natural resources whose supplies were either depleted or rapidly diminishing in dryland mines.

Although Tod and Lisa were engaged in an unsupervised training mission, the primary purpose of the underwater base camps that dotted the submerged perimeter of the Antarctic continent was to locate metal-rich deposits for underwater strip-mining operations. Biological studies were of secondary importance when weighed against more essential needs and considerations.

Darkness fell again. They took another extended power nap in the middle of the night. Dawn arrived bright if not cheery.

"Hunk, do you think Prof is worried about us?"

"He shouldn't be. He knows how these missions can encounter unexpected diversions. Our return time was based on Denny's artificial timetable, not on mission parameters. Now Denny, on the other hand – "

"Won't be worried. He'll be irate."

"That's putting it mildly."

"I estimate that we'll be about thirty hours over Denny's due time of return."

A few hours later they reached the transponder zone. Surface transponders were used only in emergency situations, in which the emergency equated to imminent demise – this because the Persians could triangulate the position of any transmission signal. Underwater base camps kept a receiver afloat above the station so that emergency signals could be intercepted. Receivers could not be detected by electronic means, only by optical scanning systems. The receiver unit was too small to be sighted from an orbiting satellite. An enemy vessel would have to pass within a few hundred feet for a sharp lookout to spot it. Atmospheric transponder silence was a strict protocol.

Surrounding each base camp was a series of transponders that were hard-wired to each other and to the receiving station. Lisa enabled the saucer's transmitter. She reduced amplification to extreme low-range, selected the appropriate calling frequency, input the authentication code, and switched to voice transmission.

"*Reef Cruiser* calling base."

The response delay was momentary. "Base here."

"Require two airdocks for immediate disposal."

"Repeat, please. *Two* airdocks?"

"Correct. One for the *Reef Cruiser* because of extensive hull damage, and one for our tow."

"What is your tow?"

"You're not going to believe this, but it's a captured Persian submarine of the *Scheherazade* class."

Chapter 5

Lisa's announcement unleashed virtual chaos in Benthocity 3.

Despite her calm assurances that there were no enemy agents still alive on the submarine, the base went into immediate lockdown mode and implemented full-scale repel-attack measures. Automated armament devices were activated; these consisted of camouflaged mines whose explosive charges were triggered by the proximity of large moving objects that were not programmed with the proper authentication code. (More than one whale had been blown to smithereens.) Armed patrol subs were launched, and their torpedo tubes were loaded and put on ready status. Subsuited personnel swarmed from airlocks like disturbed carpenter bees.

The Persian submarine was soon surrounded. It was far enough away from the base that it could do no harm in the event of self destruction.

The *Reef Cruiser*'s computer was unable to translate all the technical language in the submarine's communication circuits, so Tod had to patch through the transcriber. Again despite Lisa's assurances, base marshal and vessel dispatcher Denny Harker worked on the presumption that Tod might be giving false information under duress. Harker coordinated the base offensive posture, then took it upon himself to enter the submarine in order to ascertain the facts.

Tod stood outside the subsuit chamber to greet him. "Welcome aboard," he said in a tone that was guaranteed to ruffle Harker's figurative feathers.

Harker cradled a rifle-sized stungun with a high-energy battery cell for a stock. As soon as the chamber door opened, and there was room to swing the barrel, he panned the compartment as if he expected attack from every quarter at once. He pointed with his chin. "Who are they?"

Tod looked down at the two deceased Persians he had dragged into the compartment. "They were on board when I entered." Then, as an afterthought, "They were already dead."

"Humph." The treadmill pulled Harker's subsuit into the compartment. He was taking no chances of an ambush. "Close the hatch behind you. And the one at the other end."

Tod nodded at the precaution, then complied with Harker's request. He closed both hatches, fore and aft. This would give Harker time to climb out of the subsuit before an unseen enemy could open the hatches and catch him unarmed. Harker removed the stungun from the manipulators.

"You've created a fine mess."

Tod grinned. "Just doing my job."

"You don't have a job. You're still in training."

Tod shrugged.

Harker checked each body for signs of life. "How did these blood stains get there?"

Tod shook his head. "I don't know. That's the way they were when I found them. Projectile rifles are missing from the armory. They must have been shot."

"Mutiny?" The question was rhetorical. "All right. Let's inspect the vessel."

Tod took Harker on a guided tour. There weren't many places where a person could hide aboard a submarine, not even if he were undersized. Harker was soon satisfied that there were no living Persians concealed in any nooks and crannies.

"Did you check the reactor for sabotage or explosive devices?"

"Uh, no."

"Did you check the missile silos for timers or remote detonators?"

"No."

"Then how do you know this outmoded sub isn't a concealed weapon that the Yupers sent to destroy one of our underwater bases?"

Tod was suddenly horrified. Because his mental

processes didn't work the same as Harker's, the idea that the submarine could be a delayed action bomb had never occurred to him. He was speechless.

"You idiot, they could have rigged the reactor rods to fail and cause the core to go critical. Or they could have set the nukes to detonate after a certain lapse of time. What the hell were you thinking?"

Tod was nonplussed. He realized that Harker could be right.

"So they put some corpses in here to make it look like an accident. And you fell for it, you ignorant fool."

"Well, I never thought – "

"That's your problem, Mallory. You never think."

"Well – "

"We're at war, in case you didn't know it. At war with a bunch of fanatics – fanatics who wouldn't think twice about committing suicide just to kill a couple of God-fearing innocents. You can't trust Yupers even when they're dead."

"But given the circumstances – "

"The circumstances deluded you – "

"That is quite enough, Denny." The smooth baritone voice emanated from Tod's audiotab at the same time it was projected from the communication link in Harker's open subsuit. Stereophonic sound added emphasis to a voice that was soft but authoritative. "I think we can dispense with the personal derision. It is out of place."

Harker fumed and grimaced, but did not reply.

"Let us proceed with the investigation in an orderly fashion and without recriminations."

Harker sputtered, but yielded to compliance. "Prof, I want a six-man tactical team to check for scuttling charges."

"Prof" was Professor Augustus Pembroke, Chief Administrator and Science Advisor in charge of Benthocity 3. The only people in the world who did not call him Prof were his close relatives. Once someone jokingly called him Augie, and lived to regret it.

"That is sound advice, Denny. I will dispatch a team at once."

Harker glowered at Tod but said not a word. Even subvocal mutterings were received and transmitted by the sensitive comm links. In due course the tactical team arrived in subsuits, entered the chamber one at a time, and commenced their examination.

"You can go now," Harker commanded.

Tod treadmilled his subsuit into the lockout chamber and exited the submarine. Lisa had already docked the *Reef Cruiser*, so he propelled to the nearest airlock and cycled into the base camp.

Benthocity 3 was one of six underwater science labs that contraPersia nations supported in Antarctic waters. It consisted of a sprawling network of hemispheres that were interconnected by watertight "breezeways," each of which was sealed by a hatch at either end as a safety measure against widespread flooding. The five administration hemispheres that constituted the central cluster were arranged in the form of a pentagon. Breezeways connected each hemisphere to its two adjacent neighbors. Each hemisphere had a breezeway that led inward to the small central node, which housed the nuclear reactor that generated electricity for the base. Pundits liked to compare the geometry to a pentagram, which the pentagon closely resembled, and claim that its purpose was to protect the inhabitants from evil spirits that were conjured in the form of radioactive particles inside the reactor. Because of the appearance of the auxiliary shielding that separated the inner facing of the five hemispheres from the reactor chamber, they were not far off the mark.

Each of the pentagon's hemispheres had two outward breezeways that led to encircling hemispheres. Those hemispheres were interconnected to their neighbors, and had their own outward breezeways that led to the next circle of hemispheres. The hemispheres in the second and third circles enclosed laboratories. The fourth circle of hemispheres consisted of living quarters and commissaries. The fifth circle was a ragtag collection of lozenge-shaped airdock hangars for submersibles of all shapes and sizes. Only submersible accommodations exceeded fifty feet in diameter.

The population of the complex averaged one thousand individuals, not counting transients.

The airlocks were numbered sequentially in clockwise rotation. Tod selected Lisa's personal frequency and told her where he was docking. Although the saucer required extensive repairs to the damaged hull, she still had to perform standard lockdown procedures: securing the reactor, copying the transcriber chip, refilling oxygen tanks, replacing scrubber canisters, and so on.

Tod did much the same for the subsuit. The most important item on his punch list called for plugging the batteries into charging ports.

He was still steamed by his confrontation with Harker when he met Lisa in an empty canteen.

Lisa was the exact opposite of Tod in size. She stood four-feet-eleven inches tall in her padded booties. Like all subaqueous females, she wore her hair in a bush cut that was only slightly longer than Tod's crew cut. Her nose pressed against his sternum when they hugged. Her voice was high-pitched and squeaky compared to Tod's deep base. "That was a mission we'll never forget."

"Neither will anyone else."

"Not many people can say they captured a Persian submarine single-handed."

"I don't know whether to be ecstatic or despondent. That Denny makes me so sore, I'd like to punch him right in nose."

"I know. I know. He's a jerk. But don't let him get to you. That's exactly what he wants."

"He tells me we're at war. He forgets that we're at war with Persia, not our own people."

"Forget it, Hunk." When she grabbed his clenched fist it was like a mouse trying to shake hands with a bear. She dragged him toward the nearest hatch. "Let's forget about it and go to bed. I'm too tired to eat. Prof said we can debrief on the next shift."

Tod grumbled, but let Lisa lead him to the breezeway. Perfunctorily he checked the pressure gauges, spun the handwheel, and swung open the hatch. Lisa entered first. Tod closed the hatch and sealed the compartment. They were halfway along the breezeway when the klaxon sounded.

Instinctively they parted. Lisa ran to the hatch at the farther end, while Tod returned to the hatch that he had just closed. The sign above the hatch flashed "No ALARM. THIS IS A TEST." He switched off the klaxon, then pressed the button to initiate the automatic diagnostics.

He studied the gauge panel for pressure drop and oxygen depletion. Everything showed normal except for an annunciator bulb that indicated carbon dioxide content; the bulb was illuminated but the digital readout showed that the concentration was within acceptable limits.

Tod opened the emergency toolbox and removed a continuity tester. He touched silvered prongs to exposed contacts.

Lisa stood beside him. "No leaks at my end. What's wrong here?"

"Looks like a short circuit."

"That circuit looks long enough to me."

"Very funny." He replaced the tester and removed a Philips screwdriver. It took but a moment to separate two loose wires that had vibrated together, and to tighten their bolts. The annunciator bulb winked out. "Now are you as de-lighted as that annunciator?"

Lisa winced. "Very funny."

Tod replaced the screwdriver and closed the toolbox lid.

Lisa pressed the comm button. "Safety Control, this is breezeway four-two. Have just repaired circuit on CO_2 analyzer on hatch four-two-A. No further repairs necessary. Out."

As if nothing untoward had happened, they continued on their way through the far hatch into their berthing hemisphere.

"I hate Denny. I just hate him."

"You're not alone. So does everyone else he ever met. Now forget about him."

They stopped at a door that led to a berthing cubicle with two name boards. One read "TOD MALLORY." The other read "LISA MALLORY."

Tod said, "Would anyone care if I stungunned him?"

"Care? People would cheer."

Tod and Lisa entered the cubicle that they had shared for the past two years.

Chapter 6

Tod and Lisa slept straight through two eight-hour shifts. When they finally awoke, they drank coffee in their cubicle as they collaborated on writing their mission report. After submitting it electronically, they called Prof on the intercom.

Professor Pembroke was always on call. He worked essentially around the clock. Instead of being assigned to every third shift on a rotating basis, like the rest of the base personnel, he catnapped on a sofa in his office whenever he had the opportunity to do so. He had the ability to fall asleep at a moment's notice, and wake up fifteen minutes later without feeling groggy.

"Have you two caught up on your rest."

"Pretty much," Lisa said.

Tod chimed in, "We sent a rough draft of the highlights of the mission. We'll do a detailed report later."

"That is fine. Let me start by congratulating you both on an exceptional achievement. What you have done is an historic event that has Grand Intelligence positively enthralled. Examination teams are working extra shifts, and we are transmitting information continuously as soon as new facts become available."

Aerial transmissions could be intercepted by enemy surveillance systems. Encryption devices prevented unauthorized access to data, but it was even more important to keep the enemy from learning the locations of underwater bases by triangulating the transmission sources. Data were transmitted by a network of fiber-optic cables that lay on the seabed like nineteenth-century transatlantic telegraph cables. These fiber-optic cables connected the Benthocities to each other, but not to the outside world.

"I daresay that you will both receive commendations no matter how you do on your qualification tests. Grand Intelligence was not even aware that a Persian submarine was reported missing. A discovery of this magnitude is of the greatest importance to global security. Each revelation is more revealing than the previous one. In short, you have struck an intelligence goldmine that could greatly facilitate a shift in the balance of worldwide power."

Neither Tod nor Lisa knew quite what to say.

"Take off the rest of the shift. I am holding a special meeting that is scheduled for shift-two hour-one. I want both of you to attend. Out."

Tod's gray eyes widened. "Looks like we opened a can of sea worms."

"Or Pandora's box."

Tod nodded slowly. "Could be that, too."

"I'm famished. Let's go to the canteen and do some serious chowing down."

"I'm with you on that."

Chowing down was more difficult than they anticipated. In a small community, especially one in a confined space such as Benthocity 3, word of their accomplishment traveled only a binary digit slower than the speed of light. They were so busy answering enthusiastic questions that they hardly had time to chew, much less swallow. Hours passed before they drank and consumed their fill.

They slept in their cubicle for the remainder of the shift. When they awoke, there was barely enough time to spongebathe before they had to rush to the meeting.

The conference cubicle was sealed the same as every other compartment. This was done as a routine safety measure again implosion or flooding from adjacent compartments, not to keep out uninvited personnel. There were no secrets in Benthocity 3. Audio and video monitors were in operation to record the meeting and to transmit its proceedings throughout the base to anyone who was interested.

Everyone was interested. Nearly all work ceased for the duration as nonessential personnel watched private screens in their cubicles, or gathered in public compartments to watch community screens. Essential duty personnel watched on handheld screens.

The conference cubicle was strictly utilitarian, like every other one on base. The bulkheads were bare metal shorn of adornment. Surface-mounted conduits led to gas-tight electrical panels, overhead cage lights, quadruplex outlets, computer consoles, and communication instruments. Pressure gauges and gas analyzers were grouped on either side of the hatch. Fire extinguishers and oxygen kits were placed strategically within easy reach.

Tod and Lisa were given seats on either side of Professor Pembroke. Fourteen other people sat shoulder to shoulder around the oval-shaped table that was crowded with keypads and screens.

Prof was not imposing in either height or shoulder breadth. Fluorescent lighting reflected harshly off his perfectly bald head. He seldom took time to trim his black scraggly beard. His dark brown eyes never seemed to rest, but darted from his screen to people around the compartment. His bulbous nose stood out like a stone promontory.

"We have so much information to disseminate and collate that I hardly know where to begin. Thank you all for attending. I do not need to remark upon the extraordinary event that has brought us here this shift. You all know that our prize pupils Lisa and Tod Mallory captured – or perhaps, recovered is a better word – a Persian submarine in our operational theater. What everyone does not yet know is what our specialist teams have to report about the submarine. I daresay that their examinations have uncovered information that will come as somewhat of a shock. Rather than give away the end of what I am certain will be a dramatic performance, I will let the experts speak for themselves about their areas of expertise. Charles Medford, would you be so good as to take the lead?"

Despite the usual informality of the proceeding, Prof clearly pronounced the surname as a matter of record, for outsiders and future generations to whom the first name Charles would be meaningless.

"Of course." Medford acknowledged himself with a

flick of the finger. "Although I don't know how good I can lead. Or how well."

A smile cracked on every face except that of Denny Harker.

"Well, to begin. After determining that the Persian submarine was not rigged to explode, and did not carry biohazardous materials or airborne pathogens, my crew disengaged the propulsion machinery and used towsubs to push and pull the vessel into an airdock hanger. After dewatering, we opened the hatches and refreshed the air with standard processed breathing mix.

Sarah Simpson interrupted. "Excuse me, Chuck. Did you test the air before you recycled it?"

Charles nodded. "Tod had already done that, but we collected samples for more detailed analysis. It was ordinary atmospheric air. Denise, would you like to comment on the, uh, abnormalities?"

Denise Meyers temporarily took point in what was already becoming a round-robin discussion. "Prof, do you mind?"

"Not at all. I have outlined a chronology for this inquiry to follow, but strict adherence to sequence is not necessary. Eventually all relevant information must be imparted. We can go out of order as circumstances warrant. Denise Meyers, please proceed."

"Thank you. My laboratory conducted microscopic studies and spectrographic analysis of the reclaimed air. It contained no toxins or harmful contaminants, but we did find some unusual . . . botanical artifacts." Denise paused, puckered her lips, and pinched her eyebrows. "We found pollen which so far we have been unable to identify. A full search of our databank leads us to believe that it is pine pollen, but of a species that we do not have on record."

Quiet inhalations suffused the compartment.

"We're still working on it."

"Thank you, Denise. Charles?"

Charles cleared his throat. "Yes, well, as I was saying, after we airdocked the submarine and while the air was being refreshed, we examined the exterior of the hull. In particular we concentrated on examining the holes that caused the flooding. These holes have a curious pathology. Here is a close up."

He tapped several keys on the keyboard in front of him. Everyone's screen showed the image he selected.

"Each hole measures approximately one-quarter inch across. The diameter cannot be measured with precision because the perimeter is distorted and asymmetrical. As we zoom in – " He keyed for enlargement of the image. " – you can see the minute bloblike protrusions and indentations that deform the circumference. This gives the appearance of direct contact with a source of intense heat, say, that produced by an oxyacetylene torch or the disintegrating rod of an exothermic burning tool. At least, that was our initial interpretation."

"Pardon me for interrupting, Charles." Prof wet his lips with his tongue. "Is this one of the holes that Tod Mallory patched?"

"Yes, it is. We removed the patch resin with a chemical reducing agent. The agent did not affect the steel."

"I understand."

Charles used a computer generated pointer so that everyone could see what he was indicating on his screen. "Notice that there are no scorch marks surrounding the hole. The metal surface is completely unaffected, both inside and out. Pressure hull steel is half an inch thick. To burn through that much steel would require high heat for long duration – say, thousands of degrees for several seconds. Waste heat should have singed and darkened nearby surfaces. While it is true that water acts as a heat sink, water can dissipate some heat but not all of it.

"Acids can dissolve metal without generating great quantities of heat. But acids are diluted in water. Furthermore, acids take a long time to dissolve even thin sheets of base metal, much less hull plate steel.

"Laser beams can burn through metal in a vacuum or in a thin gaseous medium such as the atmosphere, but the energy is absorbed by water long before the kindling temperature of steel is reached. Many of the holes were located below the waterline.

"As Tod noticed when he patched these holes, each one was attended by a commensurate hole in the outer skin. The implication is that whatever mechanism was used to make the holes in the pressure hull was not in direct contact with the metal, but was generated at a distance – at the very least, from the distance of the outer skin. This led us to speculate that a boring tool was used. Even so, we still have the same problem of waste heat dissipation, because boring generates heat by means of friction. Furthermore, drill bits do not leave a ragged edge such as we have here. Not only that, but boring takes time. We can't imagine a situation in which a submarine stayed immobile while an exterior agency drilled holes through its hull."

Lisa raised her hand like a student attracting the attention of a teacher. "I know this sounds farfetched, but is it possible that some species of marine organism bored the holes?"

Charles smirked, but it was not a smirk of derision. "I have to admit that after reading the transcription of your, uh, adventure, I entertained the same notion myself. It's easy to imagine a swarm of starfish crawling over the hull and disgorging stomach acid that dissolved the metal. That could account for the pockmarked appearance of the exterior. But . . . "

Charles paused to take a deep breath. He glanced around the compartment at the eager attendees.

"To complicate matters, we found that partitions and equipment inside the submarine were also pierced. These interior holes were not readily apparent because, obviously, they didn't leak. The interior holes were the same size as the exterior holes. Furthermore, the interior holes were in perfect alignment with the exterior holes."

The overall silence was as audible as a collective gasp would have been.

"In other words, some mysterious force or unknown

mechanism was used to pierce the outer skin, the pressure hull, all interior barriers, and the pressure hull and outer skin on the opposite side. I have no idea what kind of device could have done such a thing."

Chapter 7

Prof leaned back in his seat and let the hubbub proceed until it nearly wore itself out. Finally he called the meeting back to order by gently rapping on the table with his knuckles.

"Thank you . . . Thank you . . . Thank you, Charles . . . " He finally got everyone's attention. "Do you have anything else to report?"

"Not as far as explanations go, no. But I would like to mention that the exit holes were identical to the entrance holes. In fact, we could not distinguish between the two. As far as we were able to determine, the submarine could have been pierced from either direction."

"Thank you, again. Now I would like to ask Meredith Chambers for her report."

No one in Benthocity 3 used titles, degrees, or identifiers of any kind. Augustus Pembroke was called Prof out of respect for his leadership as administrator, not because of his educational attainments, which were numerous.

Chambers was the base doctor, chief surgeon, and when necessary, coroner and medical examiner. "My team conducted autopsies on all three Persian males. A full report has been posted on the electronic bulletin board, except for toxicology, which has not yet been completed. For now I will deliver only the highlights of the examinations as they pertain to the peculiar condition of the bodies and the cause of death.

"All three men were killed by penetration. By that I mean that some force or object invaded the body at one point and exited at another in a straight line. External marks give the appearance of puncture wounds: minimal bleeding, little gross tissue damage, and partial closure from epidermal contraction. In lay terms, the wounds resemble deep pin pricks, or perhaps ice-pick stabs, but definitely not conventional projectile wounds because the breadth of the holes was less than the smallest caliber projectile.

"There was no deflection from hard tissue or bone as we would expect to result from a projectile, and there was no adjacent tissue shatter damage. There was no cauterization of blood or tissue as we would expect to result from a heat weapon.

"Most of the bleeding was internal. One man must have lost consciousness almost instantly and died within seconds when the penetrator – as I will call the unidentified cause of penetration – passed through the aorta: a gross insult that the system cannot tolerate for very long. This was the man who was found in the bunk."

An image of the man appeared on all the screens. He was shorn of his uniform to expose one of the wounds.

"For reasons that will be explained later, I suspect that he was penetrated elsewhere and was either carried or dragged to the bunk by his companions. There were no blood trails because of the limited external bleeding.

"The other two men survived their penetrating wounds much longer, perhaps for several minutes, perhaps for half an hour. In each case the penetrator did not pass through major arteries. One man was penetrated through the right lung, the other through the lower abdomen. These wounds would have been painful enough to distract them from their occupation."

Ever inquisitive Sarah Simpson asked, "Merry, have you ever seen wounds like these before?"

"Never. Nor have I found anything like it in the medical references. I can't even hazard a guess. Although, I suppose it has occurred to everyone that the same mechanism that penetrated the submarine's hull also penetrated the men inside. There is strong evidence that the man in the port command seat was penetrated where he sat. Charles?"

"Yes, that's my belief. Tod moved the bodies because they were leaning against the controls, so we

can't be absolutely certain, but one of the hole align-
ments enters (or exits) the hull above the control room,
passes through the port seatback and the lower portion
of the control panel, and through the bilge. It's as if the
penetrator beam – or whatever it was – went right
through the submarine and everything that was in its
path."

"That's why I deduced that the man in the bunk
was penetrated elsewhere. There were no hull penetra-
tions around the bunk."

"Thank you, Charles, Meredith." Prof acknowledged
their contributions with a nod of the head.

"Now, Denny Harker will tell us what his team sal-
vaged from the submarine's data banks. Denny?"

Harker took a deep breath and puffed up his chest.
Even in his padded garment he looked thin and lithe, if
not gaunt. "I tried to download the Yuper mainframe.
Everything was encrypted, and different ciphers were
used for different components. Some of the information
was permanently destroyed by the penetrator ray, er,
that is, whatever it was that went through the submarine and made those holes. Still, there are billions of
bits of data that were not destroyed and which we
already have decryption codes for from Grand Intelligence. I'm still decoding, and will be for quite a while.

"A lot of the data has to do with operational instructions for the submarine. That's interesting, but not
really useful. To us. The tracknav unit was working,
but because a lot of the sensor heads were smashed or
broken off, there are gaps in the plot that we can't piece
together. I did find that at one point the submarine
exceeded its designed operational depth – although not
its crush depth – for a *Scheherazade*-class submarine.
Oh, by the way, its name is the *Serendib*, which figures
somehow in the legend about Sinbad the Sailor. Anyway, its design depth is one thousand feet, which is
nowhere near the design depth of our tactical subs – "

"Denny, will you please keep focused on relevant
information?"

"Sure, Prof. Okay. Anyway, a lot of the mainframe

chips were damaged by, uh, penetrators. I don't know exactly where this sub had been before it came out of the Blue Hole. There is some satellite tracking data from when it was on the surface, but that was several weeks ago. At that time it was on the other side of the continent. Not diametrically on the other side, but in the Weddell Sea. We have no information on when it circumnavigated the continent, not even from our own tracking systems, which is a real puzzler. If it had traveled on the surface, our satellites should have spotted it visually. Under water, we have remote sonar pickups that should have detected its cavitation signature as soon as it entered the AEZ."

Harker shrugged. "I believe it was either on a reconnaissance mission in advance of a major attack against the Benthocities, or it was on a solo search and destroy mission, maybe a suicide mission. It could be – "

Prof cut him short. "Let us stick with the facts for now, and withhold speculation until we have more information. Please tell us about the *Serendib's* armament and weapons systems."

Harker was flustered at the interruption. He wore his discomfiture on his face. "Yes, well, I looked over all the – "

"Did you do this alone?"

"Well, uh, no. I had some help – "

"So this was a team effort?"

"Uh, yes, to a degree. I organized the inspection and took charge of everything. What I discovered was that some of the small arms were missing from their racks. Since this is an assault sub, and none of the marines were on board, I'm guessing that a landing party was put ashore somewhere – "

"Land bases have been alerted to that possibility."

" – Two reserve torps were missing from their racks. This suggests that two torps were fired and reloaded, which might account for the disappearance of surface vessels off the Falkland Islands. Worst of all, one nuclear warhead has been removed from its missile. I didn't find it anywhere on board. The Yupers must be carrying it over the ice, maybe on a sled – "

"To get back to the computer data, you said that you had downloaded and decrypted some of the files. Can you elucidate on what you learned from the decrypts?"

"Well, I didn't actually do the decryption personally. I had some help from the Communications Department – "

Prof interrupted. "Sarah Simpson, as head of the Communications Department, would you care to tell us about what you have ascertained with regard to coded data?"

Harker exhaled sharply and twisted in his seat like a chastised child.

"Of course, Prof. To recapitulate from where Denny left off – " Here she was unable to conceal a barely noticeable smirk – "Some of the *Serendib's* mainframe chips were damaged, and most of the others were encrypted, in both cases limiting the amount of data that my team was able to recover. The downloaded data are being decrypted, but decryption will take some time yet, even though Grand Intelligence had supplied us with codes for some of the file encryptions.

"Our first priority is to separate operational data from mission data: that is, data that pertain to physically operating the submarine from data that pertain to the submarine's mission in Antarctic waters. To use the human brain as an analogy, this is equivalent to separating involuntary mechanisms, such as those that regulate the heartbeat and the release of hormones and enzymes, from facts that a person has learned during his lifetime. As Denny suggested, we really don't need to know how to operate the submarine. At least, not at this time.

"Mission data are the most difficult to decrypt because Grand Intelligence doesn't have codes for many of those files. As you all know, GI constantly intercepts and decodes transmitted messages. Spies in Persia smuggle codes out of the UPR whenever possible. Our cooperation with GI is hampered by our communication isolation, to keep the UPR from discovering our location. We have dispatched a fast courier sub with all our downloaded data. When it reaches a position that cannot be traced back to base, it will deploy a surface transponder to transmit the data via uplink to a satellite. The sub will keep moving submerged, so that Persian offensive systems can't locate it and attack it. Then the sub will make periodic checks from randomly chosen locations in order to listen for advices from GI.

"However," Sarah paused not for dramatic effect, but so she could press a sequence of keystrokes and place an image on everyone's screen. "However, we have retrieved some hardcopy data that you will find particularly interesting. This first picture shows a stowage locker in which we found a brass container that is fashioned in the shape of an ancient Persian oil lamp." Sarah smiled peevishly. "For reasons that will soon become apparent, we're calling it Aladdin's magic lamp."

Several people snickered at the allusion.

"I was the first to find it," Harker interjected.

Sarah nodded in agreement. "Before I continue, I would like Harris to give us his findings about the material composition."

For the record, Prof pronounced, "Harris Copeland, head of our chemical lab."

"Yes, of course." Harris nervously shuffled his hands over his lap. He glanced around the compartment but was too shy to make eye contact with anyone. "We subjected this so-called lamp to various standard chemical analyses. We found it to be made of an extremely high quality grade of brass, consisting of 69 percent copper and 31 percent zinc, with absolutely no impurities of any kind."

He looked as if he had more to say, but refrained from doing so.

"Tell us about the embedded dirt, Harris."

"Yes, of course. The lamp appeared to have been buried for quite some time. The top and sides had been polished, but grains of sand and particles of soil were found clinging to the under side of the base." He paused to gather his thoughts. "I don't want to sound pedantic . . . "

Prof spread out hands. "Please lay the groundwork."

Harris's head bobbed wildly. "Yes, yes, of course. Well, most people think of sand as pure silica, or silicon dioxide, which is a crystalline compound that is the basis of many minerals such as quartz and chert. If silica is melted and cooled rapidly, it fails to crystallize, and becomes what is commonly called glass. Silica, and the glass that is made from it, is seldom found in pure form. It generally contains mineral intrusions that vary from locale to locale.

"Some of these impurities may be other minerals, and some may be particles of diatomaceous earth: sediment that consists of the fossilized remains of hard-shelled algae known as diatoms. The origin of sand and diatomaceous earth can be established with a fair degree of accuracy by their constituents.

"Soil is a highly complex ecosystem of minerals, nutrients, and an incredibly vast variety of biological ingredients, all of which react chemically in different ways in accordance with their concentration and placement within the matrix. Soil can be traced to its geographic origin even easier and with greater precision than sand. Long story short, all these samples originated in the same region: the land that surrounds the Persian Gulf."

Sarah tried to calm down the chatter. "Let me connect the dots by saying that, according to recent intelligence reports, the lamp appears to have been excavated from a newly discovered archaeological site in the desert north of Bandar-e-Abbas. It is only one of a number of artifacts that are known to have been unearthed in a cave that until recently was closed by an ancient rock fall."

The chatter continued.

Tod and Lisa looked at one another past Prof. They were so in tune with each other that their facial expressions served as means of silent communication. They often thought along the identical wavelength. Tod raised his eyebrows for Lisa to take the lead.

She asked, "So how did they remove the rock that covered the entrance of the cave? Whisper 'Open, Sesame'?"

Chapter 8

Despite the significance of the evidence, almost everyone cracked a smile at Lisa's allegorical reference. Denny Harker fumed.

Sarah Simpson's smile was the broadest. "They used explosives rather than incantations, Lisa, but your symbolism is well taken."

Lisa winked at Tod. Tod grinned back at her.

"To get back on a more serious track . . . "

Prof smiled and spread his hands again. "There is nothing wrong with a little levity to awaken the sleepyheads."

Of sleepyheads there was none.

"Okay then. To make one point abundantly clear, Harris neglected to mention that the lamp is made of brass of such purity that it would be difficult to produce today, much less thousands of years ago. Unless the ancient Persians possessed methods of metalsmithing that have been forgotten over the centuries – or millenia. Which brings us to another lost art, this one an incredible archaeological anomaly."

Sarah put another picture on the screen. "This is a thin sheet of metal that is known as foil. As you know, silver foil is used as a reflective backing on mirrors. Aluminum foil is used to wrap food products in order to maintain freshness. This foil is made of gold. Almost pure gold. It was found pressed between two thin boards that kept the foil flat and prevented it from getting bent or crinkled. Harris?"

"Uh, yes, of course. Obviously we don't have any stratigraphic data. Neither do we have enough of a baseline to utilize the dendrochronology technique. So we subjected samples of wood to various dating processes: radiocarbon, using both the scintillation method and accelerator mass spectrometry, and amino acid racemization. We arrived at an approximate age of eight to ten thousand years before present. Give or take a thousand years."

Sarah waited for the usual clamor to die down before proceeding. "Good work, Harris."

Harris shrugged.

"We found seven foils inside the lamplike container. Each one was protected by two boards. Now, if you look closely at this enlargement. . . . First I am showing you the reverse side of the foil, which is blank, so you can observe the smooth quality of the facing. This foil is thin enough that it qualifies as leaf, which is commonly used for gilding. Using a micrometer, Harris measured the thickness at about one-thousandth of an inch. With modern technology, this foil is easily fabricated using the rolling method or the continuous casting method, but thousands of years ago the only way to make foil was by pounding metal between two flat surfaces. To achieve this degree of smoothness requires equally smooth surfaces on the pressing medium. Obviously these foils were not pressed between wood, or striations in the grain would have been impressed upon the foil.

"Now this picture . . . is the obverse, or front, of the foil. What at casual glance appears to be texture is, upon close inspection, shown to be inscription." Sarah selected another picture. "In this closer enlargement you will notice the resemblance of the calligraphy to Farsi and Old Persian. . . . I'm sorry. I'm being presumptuous. Probably very few of you can make that distinction. As you know, by the nature of our job, it is a prerequisite for those of us in Communications to speak, read, and write both Farsi and Old Persian. Otherwise we would not be able to decrypt their messages. Anyway, my point is that this script is neither Farsi nor Old Persian. So far, we have been unable to translate what is written on this foil.

Tod interjected. "Sarah, I'm one of those who can't tell the difference between Farsi and Old Persian. It's all Greek to me." Most people grimaced in acknowledgment of the standard joke. "All those whirls and loops look pretty much the same. So, are you saying that this is a new kind of code?"

Sarah smiled benignly. "It's not a code. It's a language."

The compartment was so quiet that the faint hiss made by the air circulator was annoyingly loud.

"Then I'm confused. Very confused. I can understand why the Persians would create a new language that we can't read, but why would they etch it on gold foil, place the foil between boards made of antique wood, then put the packaged foil into an archaeological relic? It doesn't make sense."

"Harris, would you mind talking about the gold?"

"Yes, of course." Harris fidgeted in his seat. "We used the thermoluminescence dating process to obtain the age of the gold. The radiation dose that has accumulated since the gold was last heated and formed into leaves yields the same figure that we obtained for the age of the wood."

Sarah completed the logical deduction. "In other words, the gold foil and the boards are contemporary with each other. If Prof will permit me to step out of the bounds of verifiable fact for a moment . . . "

Prof made a single nod of the head. He had already read the departmental reports, so he knew where the discussion was going.

" . . . This is not a *new* language. It's an *archaic* language. And I believe it's a language that predates Old Persian by several thousand years."

There was a collective gasp of astonishment around the table – a gasp that pervaded every occupied compartment in Benthocity 3.

"So . . . " Tod scratched his ear. He did not know quite what to make of Sarah's confusing dissertation. "What is your interpretation of this – antediluvian language?"

"That's an excellent description in light of the apparent age of the artifacts. According to circumstantial evidence, it's a language that was used before the existence of Babylonia, before the existence of Sumeria, even before the existence of Mesopotamia. Perhaps it is the first language from which all other languages evolved."

This revelation came as a shock, as the buzz and facial contortions demonstrated.

Prof waited for a minute before assuming his job as moderator, and rapped on the table with hairy knuckles. "People. People."

Sarah once again took the torch. "As everyone knows, archaeology is not an exact science. Some might argue that archaeology is not a science at all, but rather a crude method of interpretation. Archaeology is bereft of a laboratory in which experiments can be controlled, repeated, and tested for accuracy and redundancy. Instead, archaeology is a discipline of reasoned conjectures that are held as fact until other conjectures appear to hold greater validity, or are accepted by a majority of archaeologists. What starts as an unorthodox view, or personal opinion, is generally opposed vigorously until the opposition is overwhelmed by rhetoric. In a sense, archaeology is much like a democracy, in that the majority rules."

Sarah smiled at her audience. "I would never be able to get away with such statements if we had any archaeologists on the base." She waited for the gratuitous guffaws to abate. "Anyway, I would like to point out that it takes an extremely fine instrument to cut or etch lines on foil without puncturing the material. This gold leaf is flawless."

Tod said, "Sarah, have you been able to read or decipher any of this language?"

"No. It's far too different from anything we've ever encountered. Although some of the script resembles other Persian languages, the resemblance is superficial. Lacking the equivalent of a Rosetta Stone, I doubt that we will ever be able to translate what is inscribed on these foils."

Tod nodded slowly, his eyebrows pinched. "Okay, so we can't translate it – *you* can't translate it. And I presume that Grand Intelligence won't be able to translate it – "

"Not even with the most advanced decryption programs and the most highly skilled cryptanalysts in the world. We need a key, a codebook, a starting point that we don't have. Even with the Rosetta Stone, it took scholars more than twenty years to translate Egyptian hieroglyphics from their Greek analogue. Perhaps the Persians have something in their history that has enabled them translate the inscriptions. We don't know.

"But the overriding question is: why was a Persian warship carrying priceless antiquities on a military mission to the Antarctic?" She shrugged. "You would think that such an important piece of their cultural heritage would be kept in a vault in a national museum." She shrugged again.

"Well, now for my denouement. I have saved the best, or the most perplexing, for last." Sarah's fingers drifted across her keyboard. "This picture is an overview showing all seven foils. Each foil measures about four inches in width by eight inches in height. That's assuming that we have the correct orientation for the script. You will notice that the etching on each foil is divided into two halves. The top half is etched with script; the bottom half is etched with convoluted lines that either meander aimlessly or that enclose amorphous plane figures.

"In cryptanalysis we sometimes learn as much from pictures as we do from text. So we studied the geometric figures and ran constructs through outline recognition software, both individually and in groups, looking for recognizable patterns or graphic interpretations. So far we have been stumped by all but one."

Sarah zoomed in on the bottom half of an individual foil. The large central figure resembled the silhouette of an amoeba gone wild. Surrounding the central figure were small plane figures in a variety of shapes. Some were long and jagged; others were nearly circular, like droplets of ink that had been dropped from a height.

"Does this look familiar to anyone?"

Sarah looked across the table at Prof. He nodded once but kept his own council, not wanting to weaken the dramatic effect of the climax.

"Think hard, people."

Eyebrows pinched and foreheads wrinkled in silent concentration.

"Reason abstractly."

Lips pursed. Heads shook slowly.

"It's something that you've all seen. You just don't remember it in this form."

The tension in the compartment was almost palpable.

Suddenly Lisa gasped and flung her hand to her mouth. She looked up from her screen and stared goggle-eyed at Sarah.

"Yes, Lisa, you're young enough to have studied this in school not too long ago."

"It's – It looks like – It reminds me of – a map of the way Antarctica would appear without the snow and ice and glaciers."

"Bravo!" Sarah glanced around the room. "Don't feel bad, people. None of us in Communications figured it out either. And it took the computer nearly an hour to recognize the continental perimeter."

Prof showed two rows of uneven teeth. "Perhaps Lisa should study cryptanalysis instead of submersible vessel design and construction."

"We can always use someone with nonobjective ability."

Once Lisa made the conceptual breakthrough, others were able to recast their mindset so they could picture the scribed outline for what it represented.

"But how – " Lisa kept looking back and forth between Sarah and her computer screen. "How could a pre-Mesopotamian civilization know about Antarctica? And how could they know what it looked like under the ice?"

Sarah humphed. "I wish I knew."

"The detail is astonishing," Denise announced.

"Like a rough geological survey map without topographical features," Charles noted.

"Here's a high-resolution thermal image that was generated by one of our science satellites." Sarah grabbed the thermal image with her cursor, and dragged it on top of the outline that was scribed on the gold foil. "I've pre-adjusted the scale."

Lisa gasped. "It's a perfect match."

"Line for line, curve for curve," said Meredith.

"Even the surrounding islands are the right size and shape, and in the right position and orientation," added Denise.

People oohed and ahed.

"But – what's that squiggly line that passes South Georgia and the South Orkney Islands, then terminates in the Weddell Sea, uh, where the Ronne Ice Shelf should be?"

"Nice going, Tod." Sarah waited until she had everyone's attention before elucidating. "That is the track that we believe the *Serendib* was following."

Denise's jaw dropped. "Is this a – treasure map?"

Sarah shrugged. "I would be going too far beyond verifiable fact if I were to make such a conjecture. But you can draw your own conclusions."

Tod's head was bobbing slowly. "Do you think the lines and geometric patterns on the other foils represent tracks and landmasses?"

"That's a good inference in my opinion."

"And the six other foils are similar in design?" Tod stated it as a question but intended it as an observation.

"Yes, that's correct."

Tod didn't know whether to smile or frown. He did both. "Then they aren't maps. The inscriptions are either sailing directions, or legends that explain the graphics. The gold foils are ancient nautical charts of the seven voyages of Sinbad."

Chapter 9

Benthocity 3 was an underwater beehive of activity.

To the uninformed eye, this activity held the stark appearance of disorder. Overall purpose and productivity were not expressly apparent. While some people worked furiously at computer consoles, others were in constant motion between domes on a variety of tasks.

Organizing this activity and coordinating purpose was a fulltime job for Professor Pembroke. His catnaps became shorter and more infrequent as the general workload intensified. Helping him in his multitudinous labors were Tod and Lisa, both of whom felt way out of their depth in handling administrative chores.

Prof scratched the skin beneath his scraggly beard. "The job of a scientist or engineer is not only to conduct research in the laboratory, on the drawing board, or in the field, but to follow that research with practical application. You were sent here to learn every aspect of science and engineering. Assisting me is providing you with an appreciation of the true role of scientific method and design criteria."

Lisa was not mollified by Prof's philosophical notions. "But I've never done this kind of work before."

"And you never operated a submersible by yourself – until you went on your first solo mission."

"That was different. I had a number of prior missions with an instructor by my side in case I miscalculated speed or lost depth control."

Prof splayed his palms upward. "Consider this as on-the-job training with me as your instructor."

"But I haven't had any courses in administration."

"There *are* no courses in administration. It is a facility that you learn by doing. You are doing a fine job – both of you."

Tod humphed. "I wish I had your confidence."

"Confidence is a function of learning from mistakes. I have made my fair share of mistakes, and I have learned not only how to avoid them in the future, but how to correct mistakes after I make them. It is all part of the process."

Tod grimaced in his casual good-natured fashion. "Okay, but if I start to do something wrong, stop me before I make a complete fool of myself."

"But do let him make a partial fool of himself." Lisa grinned broadly at Tod. "It's part of the learning process."

Tod grimaced and humphed.

The hatch to Prof's office cubicle burst open. Denny Harker glowered as he swept into the crowded compartment. He violated protocol by neglecting to close and seal the hatch. "What's this I hear about the kids taking out the *Benthic Explorer*?"

Prof looked up at Harker's outburst, his eyebrows raised in an attitude of calm. "That depends upon what you have heard."

"I heard that these two – " Harker sneered at Lisa and Tod. " – trainees, were planning on taking the *Benthic Explorer* back to BH-14."

"That is not entirely correct." Prof shifted easily in his seat. "The *Benthic Explorer* has never been to BH-14, so it cannot go *back* there."

"You know what I mean."

"I know only what you said."

"Then let me say *this* in no uncertain terms. The *Benthic Explorer* is a sophisticated and complicated deep-water submersible that requires an experienced pilot to operate. The control surfaces perform differently from the *Reef Cruiser*, and the control mechanisms are difficult to handle without extensive training and practical seamanship. You can't turn over a vessel like that to a couple of – of – apprentices who are still wet behind the ears."

"Your observations are duly noted."

"Furthermore, I won't authorize dispatch of the *Benthic Explorer* under any circumstances. I haven't even taken it out for sea trials yet, other than to drive it around the base a couple of times to get the feel of it."

"I would think that its passage from the States would constitute a fair sea trial. After all, it traveled halfway around the world to get here. Exploration of a Blue Hole will be an excellent test of its maneuvering capabilities."

"The delivery pilot never took it down to depth. It's rated for fifteen thousand feet, and she didn't exceed two *hundred* feet."

"BH-14 is at least five hundred feet deep. Such a descent will add another increment to its depth testing, as well as provide an occasion to determine its turning radius and buoyancy capability."

"The *Benthic Explorer* can spin on a point and change depth in one-inch increments with perfect hovering stability. It can go to any depth that the Yuper submarine went. But it can only do these things in expert hands. Right now, I'm the only man on base who can pilot the thing with any degree of competence."

"Very well. I accept your offer to volunteer."

Harker was momentarily struck speechless. His face was a picture of astonishment. He sputtered, "I didn't – "

"Of course I cannot force you to go. Perhaps the delivery pilot can undertake this potentially perilous mission." Prof was well aware that the delivery pilot had already returned to the shipbuilder's yard. "Do you think that she has any qualms about facing imminent danger?"

Harker sputtered again. "She's gone. And danger isn't the issue. The *Benthic Explorer* has kinks and quirks that I need to work out – "

"Then this mission constitutes the supreme opportunity to learn the submersible's eccentric characteristics before taking it to its extreme design depth."

"Yes, but – but – "

"You *are* the best person for the job, are you not?"

"Yes, but – "

"Yes but what? Are you or are you not the best person for the job?"

"I am, but – but I can't go traipsing all over Antarctica on a senseless science mission when there may be Yupers at our hatches."

"Oh, come now, Denny. Surely you exaggerate the threat of attack. All indications from local intelligence concur that the Persian submarine had military objectives that did not concern this base or any other scientific outpost; that it was off course, lost, and out of control; and that it ran afoul of some as-yet unexplained phenomenon that is imperative for us to investigate. I would be derelict in my duties as Chief Administrator and Science Advisor if I ignored the enormous potential of the discovery that the Persians have made, and that Tod and Lisa have brought to our attention."

"But the base must be protected – "

"This base is surrounded by every available submersible that is armed with weapons of offense. Along with its defensive measures, Benthocity 3 is secure from enemy assault. There is no reason not to pursue a scientific research mission that lies within the perimeter of our secure area of operations. Our function here is not to wage war against Persia, but to search for natural resources."

"But the *Benthic Explorer* is indefensible. It – "

"Believe me, Denny, I understand the military mindset of a trained combatant like you. I fully appreciate that your prime directive is the defense of this base and the protection of its submersibles. Your conduct in those regards is admirable. Now that you have tightened security to its highest level, your subordinates can assume control for the duration of your absence.

"We have many questions that must be answered. What were the Persians doing in BH-14? How did they get there? Does BH-14 connect to another Blue Hole by means of a navigable tunnel? If so, this might enable the Persians to breach our outer perimeter undetected. What is the source of the penetrating force that pierced the hull of the Persian submarine? What happened to the rest of the occupants? These are matters not only of scientific importance, but of military urgency. This is a two-pronged mission of the highest priority."

Harker ran thin fingers through close-cropped blond hair. "I hadn't – I hadn't considered the military aspect."

"Of course. You have been consumed by your priority to establish an impregnable defense for this base. I understand that."

Harker breathed deeply. He jerked a thumb in the direction of Tod and Lisa. "But why them? And why the *Benthic Explorer*? Why not the *Reef Cruiser*, and someone more experienced to pilot it?"

"I did not intend for them to go unsupervised. I chose the *Benthic Explorer* not because of its depth capability, but because of the thickness of the hull that allows it to reach extreme depth, in the surmise that the penetrating force that pierced the hull of the Persian submarine may not be able to pierce the hull of the *Benthic Explorer*. Additionally, the *Benthic Explorer's* advanced self-sealing mechanisms that are inherent in its double-hull construction will provide another measure of safety."

Harker ruminated.

"In my estimation, the potential for discovery outweighs the risk of the venture."

Harker glared sullenly at Tod and Lisa. "I'm a marine, not a babysitter."

"Another individual will be assigned as supervising science officer and expedition leader. I would like to have you as the pilot."

Harker breathed deeply again. "I'll think about it." He turned on his heel and took one step that placed him in the hatchway. Looking over his shoulder at Tod and Lisa, he said gruffly, "Don't forget to bring a magic genie." Then he strode out of the compartment. He sealed the hatch behind him.

Both Tod and Lisa sighed in evident relief at his departure.

A smile spread slowly across Prof's jagged features. "There is your first lesson in personnel administration. Notice that I did not pull rank on him. I appealed to his ego."

Lisa scowled. "That's great, Prof. Really great. Now we've got to be cooped up with macho man in the hull of a submersible. I don't mind being supervised, but couldn't you find someone who's a little more amiable?"

"Granted that Denny has an abrasive personality, but he *is* the most skilled pilot on the base. This mission is not one for half measures. In case of dire straits, the person you will want at the helm is the one with the greatest amount of experience."

Tod humphed. "I follow your logic, but I'd rather have the second best pilot at the helm. Denny will harass us to no end. He enjoys it. Without a moderator – "

There were two light taps on the hatch. The oversized hand wheel spun, the hatch opened, and Sarah Simpson slipped into the compartment. She closed and sealed the hatch behind her. She stared at Tod and Lisa. "Why the pouty faces?" When neither Tod nor Lisa answered right away, she glanced at Prof. "Have you been giving them the glum treatment?"

Prof grinned and splayed his hands palms upward. "Denny just volunteered to pilot the *Benthic Explorer.*"

"He didn't volunteer. You volunteered him with suave psychological doubletalk." Lisa stabbed an index finger in Prof's direction. "This man is a menace. Beneath that ugly face lies a heart of evil."

Prof did not defend himself. "You need a lesson in anatomy. The heart is not located – "

Lisa was only half serious. "I know where the heart is, and that isn't the point. The point is – "

Tod interrupted. "The point is that . . . Hey, wait a minute. He didn't volunteer. He only said that he would think about it."

Prof raised bushy eyebrows at Sarah. "He volunteered. He simply does not realize it yet." He changed the subject abruptly. "What progress have you made with the translations?"

Sarah shrugged. She sat on the corner of the desk and laid down a sheaf of papers. "I'd say very little but that would be an exaggeration. I'm afraid that we just don't have enough background material to go on." She addressed everyone. "Not to make excuses, but the purview of my group is to intercept and decipher coded transmissions. We integrate with Grand Intelligence whenever the Persians change their codes. So far we've been fairly successful. By 'we' I mean Grand Intelligence. My personal group has helped to a slight degree.

"I'm quite proud of one of our coups. We took a lesson from World War Two. When American code breakers couldn't figure out which Japanese code words referred to which American bases, they transmitted a fake message in which they stated that Midway Island was running out of water. The Japanese intercepted the message and forwarded it to Tokyo in naval code. The American code breakers intercepted the Japanese message, most of which they were able to decrypt. The message referred to an American base that was running out of water. Thus the code breakers learned the code word for Midway.

"My group tried a similar trick by remote transmitting a fictitious emergency message in the clear, in which we informed the Pentagon about a bulkhead breach in Benthocity 3, and the fatalities that resulted from flooding. The Persians intercepted the message and transmitted it in code to Baghdad. Now we know their code word for Benthocity. They use the word followed by numbers to distinguish one base from another, the same as we do."

Sarah brushed an errant hair off her forehead. "Anyway, I'm getting rather far afield. My point is that breaking codes is an ongoing process. We may break part of a code but not be able to read an entire message. Some messages we cannot intercept because they are transmitted via focused beams to a communication satellite, which retransmits them to designated Earth stations via focused beam. Sometimes atmospheric interference corrupts part of a high-speed blip message. And so on, and so on. There are always problems, but there are not always solutions.

"The problem we face with the gold foil script is far more complicated. Did you know that only three percent of the ancient Mayan language has been translated? And there's no guarantee that the ideographs that *were* translated were interpreted correctly. Yet scholars have been studying Mayan hieroglyphics for more than a century. There exists a wealth of ideographic symbols on the walls of ziggurats, on stones, on artifacts – but no key to relate them to any other language. Even with modern computers that operate at nearly the speed of light, and software applications that contain billions of bits of data, no one has made any progress in the last fifty years.

"You might think that the language on the gold foil could be compared to Old Persian with some moderate degree of success. True, we have found some similarities between the antediluvian script and Old Persian cuneiform script – even with the phonetic characters and logograms of modern Farsi – but when we correlate those similarities we generate nothing but gibberish. Some of the script *looks* the same, but it doesn't *mean* the same.

"Literal translations from one language to another generally yield somewhat garbled connotations, if not outright garbage. That's because human language is not just a string of words, each with a unique definition, but a complex arrangement of grammar, syntax, idioms, and multiple definitions. Did you know that the word 'run' has more than one hundred fifty meanings? It is used as a transitive verb, an intransitive verb, a verbal phrase, a noun, and an adjective. The intended meaning can be understood only by the context in which the word is used. A jogger runs, a vehicle runs, a machine runs, a stream runs, solder runs, dye runs, and a nose runs, but all in different ways. Without multiple definitions there would be no such thing as a pun. Such are the foibles of linguistics.

"Now, to give you some idea of the semantic issues that we're up against, let me cite some examples of problems that were encountered in early computerized translation programs – keeping in mind that the languages to be translated were perfectly understood, so that the translations could be compared by human analogues for accuracy. Or inaccuracy, as the case was more often. Programs were tested by having them translate English into Russian, then translate the result back into English.

"The phrase 'like a bat out of hell' came back as 'like a winged mouse from the cave.' The *Bible* verse 'the spirit is willing but the flesh is weak' came back as 'the wine is agreeable but the meat has spoiled.' My personal favorite is the engineering term 'hydraulic ram;' it came back as 'water sheep.' Now imagine that we don't even know the meaning of what we're starting with, and you can begin to understand some of the complications of translating the gold foil script."

Sarah apologized. "I didn't mean to babble – if you will pardon a pun on the biblical Tower of Babel."

"Quite all right, Sarah. Quite all right." Prof scratched his face. "I called you here precisely so we could all benefit from your insights."

Tod reversed his crossed legs. "Have you been able to match any of the other maps or charts."

"I'm afraid not. We believe that the drawings on the foils might not represent only geographical features, but also political borders. That could explain the lines that are drawn within the outline of the Antarctic continent."

Tod nodded. "You know I wasn't serious about the seven voyages of Sinbad."

Sarah smiled and shook her head. "It's as good a guess as any. Persian artifacts on a Persian submarine would naturally lead to Persian allusions." She pulled a memory chip out of a hip pocket of her one-piece thermal garment. "I don't know what you might encounter on this mission, so I took the precaution of loading all the data that we retrieved from the *Serendib* on this chip. If you meet any more Persians – perhaps the missing occupants – the information might come in handy."

She placed the chip on the desktop. "I've also loaded everything we have on Farsi and Old Persian: dictionaries, encyclopedias, usage and grammar texts, and so on. And – " She looked hard at Prof as she produced another chip from a different hip pocket. " – this chip contains literally every bit of decryption software that we possess. If it were to fall into enemy hands . . . " She didn't need to complete the sentence.

"In addition to being password protected, the code-breaking chip is programmed with a transfer prevention protocol. The transcriber that you will take with you is keyed to *read* the data but they cannot be transferred to the computer on the *Benthic Explorer* – or to any other computer for that matter. Each time you access the program, you must activate it by tapping the transcriber's scroll button in a coding sequence of taps and spaces: for example, one tap, space, two taps, space, three taps – simple but effective and not intuitive for someone who is not conversant with tap codes. The program times out after five minutes of disuse.

"This – " Sarah removed a digital readout disk from a breast pocket. It was smaller than a coin. " – is a miniature random number sequencer. It can be concealed but it must be within range of the chip in order to register the transmission – say, five to six feet. If the transcriber is removed from your person or is taken out of range of the sequencer, the program cannot be activated. The four-digit number changes every sixty seconds. The current code number must be tapped on the transcriber to unlock the numerical coding program, whose integers I have printed for you. It's what we call a double code input. If the wrong number sequence is input, the program automatically locks up until the next sequence appears. As an added safeguard, when not in use, keep the chip stowed in this security device."

She pulled a flat, square electronic plug-in capsule out of her other breast pocket. She inserted the decoding chip into the capsule. She pressed a rectangular button on the side of the device. "I have just activated the self-destruct mechanism. To release the chip, you must tap this button in accordance with the *reverse* of the numbers that are displayed on the sequencer. If you make a mistake, or try to forcibly remove the chip from the security device, a heating element ignites and melts the chip. Don't worry – it won't explode and blow off your hand."

She indicated the sheaf of papers. "The instructions are all there. Read them, memorize them, destroy them."

Prof picked up the sheaf. "These papers will not leave this compartment unshredded."

Tod said, "Thanks, Sarah."

"Thanks for the help."

"Now, no more pouty faces." Sarah departed quietly.

For several seconds, the only audible sound in the compartment was the soft hush of the circulator pushing air through the vents.

Prof shuffled the papers in his hands, glancing at each sheet for the barest moment before moving on to the next. In those brief glances he read, processed, and memorized the coding instructions. "After taking care of a few more minor details, I should think that we will be ready to depart."

Lisa asked, "Have you decided on a mission control officer?"

"Someone with a strong enough personality to keep Denny in his place?" Tod added.

"Quite assuredly." Prof pursed his lips in an expression that could be interpreted as a grin. "Rank does have its privileges. This allows me to select the individual I deem to be best suited for the task. I would not miss this opportunity for the world. Therefore I have nominated myself for the position, and I have accepted the nomination."

Part Two

In Xanadu did Kubla Khan
A stately pleasure-dome decree
Where Alph, the sacred river, ran
Through caverns measureless to man
Down to a sunless sea.

Kubla Khan, by Samuel Taylor Coleridge

Chapter 10

In a world in which most coral reefs were either dead or dying as a result of global warming and loss of the ozone layer, Blue Holes harbored the last refuge for shallow-water organisms that were not directly dependant upon sunlight for their survival. Filter feeders could live anywhere that had a strong reversing flow that enabled them to siphon sufficient nutrients from passing water.

Melting polar ice caps added to the problem of survival for light-dependant organisms. Light penetrated the top layers of the ocean the same as it had always penetrated, but due to the rising sea level, the additional height of the water column meant that more sunlight was absorbed before it reached the seabed where sessile organisms, which required solar energy for metabolic purposes, had their niche.

Plankton blooms were a phenomenon of the past. "Happy as a clam" was an outdated expression. The world's oceans were in dire straits. Nature was out of balance.

Submersibles were the seven league boots that enabled humanity to stride across the briny deep in a desperate search for life-sustaining resources that occupied Davy Jones's locker. So far, no one had located the key to open that locker.

These thoughts passed idly through Tod's mind as he sat in a rear seat of the control room in the *Benthic Explorer*, keenly watching the viewscreens. Denny Harker was piloting the submersible into BH-14. Lisa navigated. Prof paced the compartment like a caged animal in a zoo; or, more appropriately, like a large fish in a small aquarium.

The *Benthic Explorer* was equipped with six viewscreens, one for each direction: fore and aft, port and starboard, above and below. Banks of floodlights illuminated the rock walls of the Blue Hole with far greater candlepower than the subsuit lights that Tod had used on his previous study mission. The extra luminosity enabled him to see facets of the walls that he had not noticed before under dim viewing conditions.

Only the downscreen was virtually blank – this because the floodlights were not powerful enough to reach the bottom of the Blue Hole from the midpoint of the descent. Particulate matter in the water created a backscatter effect, much like headlamps in fog. Tod tried to peer through the reflecting particles in hopes of discerning recognizable shapes or patterns in the abyss. His imagination ran riot.

The *Benthic Explorer* was shaped like a blimp that was short and fat, except that there was no control car slung underneath, or engines on sponsons. Instruments, sensors, and transducers sprouted from the exterior of the hull like so many porcupine quills. Along with digicam recorders and floodlights, the outer hull appeared fuzzy instead of sleek and hydrodynamic.

Unlike a submarine, whose smooth and narrow hull was designed to carve through the water at flank speed, the *Benthic Explorer* was intended to move sluggishly in order to make scientific recordings. In that regard speed was not a virtue, but a detriment.

Instead of propellers and rudders, thrusters were used to drive and turn the submersible. Pivot mounts on stalks made it possible for the thrusters to rotate nearly three hundred sixty degrees in all three dimensions. This enabled the submersible to move in any desired direction without the need to change the attitude of the hull. The vessel could be pushed sideways as well as up and down. Thrusters could be used as brakes to stop momentum. The turning radius was the length of the hull.

The impellers were protected by shrouds whose close tolerance to the blades increased efficiency. Spin rotation could be reversed for extra maneuverability. Fine mesh screens at both ends of the shroud prevented large objects from being sucked through the nozzle.

Harker's opinions were that the mission was a waste of time; that the Persian submarine must have been pulled into the Blue Hole on an incoming tide; that lateral tunnels would prove to be too small for the passage of a submersible much less that of a full-sized submarine. He agreed to pilot the *Benthic Explorer* into BH-14 only because he didn't want Tod and Lisa to have the privilege. Now that the submersible was making its descent, he kept his opinions to himself.

Lisa announced the depth readings. "Three hundred feet. . . . Three ten. . . . Three twenty. . . . Three thirty."

"Here comes the ledge at three forty-five," Tod sang out. "That's where I was when the sub first showed up on sonar."

"It appeared on the screen suddenly. That's why I think the tube must be curved deeper down. It's the only way to explain why sonar didn't detect it as soon as I nosed the *Reef Cruiser* over the lip."

"When it first came into visual range, it was ricocheting from wall to wall like a billiard ball."

Harker was tight-lipped. He ignored their enthusiastic comments, and concentrated on manipulating thruster controls that he had not yet mastered.

"This Blue Hole looks like the throat of a volcano," Prof observed.

"Extinct, I hope," Lisa commented dryly.

The *Benthic Explorer* passed the ledge on which Tod had settled for his biological studies. "I see that my friends are alive and well."

"Four hundred feet. . . . Four fifty. . . . Five hundred."

Tod sat upright. "Here comes the curve."

The vertical tube curved slightly, like a bent straw. The diameter remained around two hundred feet. As the submersible descended deeper, the curvature became more pronounced.

"Five fifty."

Tod glanced at the viewscreen for the upward-facing digicam recorder. The circle of sunlight was flattening on one side as the *Benthic Explorer* moved laterally out of vertical alignment with the mouth of the Blue Hole.

Harker reduced the speed of descent. He powered the thrusters in such a way as to vector the submersible onto a more horizontal plane.

"Six hundred."

Prof scratched his face. "No more granite. The rock now looks like pure basalt."

Tod noticed that overhead sunbeams passed from view. "We're out of the light zone."

Instead of narrowing, as Harker had predicted, the tunnel broadened as it gradually turned into a horizontal tube. Flow meters showed that the submersible was bucking an outgoing tide that was diminishing progressively.

Harker leaned back from the controls. "The restricted entrance tube created a venturi effect. In here the water flow is barely negligible."

Suddenly the bottom dropped out from beneath the submersible.

Lisa pointed a finger at the viewscreen for the downward-facing digicam recorder. "Look at that!"

There was nothing to see on the viewscreen. The abyss appeared to be bottomless.

Although the submersible maintained its depth, Tod felt his stomach twist at the mere thought of so much empty space beneath him. "I – I can't see the floor – or the walls."

The cavern was so vast that the only points of reference were the rock overhead and the wall astern. All the other viewscreens showed unfathomable blackness: a maw of such immensity that it defied imagination.

"Aw, it's prob'ly no bigger than the caldera of a topside volcano," Harker scowled. "Like Crater Lake. Or Kilauea. Or Mauna Loa. This one just happens to be subaqueous."

"I'm changing the scale of the sonar scope from five hundred feet to one thousand." Lisa rotated the dial that increased the scale. "The definition won't be as good, but we'll get some idea of the size of this hole from the signal return."

There was no return signal. The hole was larger than a thousand feet across and deep.

"So this is what the Persians discovered." Prof stopped pacing long enough to stare at the various viewscreens. "There must be another tunnel that leads out of this vast volcanic cavity – one that leads to another Blue Hole that the Persian submarine entered."

Harker was ever the pragmatist. "That means they found a way to bypass our perimeter alerts."

"Not really. Remember that those who escaped from this submerged labyrinth did not survive to tell the tale."

"Increasing scale to two thousand feet."

This time Lisa was rewarded with a return signal from below and to the right.

"Bigger than Kilauea, but still not as big as Mauna Loa or Crater Lake – and a lot of other calderas around the world." Harker was emphatic. "The underwater caldera on Thera is ten times this size and twice as deep."

Harker's knowledge of volcanism was deficient. He was a marine, not a marine scientist. Prof, Tod, and Lisa knew better, but did not bother to contradict the irascible pilot for fear of sending him into a voluble tirade.

Thera was a volcanic island of the Santorini archipelago, located in the Aegean Sea off the coast of Greece. The so-called Minoan eruption, which occurred some sixteen hundred years Before the Current Era, was the largest volcanic eruption in mankind's recorded history. More than twenty-five cubic *miles* of ejecta – enough to fill the Grand Canyon and then some – spewed into the atmosphere and landed hundreds of miles away. The volcanic cone disappeared, leaving behind a caldera that measured four miles in length by eight miles in breadth. The bottom of the caldera lay thirteen hundred feet below the surface of the sea, while the one remaining wall of the volcano rose to one thousand feet above sea level: nearly half a mile from top to bottom. The island was covered by ash that lay two hundred feet thick.

Seventy miles away, the north coast of Crete was inundated by a seismic wave that measured some five hundred feet in height; coastal communities were wiped out. Tsunamis caused devastation throughout the region. The Minoan civilization, which was centered on Santorini, was totally obliterated. Compared to other volcanic events, the eruption of Vesuvius was a mere hiccup, and Krakatoa was an ugly burp.

"BH-14 is nothing more than a steam vent," Prof temporized. "We are now inside a magma chamber, left vacant after the volcanic edifice solidified overhead, and the still-molten magma subsided."

"Increasing scale to four thousand feet."

Tod rotated his seat and faced the adjacent computer console. "I'll switch on the graphics program."

"Good idea, Hunk."

After the program loaded, the screen displayed a three-dimensional representation of the interior of the cavern as the returning sonar signals drew it. The resulting image was a virtual line-drawing that was reminiscent of a chain link fence enclosing a columnar space. Distances were denoted on vertical and horizontal axes. The bottom was shown at twenty-two hundred feet, but the side walls were incomplete and the far wall was not shown at all.

"Increasing scale to eight thousand feet. . . . Sixteen thousand."

The image was now complete. The cavern looked like a distorted drinking glass with a no-spill lid that was shaped like a dome: approximately cylindrical except where one wall was pinched inward. The cavern measured two and one-quarter miles at its broadest beam, and one and a half at its narrowest. The depth recorder registered 1,753 feet."

"Deeper than Thera but with a smaller circumference," Harker said.

"Actually not as tall as Thera," Lisa countered, "if you factor in the height of the island."

Before Harker could offer a rejoinder, Prof said, "Definitely smaller with regard to overall volume. Denny, would you take us to the center of the chamber and commence a slow descent? I would like to get a sonar picture beyond that bulge."

Harker acknowledged with a grunt. He manipulated the thruster controls.

"Prof, why didn't the ceiling cave in when it lost its support as the magma receded?"

"You have overlooked your basic physics, Tod. Water, as you will recall, is incompressible. I surmise that the magma did not subside until after the overlying lava cooled and solidified, similar to the principle that creates lava tubes. As the molten magma sank back down the throat of the volcano, seawater poured into the void through the steam vent. If we were to drain this chamber of water, or even reduce the water level by the slightest amount, I have no doubt that the ceiling would collapse."

Harker brought the submersible to a hover in the approximate center of the chamber, at a depth of one thousand feet. "This is the design depth of the Yuper sub."

"But far short of its crush depth," Prof noted. "Let us proceed downward. I have a feeling that the *Serendib* must have emerged from a tunnel that is somewhat deeper, and that the sub was drawn into that tunnel involuntarily. I expect that we will find a current that flows back and forth in that tunnel and through this chamber to BH-14."

Lisa activated the directional sonar. "I'm seeing dimples in the walls from the uneven surface, but nothing yet that looks like a tunnel. The sonar beam has to be pointing almost straight into a tunnel for it to show up as, well, as a tunnel."

The sonar sweep was integrated with the graphics program in real time. The virtual image changed incrementally as incoming data constantly updated the output to the screen.

"Twelve hundred feet. . . . Thirteen hundred. . . . "

"There's a big indentation," Tod said enthusiastically. "I mean, a deep indentation."

Prof studied the display. "It is one mile away, on the opposite side of the chamber. Denny, proceed in that direction."

Harker aimed the submersible's stubby prow toward the deep indentation that was shown on the screen. He aligned all the thrusters so that their backwash pointed in the opposite direction.

"Full speed ahead," Lisa taunted.

Harker scowled at her but didn't say anything.

Tod scaled dimensions off the readout on the computer screen. "It's a big tunnel. I mean, a broad tunnel. Just under three hundred feet in width, and slightly more than two hundred feet in height. Easily large enough for the Persian sub to transit."

Harker reduced speed as the submersible approached the tunnel entrance. He reversed thrust to bring forward motion to a halt. The sonar signal return stabilized, indicating that the submersible was hovering at a standstill. A moment later, the distance between the submersible and the tunnel increased.

"Outflow," Harker remarked.

"That is consistent with the outflow of BH-14." Prof pointed an index finger at the chronometer. "Slack tide should commence in another twenty-three minutes. Inflow should commence thirty-two minutes after that."

A hush engulfed the control room.

Tod's stomach turned again as he contemplated the unknown.

Prof said softly, "Proceed with caution."

Chapter 11

The floodlights did much to dispel the unaccustomed gloom that Tod was feeling. Every nick and cranny in the broad passageway was illuminated brilliantly. He checked that the tracknav unit was functioning properly. As long as it was maintaining a continuous plot of the submersible's course, the reverse plot could be followed back to the entrance of BH-14.

Lisa seemed unconcerned. "Looks like we got more than we bargained for."

"I am surprised that we are headed away from Erebus instead of toward it."

Professor Pembroke was referring to the largest and most active volcano in Antarctica. Mount Erebus and a number of other volcanoes occupied all of Ross Island, which lay less than two hundred miles from Benthocity 3. The crater was filled with a lava lake that measured half a mile in diameter. Eruptions were frequent. Cabin-sized lava bombs regularly disturbed roosting emperor penguins, the island's only inhabitants.

"That's comforting," Tod commented dryly. His mouth felt like a ball of cotton.

The *Benthic Explorer* proceeded placidly through the lava tube. The surrounding walls were rough-cast and devoid of identifying features. The tube maintained its approximate dimensions for more than two miles before expanding.

"Temperature is on the rise." Lisa highlighted the thermometric readout that displayed external ambient temperature. "Up a degree from 28."

Pure water froze solid at 32 degrees Fahrenheit. Seawater contained minerals and dissolved salts, such as sodium chloride, which reduced the temperature at which water could remain in liquid form.

Harker adjusted the thrusters. "The floor is rising, too."

"Six degree up angle." Tod monitored the computer

graphic image of the lava tube.

"Thirty-one degrees F. . . . Thirty-two. . . . Above normal freezing."

"Eight degree incline."

"Thirty-five degrees. . . . Forty-two."

The lava tube suddenly doubled in size, then quickly tripled. The image on the forward viewscreen shimmered.

"Sixty four degrees. It's a heat wave."

"The ceiling is more than six hundred feet overhead," Tod announced.

Prof's voice was calm. "I believe that we are about to encounter a steam vent from deep geothermal activity."

"Now you're forgetting *your* physics," Tod chided lightly. "You've forgotten that the boiling point of water is dependant upon pressure."

Prof looked chagrined.

"He's got you there, Prof," Lisa singsonged.

"Right you are, my boy. I congratulate you on your perspicacity." A grin spread slowly across Prof's bearded face. "I was just testing you to see if you were paying attention."

"You were not!"

Now Prof's grin fledged into a full-blown smile. "No, I was not."

"It was a good try, though," Lisa said.

Tod and Lisa both laughed out loud. Harker remained grim.

Water boiled at 212 degrees Fahrenheit only at sea level. Mountain climbers were more aware of this fact than undersea dwellers. High in the Himalayas, the reduced atmospheric pressure allowed water to boil at less than 180 degrees, making it impossible for mountaineers to drink a truly hot cup of tea.

The atmospheric pressure at sea level was 14.7 pounds per square inch. This pressure doubled at a depth of 33 feet under water, and doubled again at 99 feet: an increase of 14.7 psi for every 33 feet of depth. The pressure at 1,300 feet was more than 580 psi. At that pressure, water did not boil until its temperature rose to more than 480 degrees Fahrenheit.

Tod said, "So that isn't steam up ahead. It's super-heated water."

"That is correct."

In purely mechanical terms, Earth was a massive heat dissipation engine. Hydrothermal venting was a global cooling mechanism.

"There's no turbulence," Harker observed.

The temperature jumped to 86 degrees, then 110, then 142.

Harker reversed the thrusters and brought the *Benthic Explorer* to a halt. "I'm not going any farther till we know what we're getting into."

"A wise move." Prof had long since quit pacing. He now stood as still as a marble statue. Only his eyes moved as he rapidly shifted his gaze from readout to readout on the various screens. "You may proceed, but do so at minimum velocity and with the utmost heed."

Harker propelled the submersible with considerable restraint. The compass needle moved with infinite slowness. "Now there are convection currents."

"No doubt caused by the extreme temperature differential."

No cracks or vents were apparent in the floor, but the origin of the rising heat was now visible in the near distance. The shimmer was caused by a heat wave – not the kind that Lisa called to attention, but the kind that appeared above a macadam road in summer. Instead of rising air, rising superheated water pushed nearby cold water out of the path of its escape to the surface.

Prof pointed to the virtual image of the chamber. "Notice that there is a volcanic chimney overhead. The superheated water must be rising up the flue and finding its way to the ocean through fissures in the basalt."

"Hey, Squirt, how about extending the thermoprobe before we get too close to those vents."

"Good idea. I forgot we even had one."

The probe was a thermocouple that was mounted on a thick monel wire, much like a horizontal antenna. Lisa actuated the servomotor that pushed the probe wire out of its sleeve into the water forward of the sub-mersible.

"Hmmnn. Variable readings, as expected . . . "

"Look at that!" Tod shouted.

Harker did not look up from his control panel. He instinctively applied braking action by reversing the rotation of the impellers. He over-corrected. The submersible stopped its forward motion, then started to move in reverse. Everyone lurched at the abrupt change of direction. Prof steadied himself by grabbing the back of a seat.

"No, go back."

Harker took time to look up at the forward viewscreen. "Now what?"

"Stop all movement," Prof stated succinctly.

Harker switched off the power to the thrusters. The submersible coasted backward for several seconds, until friction with the water brought it to a complete standstill. The submersible hovered motionless.

"Magnifying the image." Lisa zoomed in the forward digicam recorder. The magnified image appeared on the forward viewscreen. "Wow. Look at that."

The hydrothermal vents were surrounded by a forest of active biological organisms. Giant tubeworms stood five feet tall. Mobile creatures that resembled isopods walked on long hairlike legs. Albino crabs scuttled along the rocky outcrops. Tiny eyeless fish swam in lazy circles among the tubeworms. This was a complete and self-sustaining micro-environment.

Hydrothermal vents were rich in oxide ores and sulfide ores of iron, zinc, copper, and gold. These metal compounds precipitated in the water in the vicinity of the vents.

In this sunless cavern, tubeworms managed to eke out a living by means of chemosynthesis: a method of harnessing energy in the absence of sunlight. Each tubeworm sported a crown of plumes that captured hydrogen sulfide that escaped from the vent. The chemical was passed down the gullet to symbiotic bacteria that oxidized the compound either from dissolved oxygen in the water or from naturally occurring nitrogen compounds. The oxidation process resulted in excess energy that the tubeworm utilized for growth and reproduction. Associated animals metabolized natural byproducts or fed off each other. The first benthic micro-environment consisting of chemosynthetic organisms living off thermal vent discharge was discovered in 1977 in the Galapagos Rift, when deep submergence vessels were just coming into vogue.

The biologist in Tod was overwhelmed by the discovery. "This is spectacular."

"And totally unexpected," Lisa added. "Especially in a lava tube. That implies geological stability over enormous spans of time."

"Quite right, my dear."

"I hate to burst your nitrogen bubble," Harker interrupted. "But we're here to track the route of a Yuper sub."

"Technically correct," Prof responded. "But in the larger perspective, the Benthocities were established to seek new food and energy resources. I submit that while tubeworms may not be fit for human consumption, a hydrothermal vent such as this could produce vast amounts of energy if properly tapped."

Harker scowled.

"The purpose of exploration is to investigate the unknown. If we knew precisely what we were going to discover, this would not be an exploratory mission."

Harker kept scowling.

"However, you are correct in noting that the primary objective of this particular mission is not one of scientific discovery." Turning to Tod, "I know that you would like to examine these wonderful biota in exacting detail, and I will see that you have the opportunity to do so at a later date. But for now we must proceed with the task at hand."

Tod was disappointed. "Sure, Prof. I understand."

"It's not as if these tubeworms are going anywhere," Lisa added for his comfort. "They're not mobile. And besides, these thermal vents have been here for thousands of years. Tens of thousands."

Tod nodded silently.

"Denny, please circumvent this remarkable tube-worm colony with prudence, and continue on our original course."

Harker acknowledged with a single nod. He spun the *Benthic Explorer* on its axis, circumnavigated the miniature oasis, and proceeded across the tunnel that was depicted by the virtual sonar imaging software. The chamber diminished in size on the opposite side of the entry point, but only slightly.

Time dragged. Mile passed after dreary mile. The submersible encountered one fracture zone after another. It passed over great chasms that were hundreds of feet deep. There were no intersecting lava tubes, but giant rents in the sidewalls beckoned like Sirens for the *Benthic Explorer* to explore. Most were jagged and too tight a fit for the Persian submarine, so the submersible did not bother to probe them. Others the submersible penetrated until the loss of flow predicted a dead end, or shrank small enough that further passage was difficult.

On one hand Tod found the length and complexity of the subaqueous cavern system exhilarating. On the other hand he found the featureless basalt or granite walls boring. One wet rock looked like any other.

When the passageway straightened, Harker took a break and let Lisa pilot the submersible. Tod tried his hand at the controls when Lisa wanted to nap. They ate in turns on the fly, from food stores in the lockers and drinks in the bins.

The passageway continued to trend upward. A tall chimney appeared overhead at a depth of 500 feet. At first it seemed as if it might be a Blue Hole, but it topped out at a depth of two hundred feet; and anyway, the tracknav indicated that the submersible was under the Ross Ice Shelf, adjacent to the Antarctic continent, where the ice overburden was hundreds of feet thick. Some Caribbean Blue Holes had inland outlets, but only on islands with low profiles. There was no reason why there could not be a hidden outlet under the ice.

Harker took over after the submersible crossed a vast chamber whose only other exit was a tunnel of small dimensions – large enough for the Persian submarine, but small enough to require care in navigation.

"Hey, we've got some flow in here." Harker indicated the difference between ground speed and thruster revolutions. "We're being pulled along at a steady, uh, two knots."

Everyone knew that flow suggested an outlet to the sea.

"Watch the virtual sonar image," Prof cautioned.

Lisa sharpened the image with the sonar range dial, by reducing the range to the dimensions of the tunnel. "Yeah, we don't want to get banged up like the *Serendib*."

"Or shot full of holes by an electrostatic discharge beam." Tod glanced at Prof. "I know that an ionization path can't be created through water, but lava flows on the surface usually induce electrostatic discharges. I just wondered if that was what happened to the *Serendib*."

Prof arched his bushy black eyebrows. "It is certainly food for thought."

"Hey, the compass is going wacky." Harker called attention to the gyrocompass repeater on the forward bulkhead. "That's impossible. Magnetic disturbance can't affect – "

"The needle isn't moving," Lisa said calmly. "The sub is turning."

"But – "

"Trust your instruments," Prof cautioned. "Reorient your thinking."

"The floor is sloping upward," Tod announced.

Lisa decreased the sonar range again because the tunnel was growing smaller in both height and width. "Look at the viewscreens and sonar imagery. The appearance of movement from port to starboard means that the sub is rotating counterclockwise."

Harker momentarily took his hands off the controls.

"I can't – "

"Trust the instruments," Prof repeated calmly.

Harker shook his head. "Okay. Okay, I got it."

"Ground speed is increasing."

The *Benthic Explorer* seemed to be caught in a vortex that was moving upward at an angle of nearly 45 degrees. It was pulled along like a toy in a cyclone. Harker grappled with the thruster controls and ballast pumps. He was trying to straighten the submersible at the same time that he was trying to stabilize its buoyancy.

The pressure that was exerted by water was a function of depth. As the external pressure was reduced by the reduction in depth, the submersible became too buoyant: it wanted to float to the top of the tunnel. Harker was further overtaxed by trying to adjust the trim so that the bow would stand higher than the stern, in parallel with the slope. Otherwise the prow might slam against the jagged bottom, or the stern might crash against the ceiling.

"I can assume ballast and trim control – " Lisa started.

"Do it!" Harker shouted.

The submersible was badly out of control on both axes.

"There's a fork up ahead." Tod kept his eyes glued to the virtual sonar image. He saw the tunnel split into two passageways, one above and to the right of the other. "They're both large enough – "

Lisa interrupted. "We're being sucked into the upper tunnel."

Prof studied the Doppler readings. "Water appears to be issuing from the lower tunnel and entering the upper one."

"That's what I just said."

Harker was still fighting to align the submersible's prow with the direction of forward motion. "We're going too fast. I can't reduce speed and change the angle at the same time. We're being overpowered . . . "

The submersible entered the upper tunnel like a

race car skidding sideways off the track.

"Up angle increasing." Tod gulped as he watched the virtual sonar image lines converging. "The tunnel is getting smaller."

Lisa had the ballast pumps going full tilt, filling the tanks as fast as they could operate. Trying to compute the difference between the forward tanks and the after tanks was more than she could accomplish in such a short period of time. Instead she concentrated just on achieving approximate stability gauged against ambient pressure. The ceiling loomed ever closer. "It's going to be close . . . "

Each thruster operated independently. Harker managed to reduce the submersible's forward angle to 30 degrees. It was not enough. The starboard stern touched the black granite surface. Ironically, the collision and subsequent friction helped to straighten the alignment of the hull with the wall. Harker turned the thrusters on their pivots in an attempt to have the starboard units pull at the same time the port units pushed. The maneuver required quick and deft manipulation of the controls. He was partially successful.

The hull grated against the rock. The starboard viewscreen went blank as the starboard digicam recorder was scraped off its sponson. Several sensors went dead. Both starboard thrusters suffered damage: the stalk of the forward one was bent back against the hull; the after one was dislodged from its universal joint.

"Do your best, people, but remain calm." Prof's pronouncement was lost in the frenzy of activity. "The hull is extra strong."

Tod felt helpless. The rear-seat computer console did not have navigation links, so he was powerless to help Harker and Lisa control the submersible. All he could do was monitor sensors and call out depths and angles.

There was another scraping sound as the starboard hull of the *Benthic Explorer* contacted the wall. More instruments were knocked out of commission.

Despite the damage, Tod was gratified to notice that the slope of the tunnel was decreasing instead of becoming vertical like BH-14. That made it easier for Lisa to control the buoyancy and adjust the trim. The ground speed decelerated quickly. Once Harker steered the hull parallel to the bottom and side walls, he threw the thrusters into reverse. The prow bounced off a huge boulder that had fallen from the ceiling millennia in the past. More ceiling collapse was made evident by the rocks that littered the floor. The uneven bottom created an undulating flow. The submersible rose and fell sickeningly like a canoe passing through rapids in a fast-water stream.

"We're shoaling out." Tod felt nauseated by the constant agitation. "Oh, no . . . "

"What?" Lisa fairly screamed, her natural calm momentarily overcome by the tone of his voice.

"It looks like – It doesn't make sense." Tod studied the virtual image of the sonar scanner. He looked up at Prof in astonishment. "It looks like a ceiling."

"That's impossible," Harker grumbled. "All this water has to go somewhere."

Every working viewscreen went fuzzy. The tunnel walls could no longer be seen. It looked as if great quantities of oil had been mixed with the water.

"Half our instruments are either malfunctioning or completely inoperable." Lisa looked over her shoulder at Tod in the rear seat. "You must be getting false readings from a damaged transducer."

The *Benthic Explorer* stopped so suddenly that everyone was jolted upward out of their seats – except for Prof, who was tossed a couple of inches off the deck.

All was quiescent.

Tod still felt queasy.

Except for a slight tendency to roll and bob, the submersible's buoyancy seemed to be under control, and forward motion was nearly at a standstill. The compass needle moved sluggishly. The depth meter was out of calibration. The thermometric unit didn't register at all. The starboard side was a dead zone.

The working viewscreens showed a long tunnel ahead, and a distant wall to the left and behind. This was confirmed by the sonar imagery. Overhead, a large chamber was fantastically decorated with long stalactites that were suspended from the ceiling like thrusting spears.

Tod gripped his stomach. "I don't feel so well." Then he vomited.

"Congratulations, people," Prof stated flatly. "We have just surfaced."

Chapter 12

"Seasickness is a common ailment among sailors until they get their sea legs." Prof crawled on his hands and knees, swabbing the deck and cleaning up Tod's mess with a damp cloth. "Do not blame yourself."

Tod crouched in his seat with his head between his knees and his mouth over a plastic bag. "I've never been on the surface before."

The *Benthic Explorer* bobbed gently on a column of upwelling water. The vessel was badly damaged. Lisa was running diagnostic tests while Harker was attending to instrument malfunctions.

"You will get over it in time."

"How much time?"

"That is impossible to determine. It could take anywhere from hours to days. Eat more of those crackers. They will absorb stomach acid and help to make you feel better."

Tod went through a bout of dry heaves. His stomach had already been emptied of its partially digested contents. "Why isn't anyone else sick?"

"The vestibular nerve conducts impulses to the brain based upon fluid level in canals in the ear. It is the mechanism that maintains the balance of the body with reference to movement of the head. Sloshing of the fluid can cause vertigo and dizziness, especially when the nerve detects movement but the eyes do not. This conflicting information can trigger the vomit reflex. The sensitivity of that nerve is different in different people. Apparently, you are extra sensitive."

Lisa wrapped her arms around Tod's shoulders and kissed the top of his head. Because of the difference in their heights, their faces were nearly even when she stood next to him in his crouch. "Poor boy. I feel so sorry for you."

Tod responded by dry-heaving again. He was not in the mood for cuddling. He wanted to lie down and die.

"If you people can leave that sick kid alone for a minute, we've got problems that need to be fixed."

Lisa turned to Harker with fiery green eyes. "You're a mean bastard, you are."

Harker was shocked into silence by her vehemence.

"Let us calm down and take a moment to evaluate our situation." Prof stood and wiped his hands on a clean towel. "This vessel may be damaged but it is still operational. Because we are on the surface, we will not have to dry-dock it in order to effect external repairs. Furthermore, I feel confident that we have followed the wake of the *Serendib*, at least partway. The abnormal current that carried us here from the fork must have pulled the *Serendib* out of that other tunnel, and transported it in the direction from which we came. Judging by the manner in which we are now being propelled, I would not be surprised to find that this current reverses its flow as a result of tidal influence."

"No matter how big this lava tube is, I don't like being adrift. I think – "

"This is not a lava tube. Nor is it a fault zone. This cave was formed by phreatic action before the land uplifted – dissolved, as it were, from sedimentary limestone."

"Whatever." Harker shrugged off Prof's scientific discourse with a wave of the hand. "I think we should take on ballast and sit on the bottom until we get our wits together, instead of drifting along aimlessly and possibly bumping into some submerged outcrop."

"My wits are quite together," Prof said softly.

Harker scowled.

"The proximity alarm will warn us of impending collision."

Harker scowled again.

"We are not wandering aimlessly. We are exploring. We are studying. We are learning. I think it is possible that the *Serendib* surfaced in this tunnel, or one very much like it, because it was filled with atmospheric air just like the air that is circulating outside this hull. Our mission is to backtrack the route of the *Serendib*. I think that we are accomplishing that mission quite well."

Harker scowled yet again.

"Why don't we pull into the next eddy?" Lisa suggested. "Then we can all rest awhile without having to watch the instruments or listen for alarms."

"An excellent suggestion." Prof patted Tod on the back. "Perhaps we can find a place to dock, and Tod can sit on rock until he regains his equilibrium."

Twenty minutes later they encountered an area where the cave broadened considerably. A jutting wall deflected some of the water into a backwash. Harker piloted the *Benthic Explorer* into the eddy. The submersible was not equipped with anchors, or bitts for mooring lines. The mild circular current gently nudged the submersible against the limestone wall, and held it in place by means of constant pressure.

Lisa studied the viewscreens. "Not only is there a ledge, but there's a perpendicular tunnel leading up and out of the water."

"Perhaps we can conduct some dry-cave exploration," Prof suggested.

Harker switched off the thrusters. "I'll see what I can do about the damage on the starboard hull."

"I think Tod could use some food and drink. Let us take a satchel with some provisions."

Tod groaned, but nodded acquiescence.

"An underground picnic." Lisa was ecstatic. "Who would have thought?"

Prof shoved handlights and a mound of packaged victuals into a knapsack. "I do not know what you might feel like consuming, so we will take some of everything." Prof slung the single long strap over his shoulder. "Do you feel up to an excursion, my boy?"

"Not really." Tod stood slowly. He was a little unsteady on his feet. He held onto a seatback for temporary support. "But I know I should go. I'll take the transcriber in case there are fossils in the matrix."

"Ever the scientist, eh my lad?" Prof grinned as he led the way to the escape chamber.

Lisa grabbed another knapsack and shoved liquid refreshments and snack food containers into it. "It seems strange to exit a sub that's not in dry-dock without a subsuit. I mean, not that the sub needs a subsuit, but to not be wearing a subsuit and not going into dry-dock. That is – " In exasperation, "You know what I mean."

Tod managed a weak grin.

"It is a first for me, too," Prof confided in a low voice.

One at a time, all four climbed up the ladder, through the hatchway, and onto the top of the hull. The submersible's functional floodlights illuminated the vast chamber with incredible brilliance. Seventy-five feet away, a bed of stalactites that measured more than ten feet in length grew down so far that they pierced the calm surface of the water to a depth of several feet.

Prof pointed to the phenomenon. "Formations cannot grow in water, only in air. Water that filters down through porous limestone dissolves calcium carbonate along the way. The encapsulated mineral is then transported by means of gravity. When it drips into open air, the calcium carbonate is precipitated on the overhead when the water droplet evaporates. If the droplet falls before it evaporates, the calcium carbonate is precipitated on the floor to form a stalagmite.

"If a cave is subsequently flooded, the growth of formations is halted because the calcium carbonate is not precipitated, but is dispersed in the water and carried away by the current. On the other hand, if the water has no flow and maintains the same level for a long period of time, the stalactite will spread sideways across the surface. Under the present circumstances, I would venture to guess that this particular cave has only recently been flooded – by the global rise of sea level."

They stepped off the submersible onto the nearby ledge. This ledge extended scores of feet in either direction, like a rocky beachhead. Offset ledges gave the appearance of steps. While Prof, Lisa, and Harker found flat places to sit on the ledges, and started munching on their food, Tod knelt at the water's edge and aimed the transcriber into the crystal clear liquid, where he saw tiny creatures swimming haphazardly like dust motes in Brownian motion.

Tod said, "This water is teeming with life."

Each multi-legged animal was the size of a grain of rice. The transcriber tried to identify them from its newly enlarged databank.

Prof asked no one in particular, "Do you understand why the sonar return showed a ceiling?"

Lisa looked at Prof. "I didn't at first. Too much was happening at once for me to think straight." She removed a sealed package of bread and a plastic jar of peanut butter. She calmly unwrapped the loaf, sliced the bread with a foodkit knife, then used the knife to spread peanut butter on the slice. "But I realized afterward – after you said that we were on the surface – that the signal was bouncing off the water/air interface."

"Exactly. Sonar works in water the way radar works in air, but neither will work out of its element. Submersibles are not equipped with radar – "

"Prof, look at this!" Tod carried the transcriber to where Professor Pembroke was masticating thoughtfully. He held the transcriber screen so that Prof could see the captured image. "It hasn't identified the genus or species, but it says the critters belong to a freshwater family."

"Let me see that." Lisa plopped down beside Prof and turned the screen so she could see the display. "Humph." She walked to the edge of the rock, scooped up a handful of water, examined it to make certain that there were no critters in it, and touched it with her tongue. "It's fresh!" She slurped a couple of mouthfuls. "High mineral content, probably iron and sulfur, but it's potable."

Prof did not miss a chew. "That explains the fuzziness that we saw on the viewscreens. There was nothing wrong with them or with the digicam recorders. We passed through a halocline: a horizontal stratification or mixing zone where fresh water lies atop denser saltwater."

Tod stepped back in deep contemplation. "That means . . . "

"Go on," Prof urged.

"That means – it means – that this is ground water." He paused to wait for more coaxing, but Prof just stared. "It means that we've passed completely under the Ross Ice Shelf. We're under the Antarctic continent!"

Prof grinned broadly. "Well done, my lad. Well done."

"This whole area must be honeycombed with caves, like a sponge."

Harker stopped chewing long enough to scowl. "That means Yupers could be all over the place. They can sneak up on our bases and pop out of Blue Holes like a rabbit out of spider hole."

"Your tenses and metaphors are mixed but your point is well taken. Perhaps the Persians are mapping this underwater labyrinth for precisely such nefarious purposes."

"But that still doesn't explain the ancient gold foils," Lisa protested. "Or why they would bring such priceless artifacts on a reconnaissance mission."

"It explains much but not all." Prof scratched his face under his scraggly beard. "It almost seems to pose more questions than it answers."

"I'm done gabbing." Harker jumped up from his ledge and swallowed a last bite of his food. "I'm going to get this sub in order for a quick retreat – or for hostile action." He studied the damage on the hull. "By shifting ballast to the port tanks, I can careen the sub to bring the starboard thrusters out of the water."

Lisa watched him climb down the hatch. "I'd like to explore some of this dry-cave."

"It might do us some good to stretch our legs." Prof handed some pretzels to Tod. "Do you feel up to a little walk?"

"I feel fine, now that I'm standing on something that doesn't wobble." He swallowed a handful of pretzels. "I want to look for more signs of life. If this cave was carved from sedimentary rock, as you said, there might be some fossils on the walls."

Prof shouldered the knapsack. "Let us go and leave Denny unmolested. He works better on his own."

Lisa slung her knapsack over her shoulder as if it were an oversized purse. "And we're better off without him."

"Unvexed, perhaps, but not necessarily better off."

The trio trod up the series of ledges for a hundred feet. The open expanse of the cave then contracted into a tunnel that sloped upward so gradually that there was hardly any notice of ascent. The passageway was lozenge-shaped with a twenty-foot-high arch in the middle. The central arch tapered sharply to the floor on either side. Typical for erosion caves, the floor was uneven and was littered with loose rocks that had broken away from the ceiling in the distant past.

Tod stopped nibbling on pretzels so he could hold the transcriber in one hand and a handlight in the other, both pointed straight ahead. Prof and Lisa each panned the extremities of the cave with their handlights. Whenever Tod spotted a geometrical design that did not look like a pattern of erosion, he examined the area with the transcriber. The transcriber detected no fossils, just grooves and swirls that gave the appearance of embedded shellfish. He was disappointed by the lack of fossils, but ecstatic over the endless and fantastic variety of drip formations.

Speleothems grew in great profusion on the ceiling and along the walls. Most of them stood tall and stately, but some small ones looked like upside down blossoms, while others were curled in grotesque shapes much like miniature mutated feathers. A few possessed features that were so thin and delicate that light shone through them, as if they were made of tissue paper. Mineral intrusions tinted many of the formations with pale shades of pink.

The threesome walked and walked.

Lisa stood in awe. "This is like a fairyland. I never

imagined that a dry-cave could be so beautiful – and so colorful – without marine life to dress it up."

"Nice echo, Squirt." Tod gave a couple of loud hoots that reverberated half a dozen times before the repetitions receded below the hearing level. He shouted, "Hello!"

"Hunk, cut it out."

Tod looked sheepish. He avoided Lisa's glare, and returned to making a record of the profusion of speleothems with the transcriber. For those formations that stood too high to reach, he used the transcriber's telephoto capability to record images. "I agree with you. This is just incredible." It suddenly occurred to him that he had lost all sense of time and distance. "We've come pretty far . . . "

"One thousand seven hundred forty-seven paces," Prof announced. "My natural stride is thirty inches, but what with stepping around all these rocks, my average pace is probably closer to two feet."

Tod checked the plotting feature on the transcriber. "Point six nine mile." He grimaced at Prof. "How do you do that?"

Prof shrugged.

"What's that shiny spot up ahead?" Lisa pointed her handlight to a glittering pinpoint in the distance.

Tod squinted. "Reflection off something. Maybe mica?"

"Mica is found in igneous or metamorphic rock, not in sedimentary rock," Prof explained. "Quartz is more likely."

"Too small for quartz," Lisa said with a smirk. "Must be pintz."

Tod snickered. "Half pintz, like you."

Professor Pembroke groaned. "Now you know why I insisted on bringing Denny on this expedition. I needed someone to break up your repartee."

Lisa imitated the pull of a zipper across her mouth. "My lips are sealed."

"Hey." Tod kept his attention riveted on the distant dot of light. "Did you notice – turn your lights away."

Both Prof and Lisa complied.

"There! See what I mean? The reflection is still there."

"Ergo, it cannot be a reflection," said Prof. "Perhaps it is luminous biota."

"You mean bioluminescence, like in lightning bugs and glowworms?" Lisa wanted to know.

"I think a fungus is more likely. I would be astonished to find glowworms in a cave under several hundred feet of Antarctic ice."

Tod quickened his pace. "There's only one way to find out."

"Wait!" Lisa cautioned, her voice a muffled whisper. "Suppose it's a Persian campsite."

That brought everyone to a halt.

"That's impossible, Squirt."

"So's a sub coming out of a Blue Hole."

Tod pondered her reply.

"Our presence is already compromised by Tod's war whoops."

"Sorry," he whispered.

"Let us proceed quietly."

The spot of light looked like little more than a pinpoint. It was farther away than it appeared. The trio trod quietly on the uneven floor. Tod placed the transcriber in its belt loop. Lisa slung the knapsack strap over her head and on the opposite shoulder.

"I suggest that we dim our lights." Prof rotated the dimmer dial until his handlight offered barely enough illumination to enable him to pick his way through the boulder field.

Tod and Lisa followed suit. No one spoke.

The light did not grow brighter at their approach, but it grew larger – like a dilating iris. It eventually developed that the light was neither natural luminescence nor a reflection.

"It's the light at the end of the tunnel," Lisa whispered.

Tod imagined a near-death experience. "I hope that doesn't mean what I think it means."

The cave assumed approximate tubular dimensions. The pinpoint grew to the size of a baseball, then a basketball, then the apparent diameter of the sun – and nearly as bright.

All three switched off their handlights. Their steps became slower, and shorter.

The tunnel was coming to an end in a dazzling blaze of light. Finally they stepped out of the dark tunnel into a cave of immense proportions – one that put the Great Room of Carlsbad Caverns to shame. Despite a distant haze, it appeared to extend forever in front and to the left and right. They stood high on a bluff that overlooked a vast area of vegetation which Tod did not need the transcriber to identify.

It was a forest of giant redwood trees.

Chapter 13

"This is – unbelievable."

Tod was too awestruck to speak.

"Seeing is believing, as the old adage goes." Prof strode across the moss-covered outcrop and peered over the edge. The ground lay some three hundred feet below. "Although I can hardly accept it myself."

The outcrop jutted outward for a distance of twenty feet from the mouth of the tunnel, and was twice as broad. The covering of moss was thick and spongy.

Tod bent down and placed his hands flat against the green sward. His words came out as a croak. "This is real."

He remembered the transcriber in his belt loop. He extracted the device and aimed it at the dull green vegetation. The transcriber recorded the image and noted distinguishing characteristics, such as stem color and branch clusters. Signal reflection provided the distance between the transcriber and the study subject, and enabled the transducer to calculate the size of each individual plant. It identified the genus as *Sphagnum*. It listed a slew of species, such as *apiculatum*, *fallax*, *mendocinum*, *riparium*, *sericeum*, and a score of others, all neatly arranged in alphabetical order. It highlighted one, then moved to another, and finally scrolled down to the bottom of the list and highlighted "Species Unknown."

"It's an unclassified species of sphagnum moss."

"Interesting," said Prof, as he continued to scan the horizon.

"Interesting?" Lisa interjected. "Is that all you can say? Interesting. This is more than interesting. This is – impossible."

"Please keep your voice down. And keep in mind that something that you can see and touch and – " Prof stooped close to the ground and placed his huge proboscis close to the moss. " – even smell, cannot be impossible."

"I don't care if I could taste it and hear it, it's still . . . " Lisa took two steps backward, lost her balance, and collapsed onto her stern. She put the back of one hand to her forehead, then fell all the way onto her spine. The bed of dense springy moss cushioned her fall.

Tod knelt by her side. "Squirt, what's wrong?"

Lisa rolled her head from side to side. She scrunched her eyes shut. "I can't . . . I feel . . . "

"Squirt?" Tod felt helpless.

"I don't know . . . This cave . . . "

Prof braced himself on one knee, next to her head. He carefully lifted her right eyelid. Her pupil was abnormally restricted.

"Don't – make me . . . " She hugged her arms around her tiny chest.

"It is okay, my dear. It is okay. You will get used to it."

Lisa shook her head and kept her eyes tightly closed.

"Used to what?" Tod wanted to know.

"She is having a panic attack, due, I suspect, to agoraphobia."

"What's that?"

"An anxiety disorder. It is fear of open spaces."

Lisa stuttered, "I – I – I've never . . . "

"A firm grip and continued exposure can help to alleviate the symptoms." Prof patted her hand. "I am confident that you are strong enough to overcome the feeling once you have gotten over the initial shock."

Tod asked, "How long will that take?"

Prof shrugged.

"Like seasickness, huhn?"

"One can never tell."

Lisa slowly raised herself to a sitting position. "Whew. I've never felt like that before." She opened her eyes the barest slit. "Is it still there?"

"Caves are not in the habit of going away."

"I feel shaky. Hold me, Hunk."

Tod put his arms around her slender shoulders. He

didn't know what to say.

"Wow. Look at that enormous cave filled with trees. It's – inexplicable."

Prof grinned. "I will give you that."

"But how is it possible?"

"For that I do not have an answer." Turning to Tod, "Can you identify the species of the redwoods?"

Tod let go of Lisa and crawled to the edge of the outcrop. He was overcome by a feeling of vertigo as he looked down into the yawning chasm below. He gulped. He turned his face away. "I think I'm afraid of heights. Do you have a name for that?"

"Acrophobia."

"Great. So we're a couple of phobias. I'm an acro and she's an agora. Do you have a phobia, Prof?"

"Harkerphobia, but I face my fear and try not to let it show."

After a moment of stunned silence, both Lisa and Tod burst into gales of laughter.

When Tod got over his spasm of guffaws, he asked, "Did anyone ever tell you that you have a dry sense of humor?"

"When you live in a subaqueous city, a dry sense of humor is the only kind to have."

Lisa and Tod laughed outrageously again.

Tod shook his head. "Here we've made the greatest discovery of the century, and we're telling jokes."

"There is nothing wrong with a little levity."

Grimacing, Tod sighed deeply. He used his peripheral vision to point the transcriber and study the readouts. "This doesn't make sense." He blinked and looked again. "It's showing *Caloplaca flavescens*, a crustose lichen."

"Hunk, if you would look where you're aiming you'd see that the transcriber is pointing to the side of the rock wall."

"Oh. Sorry." Tod looked sheepish, and hoped that it wasn't becoming a habit. He remembered Harker's earlier statement. "I must not have all my wits about me."

"Hunk, if you can manage to get fifty percent of

them back, you can be a halfwit."

"Very funny."

"Not funny. Witty."

Prof shook his head. "Denny, where are you when I need you?"

Lisa did her zipper imitation again.

"Okay, now I've got the trees in view." He leaned back on his shins and scooted away from the edge. "Looks like California redwood, *Sequoia sempervirens*. Two hundred eighty feet in height. Between one thousand and twelve hundred years old." He linked to an information screen. "Not the tallest redwood known, nor the oldest." He looked askance at Prof and Lisa. "Based on its location, it's clearly the strangest."

Lisa used Prof's shoulder to push herself to a standing position. "No more jokes." She put her hands on her hips in total exasperation. "People, can we stop the purely scientific analysis, and talk about the impossibility – " She glared at Prof. " – of a rain forest under the Antarctic? I mean, this isn't your everyday occurrence, you know. We've got an impossible – okay, an unprecedented occurrence – in front of our eyes, and I for one would like an explanation."

"I am as astonished and perplexed as you are, my dear, but unless we face this situation with scientific detachment, I doubt that any answers will be forthcoming."

"Well, okay, I understand that." She wavered uncertainly on her feet, but quickly got a grip on herself. "I just wish you two would show some emotion about this – incredible cave."

"I grant that this cavern is more incredible than benthic tubeworms and geothermal vents, but we must obtain more information if we expect to solve the mystery of its origin."

"Okay, then let's start with finding out where the light is coming from."

They all looked up at the glowing ceiling. A uniform yellowish-white light extended from the top corner of the sandstone walls as far outward as the eye could see.

Lisa flailed her arms as she felt the onset of another panic attack, brought on by the sheer immensity of the cavern. She clung to Prof for support. "Sorry."

"Quite all right, my dear. Quite all right."

Tod aimed the transcriber upward and activated the zoom control. "Well, the ceiling is one hundred ninety-seven feet overhead – making a total height of around five hundred feet – but I'm not getting identification on the light source. The readout is 'Unknown'."

"Can you obtain the color temperature?"

Tod linked to a different screen, scrolled, and tapped choice blocks as they appeared. "Sixty-five hundred degrees Kelvin." He raised his eyebrows at Prof. "Sunlight."

Lisa humphed. "Now don't tell me that's not impossible."

"Improbable perhaps, but not impossible. The source is obviously artificial. Whoever built this place did so with the intention of using it as a greenhouse."

"Built it!" Tod yelled.

"Built it!" Lisa parroted.

"Certainly you do not think that this cave is natural."

Tod thought a long time before answering. "No, I guess it isn't."

"That's a long way for a cone from California to drift," Lisa allowed. "These trees had to have been planted – Whoa! What was that?"

Tod ducked as something the size of a bullet buzzed past his ear. He ducked again as another one sped past. They did not fly in a straight line, but in slowly curving arcs. Then one circled his head in a lazy, halting pattern.

"Hunk!" Lisa yelled. "The transcriber."

Tod raised the transcriber and held it in front of the airborne intruder. He studied the readout as it scrolled through dozens of possible identifications. "*Apis.*" The transcriber kept scrolling. "*Dorsata.*" He frowned as he read the explanatory text. "It's the giant honey bee of southeast Asia."

"Peculiar," Prof ruminated, tugging on his whiskers. "Trees from North America and bees from Asia."

"One step forward, two steps back," Lisa said.

Tod spoke to himself in a voice that was loud enough for the others to hear. "That means there must be flowers."

"And birds. Oh, I'd love to see a bird."

"This cavern must house a fully developed and self-contained environment." Prof strode again to the edge of the outcrop. "How – spectacular." To Tod, "Can you ascertain the dimensions of this cavern?"

Tod stayed away from the edge. He panned the transcriber up and down, left and right. "Four hundred eighty-six feet from the forest floor to the ceiling." He squinted. "But I can't get a reading for lateral distance. There's – too much water condensation in the air."

"Yes, I can see the mist in the upper atmosphere."

"And the transcriber doesn't have radar capability." Tod peered into the distance. "Notice how the trees are bigger here than they are farther away?"

"They are all the same approximate size, my lad. The farther trees just *look* smaller because of diminishing perspective."

Lisa hugged herself again. Her eyes danced in their sockets as she stared at the enormity of the cavern. She forced herself to remain calm. "What does that mean?"

"It is depth perception: the manner in which binocular vision perceives distant objects relative to objects that are closer to the eyes."

Tod trained the transcriber at a faraway tree. "He's right. The farther trees are the same height as the closer trees. It looks so – strange."

"It is another thing that you must get used to."

Lisa stammered, "But how – how could the Persians have done this without our knowing? I mean, how could they have done this at *all*? It's impossi – it's beyond their capability. It's beyond *anyone's* capability. How could anyone carve out a cavern like this, and plant a giant garden in it?" She squeezed her eyes together to ward off another bout of disorientation. "And if those trees are more than a thousand years old . . ."

Tod heard a strange sound in the air, like a loose belt on a servomotor. He glanced around to see if anyone else showed signs of having heard it. Lisa pinched her brows at him. Prof looked all around and, as the slapping sound grew louder, finally looked toward the ceiling.

Tod followed Prof's stunned gaze. He barely had time to throw his hands in front of his face before a dark shadow appeared overhead and something hard raked across his outthrust palms. He fell back and dropped the transcriber. The monstrous flying object, twice Tod's size, passed over him.

Lisa screamed.

Tod rolled around in time to see great flapping wings beating the air above Lisa's supine form. Stretched toward her were legs the size of tree limbs, tipped with claws like scythes. Clutching talons wrapped around her torso and legs. She was lifted bodily off the ground. A series of raucous screeches pierced the air. Then Lisa was borne over the edge of the outcrop, and away across the cavern.

After Tod got over his fright, he grabbed the transcriber. He pointed it in the general direction of the figures in flight as they disappeared in the distant mist.

He scrolled back through the transcriber's memory. When he had thrust up his hands to ward off the descending blow, the transcriber had a momentary but perfect view of the creature in flight. Automatically it attempted to identify the brute in the image. It scrolled through families and genera without making any kind of match. When it exhausted the possibilities of extant genera, it searched its databank for genera that were extinct.

The transcriber let Tod know that it was uncertain of the genus and species by flashing the closest match: *Aepyornis maximus*. A link provided descriptive details.

Prof's voice crackled with an unnatural timber.

"What was it, my lad?"

Tod stared at him in disbelief. "It was an Arabian roc."

Chapter 14

According to the transcriber's background link, *Aepyornis maximus* was the largest bird that ever existed. It attained a height of ten feet and weighed more than eight hundred pounds. It was so much larger than the African ostrich and Australian emu that adults of those species could have been mistaken for chicks of the so-called elephant bird. It was native to Madagascar.

The last authenticated sighting of a living *Aepyornis maximus* was in the 1500's. The bird was flightless like its smaller cousins. Complete skeletons were on display in various museums throughout the world. Other giant birds of similar ilk were the New Guinea cassowary (which topped the scales at five hundred pounds), and the recently extinct New Zealand moa.

The Arabian roc was a bird of a different sort. This flying raptor existed in mythology rather than in human memory. The oldest and most famous account was from the fifth voyage of Sinbad the Sailor. After landing on a desert island, his starving men dispatched and consumed a hatchling while the parents were away from the nest. They made good their escape by sea shortly before the adult rocs returned and discovered the bones of their newborn progeny. Each roc snatched a gigantic boulder with its claws, flew after the fleeing ship, and dropped the boulders like bombs. The ship was utterly destroyed, and the passengers and crew were either crushed or drowned. Sinbad alone survived by clinging to a plank until he was washed ashore on a neighboring island.

Explorer Marco Polo claimed to have encountered an adult roc whose wingspan measured nearly fifty feet, and whose feathers grew more than twenty-five feet in length. This bird of prey was supposedly strong enough to carry off an elephant. Other stories from other eye-witnesses were equally as preposterous.

Prof scoffed. "The transcriber suggested a roc only because Sarah input every bit of information we possess about Persia, including its history, legends, and fairy tales."

"But you saw it. And seeing is believing, as the old adage goes."

"I know what I saw. And I believe in its existence. I simply do not believe that it was the roc of ages."

"A raptor by any other name . . . But what it's called is irrelevant. It's got Lisa, and we have to get her back."

"Did the transcriber track them?"

Tod shook his head. "Only until they vanished in the haze."

"It probably took her to its nest."

Tod understood the implication – either to eat her, or to feed her to its young. "Then it's all the more imperative that we go after her right away."

"Go after her?" Prof squealed. Then, after a moment, "Yes, of course. But how?"

Tod overcame some of his fear of heights. He dropped down to all fours where the outcrop joined one wall, then crawled around the outer edge to the opposite side. "Look at this, Prof. There's a rock ladder over here."

Tod described the breakdown in the only language he knew. What he called a ladder was actually an extension of the cliff face in which the nearly vertical slope consisted of a broad base that stepped back incrementally to create what could, by a great stretch of the imagination, be called steps or rungs. The risers ranged from two to three feet, while many of the ledges were little more than handholds or finger grips. The nearest ledge jutted out from the cavern wall some seven feet below the rim of the outcrop.

Tod felt dizzy just from looking down. "I can climb this," he said, with confidence that he didn't possess.

"But if you slip – "

"I have to try." He glared at Prof with an urgency that was borne of utter necessity. "I have to go after her. You know that. She's – she's all I've got."

Prof inhaled deeply. "Yes, my lad. I know you do."

Tod tucked the transcriber in the belt loop, then lay flat on his belly and slunk close to the edge.

"Here, take this." Prof grabbed the shoulder strap and pulled the knapsack off his shoulder. "I will – I will go back and get Denny. We will come after you with additional supplies."

Tod pulled the strap over his head. He slithered sideways until his feet found the mossy lip. Then he spun around and scrambled over the edge. He hung for a moment, bent in the middle with his feet hanging down and his toes outstretched.

Prof held onto Tod's forearms. "Easy does it, my lad. Easy does it."

Tod slowly lowered himself farther. He slid suddenly as the bulk of his weight went over the edge, but caught himself with his elbows. "Don't let go!"

Prof's grip was firm, but Tod's considerable mass was pulling both of them over the edge.

Tod squirmed downward, felt his toes touch the rock below, then grunted, "Okay," and let his full weight down on the flat surface of the rock. His fingers maintained a grip on the edge. "Okay."

Prof let go of Tod's forearms. "I hope the other steps are shorter."

"So do I."

Tod stood on a rock that measured four feet square. The top and sides were colored with green, yellow, and brown patches of lichen. He looked up at Prof. He wanted to declare some words of farewell, but did not know what to say.

"Good luck, my lad."

"Thanks, Prof."

Professor Pembroke's face disappeared as he scooted away from the precipice.

Tod was on his own. He heard some scuffing sounds as Prof scampered over the sphagnum moss and entered the unlit tunnel. Then he felt truly alone – and scared. He had never been alone before. He had never been in such a large air-filled space. He had never been at the top of such a high vertical drop in open air. But he couldn't bear the thought of living without Lisa.

He looked down from his tenuous perch. The rocky staircase bellied outward along the wall and around the base of the outcrop. There were several ways he could descend; he had plenty of choices. He saw that one flat rock lay barely two feet beneath his own. He crouched, bent down on one knee, and swung his other leg over and onto the next lower rock. From there he stepped half a foot down to an adjacent rock. Then he had to stretch three feet down to the next one.

The descent was easier than he expected – until he skidded on a slick spot, lost his balance, and fell on his posterior as his feet slid out from under him. He clung to the rock like a limpet. He suddenly found himself breathing hard and fast despite the temporary cessation of exertion. Beads of sweat broke out on his forehead. He felt faint.

After he got over his initial fright, he studied the situation before rushing headlong and possibly tumbling to the bottom head over heels. The gripsoles of his booties had never slipped before; it was a new experience for him. He proceeded cautiously, testing the footing of each ledge by gradually sliding his bootie along the surface before he put any weight on it. It seemed that rock that was dry offered a high degree of friction, while dampness from condensation made the surface slippery.

He tried not to look at the forest floor, but to limit his glances to the next narrow ledge that jutted outward beneath his feet. This system enabled him to control his fear – or at least to keep his fear to a minimum. He found that by scuttling sideways he could sometimes find a wider ledge, or one with better purchase.

Several times he was thrown off balance when the knapsack slid in front of his belly just as he was bending to step down to a lower ledge. He had to keep throwing it backward over his shoulder. He sat down on a ledge that was wide enough to accommodate most of his posterior, while his feet could rest on the next lower ledge; together the two ledges created a chair of rock. He pulled the pack strap over his head and placed the knapsack on his lap. The strap could be adjusted to fit people of different heights.

He was about to shorten the strap so that the pack would ride higher on his chest as it swung around, and not droop over his knees whenever he crouched, when an idea occurred to him. He lengthened the strap as far as it would go. Instead of slinging the strap over his head and onto the opposite shoulder, he swung it over his back, lifted the strap above his head, tucked both arms through the strap, then let the strap fall down onto his nape. With the strap tucked close under his armpits, the knapsack could not slide off his back. The knapsack rode comfortably on the middle of his spine. The weight of the pack was centered and did not throw him out of kilter.

Because the fabric of the one-piece insulated suit was elastic, it stretched easily as Tod clambered from ledge to ledge. The material maintained body temperature by keeping in warmth when it was needed, and by releasing excess heat as it was generated. Perspiration never accumulated on his skin, but was wicked through the fabric to the outer, water-resistant layer from which it evaporated without causing any chilling effect. Only his fingers were cold, from touching the naked rock.

Tod stopped on a ledge from which he could see no way to climb down. Twelve feet of sheer rock separated the ledge from the one below it. He sidestepped several feet, then had to climb up and sideways some more before he found a way to descend. He learned that it was much easier to climb up than it was to climb down; it was easier to pull himself up onto a ledge that he could see, than to support his weight as he stretched a leg down to a ledge that he had to feel for with his toes. He also learned that it was far, far easier to climb while facing the rock as if it were a ladder, than to put his back to the rock and scramble down as if the wall were a staircase.

He rested for a moment while he gauged the remaining distance to the forest floor. He stood barely fifty feet below the top of the nearest redwood. He estimated that he still had more than two hundred feet to descend. He felt as if he had been climbing for hours, yet only a score of minutes had passed. He felt numerous sharp aches in muscles that he had seldom used to such an extent.

One slip or false move could be fatal. After catching his breath, Tod resumed his downward progress at the speed of a nudibranch. Before he took a step, he stared long and hard at the ledge on which he intended to alight. He made certain that the rock was either dry or was covered with lichen. Then he turned and faced the rock wall, and slowly lowered himself down. He nearly panicked when the outer corner of one ledge broke under his weight. Loose rock chattered from ledge to ledge all the way to the bottom.

He got stuck temporarily on one ledge because the succeeding ledge, although only two feet away, was sloped. When he let some of his weight on the rock, his gripsole refused to produce enough friction to keep from sliding. He had to stretch so far down and sideways to the next suitable ledge that he nearly did a split. With his legs spread far apart, he worked his fingers along a narrow crack as he slowly shifted his body weight from one foot to the other. When he finally attained a secure position, his inner thigh muscles felt as if they had been stretched out of shape, and his calf muscles felt as if they were made of rubber; they were shaking so hard from physical strain and mortal terror that he was ready to collapse.

He shifted his weight from one foot to other and then back again, until his legs stopped aching and shaking. Then he dropped to the next ledge, quickly stepped to another one lower down, and found a suitable resting spot. He sat for five full minutes before tackling the next descent.

In this manner he worked his way toward the bottom of the cliff. About fifty feet from the forest floor he encountered a broad talus slope which, while angled gradually, consisted largely of loose boulders. Some of these boulders were balanced precariously. They rolled or turned when he put his weight on them. He judged that he could fall now without getting killed, but he would undoubtedly get seriously injured, perhaps incapacitated, by landing on sharp points or knifelike edges.

He switched from climbing on hands and feet to scooting on all five points: both hands, both feet, and buttocks. He got poked by sharp rocks several times, but he was able to plop down in a sitting position when a boulder rolled out from under him. All of a sudden there was no more rock beneath him. He stood solidly on a bed of brown needles that covered the forest floor.

He breathed a grateful sigh of relief at his amazing accomplishment.

Now that he no longer had to overcome fear in order to concentrate on climbing down a precipitous rock wall, he studied his surroundings with newfound awe. The redwoods vaulted toward the ceiling like stately monolithic monarchs. They looked much taller from his position at the bottom than they had appeared from above. The shelf from which he had begun his descent seemed like little more than a bump. In addition to cones and needles that had fallen from the redwoods, the ground was covered with ferns, shrubbery, and low-lying vegetation.

The air possessed a strange odor that was neither chemical in nature nor ozone from sparking machinery. It reminded him more of a hydroponics garden than a laboratory or motor room. Close to the ground there was a musky scent that reminded him of burning synthetic rubber, or perhaps the cloying scent of mold or mildew.

Tod noticed a dome-shaped object that was almost completely concealed by redwood needles. He dropped onto his knees, parted the needles, and saw that the object looked like a mushroom – growing wild in the undergrowth.

Hastily he pulled the transcriber from its holder. He aimed it at the mushroom and tapped the link for information. The transcriber immediately identified the mushroom as *Caulorhiza umbonata*, appropriately known as the rooting redwood mushroom: an inedible species that grew in redwood forests, and that extended a single long root deep into the soil as a way to obtain water and nourishment.

Soil! This was something that Tod had never seen. He scraped away needles to bare the ground beneath the understory. Careful not to disturb the mushroom, he scooped up a handful of loose black dirt and let it sift between his fingers. The topsoil was fine yet gritty, filled with a redolence that he now appreciated was nature's effluvium. Wonder of wonders!

Abruptly he yelped and jerked back his hand, dropping the soil in the process. A slimy earthworm fell squirming to the ground. Tod spotted ants and white grubs in the scattered earth. This soil was amazing! It was simply teeming with life forms that Tod had only read about in digital books or viewed on kinetic recordings. Flora and fauna abounded in this impossible cavern.

The rustling of dry needles and the sharp retort of a snapped twig jerked Tod out of his reverie. He looked up in astonishment at a four-footed mammal that looked like a cross between a deer and a moose. It stood over seven feet tall at the shoulders. The gigantic antler rack stretched twelve feet from tip to tip. The antler rack was part palmate and part fingerlike. The mammal worked its jaws as it peered down at him from its uncommon height.

Tod flung up the transcriber like a vampire hunter wielding a cross to ward off an undead bloodsucker. The transcriber was not much of a weapon.

The transcriber was still set on information mode. It scrolled through possible identities without locating a match. After exhausting the genera of present day mammals, it searched through its databank for extinct members of the Cervidae family. It finally settled on an ungulate known in binomial nomenclature as *Megalo-ceros giganteus.*

Its common name was Irish Elk.

Chapter 15

The first skeletal remains of the Irish Elk were dis-covered in a peat bog in Ireland. Later skeletons that were exhumed elsewhere indicated that the animal's range extended throughout northern Europe and Asia. Follow-up studies determined that the animal was not as closely related to modern species of elk as was ini-tially postulated. Paleontologists therefore decided to refer to the extinct ungulate as the Giant Deer. The radiocarbon-dating technique suggested that the most recent bones were around eight thousand years old, give or take a few hundred years.

The Ice Age animal that was staring down at Tod chewed its cud in ignorance of the fact that it was sup-posed to be extinct. At the moment, Tod cared less about these informative but useless facts than he did about whether he was on the animal's menu. He was too frightened to move under the steady gaze of those black watchful eyes.

The Giant Deer did not look away as it lowered its massive neck, and with a single bite tore a large shrub out of the ground. It took its time in masticating and swallowing the morsel. Tod gulped. The Giant Deer took two steps forward and ripped out another bush by the roots. It then turned its attention elsewhere. Not seeing anything edible in the immediate neighborhood, it ignored Tod and meandered among the redwoods in search of other succulent vegetation.

Tod heaved a deep sigh of relief at his close encounter. As soon as he regained his composure, he made certain that the transcriber was recording cur-rent events. Next he was struck by the awful realization that he could not afford to spend time on biological observations. He had a far more important task at hand. Forest denizens and environmental studies would have to wait until Lisa stood safely by his side to share the discoveries.

The Giant Deer ambled around the trees until it was lost to view. Tod rose to his full height. Despite his size, he felt like a pigmy in the realm of colossal trees and gargantuan elk or deer. He surveyed the terrain in awe.

The upper branches of the giant redwoods grew close together like overlapping umbrellas, obscuring a clear view through the canopy. The treetops were enshrouded in thin but clinging mist that diffused the yellow-white illumination that emanated from the cavern ceiling. After moving far enough away from the sheer cliff face so that the rock wall was no longer in sight, there was nothing to show Tod that he wasn't walking through a pre-glacial California forest, instead of traipsing through the interior of a mammoth cavity in the Earth's crust. The overall effect was one of virtual reality.

Tod was surely baffled. He used the transcriber's tracknav plotter to determine his present location. Before he could tap the link to follow the route that Lisa and her captor had taken through the air, the transcriber – still recording imagery of the surrounding terrain – provided best-guess intelligence as to the identity of his whereabouts. Two place names were flashing alternately: Hyperborea and Antedeluvia.

Hyperborea was a mythological place of warmth that existed in the arctic regions. Antedeluvia referred to the center of civilization in the era that preceded the Noachian or Biblical flood.

Tod pursed his lips and shook his head. No theory or hypothesis or conjecture or guesswork would bring Lisa back to him. He had to avoid intellectual digressions and get on the move.

He tapped the plotter link. The transcriber switched to a graphic representation of the roc's last recorded flight path, and extrapolated its probable course based on a straight-line assumption from the time of its disappearance in the fog. There was no way to ascertain if the roc turned after its image left the transcriber. The only thing that Tod could do was to follow the baseline, weave from side to side, look for a nesting site, and hope for the best.

He started walking.

The underbrush was thick and, in some places, impenetrable. Tod was forced to walk around mighty trees and dense stands of shrubbery. In some places, interlaced vines grew so thick and convoluted that they created a solid barrier. In other places, long-stemmed growths were studded with sharp thorns or stickers that snagged his jumpsuit or pierced the exposed skin of his hands and face.

He did his best to veer back onto the track that the transcriber laid out for him. When the real track ended, he programmed the transcriber to create a grid with the baseline extended through the middle. His own course plot was continuously input, so he could see not only where he was going but precisely where he had been. This information would prevent him from duplicating his search track, and would enable him to retrace his steps to the base of the cliff beneath the outcrop. He made certain that the transcriber lanyard was secured to the belt loop.

Occasionally he glimpsed more Irish Elk or Giant Deer. Some browsed in pairs, others grazed in herds. He stumbled onto what the transcriber called an animal trail: a passage through the undergrowth that animals had taken so often that the vegetation was beaten down and a clear route was trampled through the brush. Tod took time to wonder how the deer or elk managed to fit their enormous antler racks through tight places in the forest. The transcriber did not have an answer for that; it even refused to speculate. Tod followed the animal trails whenever they paralleled his course or did not stray far from his baseline.

He spotted other mammals aplenty: rabbits, squirrels, woodchucks, and hedgehogs, which the transcriber identified as a mix of Old World and New World species, with occasional Asian or African varieties thrown in for good measure. Innumerable birds flitted through the air in their endless quest for food. Insects buzzed, fluttered, walked, and crawled in countless numbers and variety. Tod let the transcriber record and categorize the profusion of flora and fauna that he encountered, but he did not let the biota distract him from his primary assignment.

He had to find Lisa. Persistently he shouted her name.

He persevered in the hope that she was still alive. Yet he felt despair every time he did not receive a reply to his call.

Tod skirted redwood trees whose trunks measured more than eight feet in diameter and better than twenty-five feet in circumference. They towered nearly than three hundred fifty feet in height. He almost fell over backwards when he leaned back to look up for an aerie. He wondered if the roc nested in treetops or on the ground. In a moment of idle contemplation, he opined that even if the eggs or chicks were not too heavy to be supported by a nest in a treetop, then certainly the adults that had to sit on the eggs to hatch them were far too massive. For what it was worth, the nest that Sinbad the Sailor found was located on the beach.

He walked around numerous ponds that dotted the landscape. The loam on the surrounding banks was soft and moist. Hoof prints in the mud indicated that deer or elk used the ponds as watering holes. Smaller animal tracks were mixed with the larger ones.

He continually found himself gawking at every new species of plant or animal that made its presence known. He was assailed by unfamiliar scents like nothing he had ever smelled before. The transcriber identified one particularly fragrant plant as *Lonicera japonica*, or Japanese honeysuckle, whose nectar was a favorite food source of certain Lepidoptera larvae. He was exhilarated by several species of beautifully ornate and colorful butterflies that flitted from blossom to blossom.

Lisa, he reminded himself. I must find Lisa.

"Lisa!" he yelled. "Lisa, where are you?"

His shouts rang hollow, swallowed by the immensity of the forest that filled this gigantic underground chamber. Then he wondered: How could a cavern be so extensive without collapsing from lack of support? The ceiling of a broad submerged chamber could be supported by water, but the ceiling of an air-filled cavern needed some form of underpinning to prevent it from caving in. It was yet another impossibility to add to the list, Professor Pembroke's proverb notwithstanding.

The ideation of the probability of collapse was followed by an instinctive cringe. Tod looked up, expecting at any moment to see great sheets of rock falling through the treetops.

"Lisa!"

For a moment after his shout the forest was preternaturally still. Gradually the sounds of nature returned to their ordinary cadence. Tod crouched in fear when he heard a screeching sound that reminded him of a drill press boring a hole through metal. The transcriber identified the stridulation as originating from an insect of the order Orthoptera: some species of grasshopper that created the raucous sound by rapidly rubbing its hind legs against its forelegs, like a bow across the string of a violin.

Tod slowly regained his upright posture. He scanned the forest in all directions. The scope of his vision was limited by the density of redwood trees and encroaching vegetation. He felt as if he could wander fruitlessly for days. Lisa could be anywhere in the immensity of this primeval forest, perhaps in the middle of one of the thickets that he had passed – or worse, down the gullet of an Arabian roc.

"Lisa!"

Tod felt pangs of hunger despite the gravity of the situation. He sat on the ground facing an enormous log from which small redwoods sprouted. The transcriber identified the long length of timber as a nurse log: a fallen redwood in which seedlings were nurtured and protected as the wood decayed and provided a substrate.

Tod removed the knapsack. He nibbled on preserved foodstuffs while he read about the interaction of various elements in the environment. No single plant or animal survived on its own. Each organism relied on other organisms for reproduction, growth, sustenance, or survival. The forest was not simply a conglomeration of disparate parts – trees, shrubs, birds, bugs, and worms – but a complex interactive and interdependent system.

Plants converted sunlight to energy by means of chlorophyll, absorbed water from the ground, and fed animals that depended upon plants for their sustenance. Animals ate plants, then fertilized the soil with undigested food, which in turn enabled plants to live and grow. It was an endless cycle of renewal.

Tod heard a thrashing in the brush nearby. He jumped up. "Lisa!" But it was only an Irish Elk or Giant Deer, which stared at him quizzically.

He snatched the knapsack and threw it over his back. He had no time for idle speculation. He was frantic with remorse for even taking a moment to rest. He started hiking again.

Hours passed. There was no sign of Lisa, and there was no indication that the cavern did not stretch to infinity in all directions. He stopped walking in a more or less straight line after trekking for several miles. There was no reason for Tod to presume that the roc had flown a linear route without deviation. It could have turned anywhere, at any time. It could have doubled back. It could have landed in the upper canopy of a redwood tree, where it was even now roosting quietly. Tod's unswerving course was nearly as aimless as walking in ever-widening circles.

The cavern itself was a puzzle. Perhaps if he solved the riddle of its existence, the solution would provide a clue that would lead directly to the roc's nest – and to Lisa.

It stood to reason that the roc was not the only one of its kind. There had to be at least two of them – male and female – in order to propagate the species. Just as there were herds of Irish Elk or Giant Deer, there had to be flocks of rocs. That was nature's way. Unless the roc was in fact a phoenix, the legendary Egyptian bird that consumed itself by fire and later arose from its own ashes, reproduction was the only mechanism that enabled the essence of an individual to survive its own demise.

Fraught with indecision, Tod took a long drink from his plastic canteen.

He watched a bee collect pollen from a bright yellow blossom that the transcriber identified as a nasturtium, *Tropaeolum tuberosum*. Tod ignored the information about the edibility of the leaves and underground tubers.

He was contemplating his options when he noticed a gradual dimming of ambient light. He rubbed his eyes with the backs of his hands, but that did not dispel the loss of brightness in the surrounding forest. He keyed the transcriber. The reduction in luminosity was increasing geometrically.

Tod had taken the illumination for granted. The increasing darkness made him realize his mistake. Nothing was ever static. Change was the way of the world.

At the same time, some changes were cyclical: seasons came and went, the sun rose and set, tides ebbed and flooded. Even in a subaqueous environment, night followed day.

The light that filled the cavern was probably not a natural phenomenon such as phosphorescence or bioluminescence. It had to be as artificial as the cavern: a manmade – or, Tod shuddered at the thought, an alien made – environment. In that case the loss of brightness should be temporary.

Ratiocination proved nothing. Tod had no experience on which to base a supposition. All he had was hope.

The cavern went black.

"*Lisa!*"

Chapter 16

The cavern was not totally black.

After Tod's eyes adjusted to the dark, he found that he could perceive faint shadows and vague silhouettes. A suffused glow emanated from overhead, above the treetops.

The forest grew quiescent with the onset of simulated night. Faint peeps and chirps were audible in the distance, but for the most part the animal population must have lain down to sleep.

Tod switched on his handlight. Its bright beam seemed intrusive in the surrounding gloom, like a stark invasion of privacy. He surveyed his environs. Nothing moved.

If he hadn't been able to find Lisa in the lustrous light of day, his chances of finding her in the thick of night were worse than slender. Furthermore, he was exhausted.

He doused the beam and sat on a thick bed of soft needles. He swept some cones aside to create a clear space around his body. He stretched out on his back, put his hands under his head, and gazed upward. Eventually, as visual purple flooded the photoreceptors in his eyes, his low-light vision enabled him to discern through the overhead mist what appeared to be either dim individual lights or tiny clusters of soft illumination above the canopy.

His mind was awhirl. Lisa was missing, perhaps dead. The long-time stability of his life was gone, no doubt irrevocably. His hopes and plans for the future were without tangible meaning, even if he did not perish in this impossible forest that occupied this impossible cavern. He must have dozed off as he was pondering these imponderables. He was startled to full awareness by a loud snort and a puff of air in his ear.

He jerked up to a sitting position, scrambled for the handlight, switched it on, and saw two columnar posts standing by his side. The posts were covered with coarse, light brown hair. He raised the angle of the beam. The elk or deer snorted, then bounded into the nearby underbrush in a series of long-legged leaps that would have put a pole-vaulter to shame. All was soon quiet again.

Tod switched off the handlight and sat in the semi-dark. He inhaled deeply. The air had a cool savor that he hadn't noticed before, and a sweet but biting fragrance. It was unlike the processed air of the subaqueous bases and submersibles. He let the flower-scented atmosphere infiltrate his nostrils and lungs.

Soon he noticed that the shadows were grayer and the silhouettes were more pronounced. He stared upward. Either the ceiling was getting brighter, or more individual light sources were being illuminated. The mist was thick in the treetops so that only a diffuse glow was evident from overhead. He felt refreshed after his enforced slumber. It was the commencement of another shift.

He wanted to call for Lisa, but felt that it would be sacrilege to break the pervading silence so early after shiftbreak.

He munched on some food and drained the last drop of water from his canteen. He studied the transcriber screen. According to the tracknav plot, he had walked more than nine miles since descending into the forest on the previous shift, yet he stood only five miles from the base of the outcrop. The difference in mileage was due to the circuitous route that he had been forced to take around ponds, trees, and thickets.

Instead of continuing farther into the cavern, he decided to work his way back toward the entrance tunnel by making wide sweeps to the left and right: a zigzag pattern that would increase his search area while decreasing the distance between him and anticipated help.

He packed his knapsack and recommenced his strange peregrination. The clinging mist dissipated at ground level.

The forest awoke with sights and sounds that were now becoming familiar. Animals emerged from their burrows and hidey-holes, nests and anthills. The air resonated with tones and twangs. Tod switched on the transcriber's microphone and audio circuits to record the sounds of the forest.

He felt almost like a part of the natural symbiosis.

He stopped at the first pond that he encountered. He slaked his agonizing thirst with cool fresh water that tasted unlike any liquid that he had ever drunk. It possessed a metallic aftertaste that suggested the infiltration of raw minerals. He refilled his canteen.

Tod had been traveling for a couple of hours when he heard a sound that was new to his ears. It reminded him of a blast furnace or a rocket exhaust that he had viewed on kinetic recordings, except that the bass reverberations were emitted in short bursts without recognizable cadence. The sounds came from ahead, from somewhere out of sight.

His forward progress was blocked by a nurse tree whose width rose higher than Tod's full stature. He had to walk two hundred feet – more than seventy-five paces as Prof would have measured it, using Tod's longer stride – before he rounded the massive root ball that marked one end. The vast glade in front of him was only sparsely populated by giant redwoods. Milling in the wide open spaces between the trees were large quadrupeds whose heads bore a pair of stout horns that grew downward along their ears before curving gracefully upward. The beasts wore brown shaggy coats whose long hair reached nearly to the ground beneath their hooves.

Tod ducked back behind the root ball. Without making noise or sudden movement, he eased the transcriber around the massive trunk, aimed it at the nearest creature, and magnified the image for recording and identification. The transcriber identified the mammal as *Ovibos moschatus*, commonly known as the arctic musk ox. They stood only half as tall as the Irish Elk, and did not weigh as much, but their short legs and wide midriff made them appear more massive. Still extant in the topside world, although endangered due to flooding of much of their foraging territory, they roamed freely throughout Greenland, Canada, and Alaska. The herd was grazing busily in a field of tall grass.

A few individuals were lapping water from a pond. One calf, on the far side of the pond, appeared somewhat deformed as it ambled along the bank. Tod squinted, then perceived that the animal's image was distorted, or wavy – perhaps, he reasoned, by intervening stalks of grain.

Tod read enough of the musk ox's background to learn that the mammals were nonaggressive herbivores. He also learned that his presence might trigger a defensive posture in which the adults would form a circle around the calves, and face outward. Extreme proximity could incite stampede.

Tod slunk out of visual range in the opposite direction – which soon brought him to another herd of bovines that the transcriber identified as the extinct aurochs, *Bos primigenius*. The adult aurochs stood six feet tall at the shoulders, and weighed more than a ton. It resembled the Texas Longhorn except that its horns pointed forward instead of to the sides. The aurochs frequently appeared in prehistoric cave paintings. Primitive man domesticated the aurochs and bred them into modern domestic cattle.

The aurochs was a grazer like the musk ox, and was harmless unless one happened to get underfoot or stray close enough to be sideswiped by the pointed horns. Tod snapped high-resolution stillshots for future reference.

In avoiding the herd of aurochs, Tod encountered a geological discontinuity: an uplift in the land which elsewhere had been mostly flat and level with some gently rolling hills. The rock wall rose to a height of twelve feet. It was covered with vines whose stems were so thick and dark that they resembled high-voltage electrical cables.

He could see that no redwoods grew beyond the wall, and that the open expanse was sparsely populated by small trees and shrubs. He contemplated the canopy above his head. The treetops stood so close together that it might be difficult for a roc to penetrate the foliage. He reasoned that the giant bird might choose to nest in an open and unobstructed area. This reasoning decided Tod upon his next course of action.

He wrapped his fingers around a stem as if it were a rope. He pulled himself up, reached for another handhold higher on the stem, and pulled himself up farther. The bootie's gripsoles found partial purchase on the rough bark. He climbed and walked his way up the vertical incline to the upper corner of the wall, then pulled his torso over the edge and onto the vine-covered top. He wormed on his belly and flailed with his legs until he lay firmly on the upper tangle of vines.

He rose up to his knees. He could see hundreds of feet ahead, through mist so fine that it wasn't noticeable nearby. Only where there were no monster trees or dense vegetation to obscure the far view was he aware of the ever-present shroud of condensation.

The transcriber identified an eclectic collection of well-known varieties of Pagoda dogwood, European holly, mountain laurel, rhododendron, juniper, and various grains and grasses.

The rock wall on which Tod was kneeling extended as far as he could see in either direction. The wall curved slightly inward, as if the land that he was facing was an enormous enclosure. The drop on the opposite side was only half as high as he had climbed. He eased himself down onto the green verdant sward of knee-deep grass.

He walked straight away from the wall. After a mile of easy going he came to another wall. This one stood about five feet high and was dappled with multicolored lichen instead of vine. He leaped and squirmed to the top of the rock. Coincidentally, this wall also exhibited a slight inward curve in both directions. The curve of this wall was more noticeable because of the lack of creepers and foliage. The curve was oddly uniform.

Tod was curious. He took a moment to pull the transcriber from his belt and pan the wall. As expected, the transcriber identified the rock as basalt. Basalt was volcanic in origin. It solidified amorphously, like excess concrete that was poured outside of a frame. Basalt could solidify in the form of massive blocks with sides that were plumb if the molten lava flowed against hardened rock that presented a vertical face. The lava would seek its own level in the cooling process, resulting in a flat top. If the outer rock eroded, what remained was a mass of volcanic rock that had the appearance of having been poured into a mold – which in effect it had.

There was a great deal of difference between a massive block of basalt and one that stretched from side to side like a bulwark, complete with symmetrically rounded corners. Tod ran the transcriber along the roughly formed surface. The picture on the transcriber emphasized a vertical junction that extended from top to bottom. Ten feet farther on it emphasized an identical crack.

Tod held the transcriber close to the crack, touched the tab for magnification, and watched closely as the image was enhanced and enlarged on the transcriber. The crack passed all the way through the rock. So did the next crack, and the next, and the next. The hairline cracks were evenly spaced.

This rock wall was not a single mass of basalt, but a series of blocks of identical size.

The cracks between the blocks were so perfectly matched that not even a blade of grass would fit into them.

The wall was artificial!

If the outer wall was not natural, and had the same degree of curvature as the inner wall, then a perpendicular line extended inward should lead to a common focal point.

Another mile of rolling grassland took Tod to a third concentric wall of black basalt. This wall also consisted of individual blocks that were laid end to end along an arc.

Tod's interpretive satisfaction was interrupted by a sound that he instantly recognized as the screech of a roc. He looked around for several seconds before it occurred to him to look up. The mist was thin enough that he could see the ceiling of the cavern, entirely aglow with a yellow-white intensity that prevented the casting of shadows. Against this bleached backdrop he spotted a pair of giant auburn birds that were soaring in his direction.

He sought a place to hide. He could either climb the low wall in front of him, and look for a suitable cubbyhole, or he could run back to the nearest stand of dogwoods. He chose the dogwoods. He crouched next to a slender trunk and peered through stems on which white flowers bloomed.

The rocs circled aimlessly for several minutes, not directly overhead but in the direction of the projected focal point of the putative concentric enclosures. Tod had the impression that the birds had not spotted his mad dash for safety. They dived, soared, and pirouetted as if they were searching for other game. For the briefest moment Tod entertained the crazy notion that the surest way to locate their aerie was to let them capture him and carry him straight to their nest. It did not require much reason to overrule his bravado. Besides, he weighed more than twice as much as Lisa, and was undoubtedly too heavy for a roc to lift.

He and the transcriber observed the hovering birds for several minutes, gathering information. Body length from beak to tail feathers measured twelve feet. Wingspan was twenty-two feet. One of them suddenly folded its wings against its side and plummeted like a falling stone. Tod thought that it was going to crash into the dirt, but just before it struck the ground it spread its wings as wide as they would go, stretched its legs and talons forward, turned the nose dive into a swoop, and grabbed a brown-furred animal with a long lashing tail and thrashing legs.

The distance was too great for the transcriber to

obtain a clear recording of the animal for identification. It was about the size of Tod's head, perhaps a little larger.

The roc let out a loud screech as it swerved to the side and flapped its great wings for all it was worth. It gained altitude rapidly, swung past its mate or companion, then soared away. The transcriber drew its track on the plotter. The direction of flight coincided with the projected focal point. This implied that the rocs nested in or toward the center of this megalithic compound.

The remaining roc flew lazily in precessing circles that carried it away from Tod. Keeping the distant shape in sight, he scrambled from his cover, leaped over the low wall of basalt, and raced for the nearest stand of dogwoods. The roc kept circling away. Tod ducked and dashed from tree to tree, each time keeping under cover until he was certain that he had not been spotted. Finally the giant bird vanished in the upper layers of mist.

As Tod strode through the cropped grass, he kept reminding himself to look up and around the ceiling – a behavior that was unnatural for him. Suddenly he thought: Cropped grass?

He dropped down to one knee and fondled a handful of blades. The tops were ragged instead of pointed. None had gone to seed. He was still pondering the meaning of this occurrence when he caught a movement of white out of the corner of his eye.

He crouched lower.

He watched the animal that was nibbling grass. Beyond it stood another, smaller but with horns. Then came another, and another, and another. Soon the field in front of him was filled with ambling mammals. He heard them bleating and baaing. The herd of goats and flock of sheep ignored him as they concentrated on grazing.

Tod smiled. He stood upright and recorded the scene for posterity. Several goats and sheep glanced in his direction, held their eyes on him momentarily, then returned to the task of filling their stomachs.

He waited until the bulk of the mammals passed before venturing into the open. He noticed that several lambs and kids were nestled under rhododendron and mountain laurel, and were only just now standing up on wobbly legs to amble into the open. He surmised that they had been hiding from the rocs. He spotted no small brown animals that resembled the one that had been carried aloft.

Tod took a lesson from the white ruminants. He attuned his senses to listening for flapping wings and watching overhead for rocs that were soaring silently and stalking prey on the ground. He realized that in order to survive in this impossible world, he had to be aware of the dangers that it presented.

He continued across the mist-shrouded grassland. Just as another wall of basalt came into view, he saw something gray that was fluttering in a tuft of tall weeds which stood in high relief against surrounding low grass that had been cropped by sheep and goats. It reminded him of a piece of cloth, or a torn shred of syntactic foam. His heart skipped a beat.

He gradually shortened his steps without knowing that he was doing it. He was afraid of what the grazing mammals might have avoided. He froze with fear when he saw who was attached to the bit of material.

It was a Persian marine.

Chapter   17

To be completely accurate, it was a dead Persian marine.

Or rather, what was left of one.

The only way that Tod could recognize the skeleton as Persian was by the tatters of uniform that lay around the body. Nearly all the flesh was gone. The rib cage was torn apart. The grinning skull was disarticulated and the brainpan was empty. One gold tooth crown gleamed dully in the suffused light. The white bones were deeply etched where they had been gnawed and broken.

The stench was awful. Tidbits of organs and other soft parts lay scattered about in an advanced state of decay.

It took no leap of intellect for Tod to comprehend that this was what rocs did to prey that was too heavy to carry. They tore it apart piecemeal and consumed it on the spot. It was a horrible way to die. Tod was sickened by the sight, even though the marine belonged to the armed forces that were responsible for the death of his parents.

Little wonder that the goats and sheep were so wary, and hid in the shrubbery when predators soared overhead.

Tod left the remains undisturbed where they lay. He scouted the area for weapons or supplies. He saw nothing that might have belonged to the dead marine: no weapons, no ammo belt, no supply pack, no protective head gear. He recorded everything for Grand Intelligence.

He proceeded with forlorn hope of finding Lisa alive. He climbed to the top of the low wall – and could go no farther. In front of him stretched a broad expanse of water whose opposite shore was not in sight.

Tod did not know how to swim.

Although he had spent all his life under water, he

had never actually been *in* the water except to bathe with a sponge.

After several minutes, it occurred to him that the water might not be deep. Perhaps he could wade. He jumped back down and retrieved a twisted stick from the ground beneath a juniper tree. The stick measured five feet in length. Tod could not touch bottom with the stick.

He picked a direction and started tramping along the top of the wall. It was wide enough to serve as a roadway. Patches of lichen grew on the surfaces. He spotted more goats and sheep that were grazing in the field. They seemed content to crop grass. Once he thought he heard the flapping of wings in the distance, but the mist obscured his sighting of any airborne predators. Despite the lack of visual reference, the grazers scattered for the bushes at the sound.

By and by he noticed a tall structure looming on the wall in the foreground. As he got closer, he saw that it was one of two towers that were built out of rectangular blocks of granite. A series of marble steps led to the top of what he now perceived was an abutment between the towers. A solid granite ramp led down to the field, where a fence denied access to sheep and goats. The posts and rails were roughly hewn from ancient balks of redwood.

Square granite piers were strung across the moat, each one connected to its neighbors by cut granite arches that supported a level roadway which vanished in the mist.

Tod climbed the steps. He surveyed the bridge before attempting to cross it. The road surface appeared to be in good repair. Each of the piers sported two small towers, one on either side of the roadway. The inside facings of these towers were pierced with doorways. Tod figured that he could duck into a tower in the event that a roc attacked him while he was in the open.

He ran to the nearest tower – not in a mad dash but at a loping trot. He stopped and peered inside. The interior was nothing but an empty compartment with a façade of limestone. He was about to run to the next safety structure when he noticed an inlaid slab of marble on which curved, strange-looking lines were engraved. They reminded Tod of the markings that were incised on the gold foils.

He pulled out the transcriber and took a stillshot of the slab. It took but a moment for the transcriber to confirm Tod's suspicions. The language chip was unable to translate the text; it merely substantiated the sweeps and vertical lines as being consistent with the language that was inscribed on the foils.

This was a monumental discovery. It implied that the builders of the bridge were associated with the fabricators of the foils, and that therefore the bridge and foils were of the same approximate age.

The inner facing of the opposite tower sported a similar marble slab, with different script. Tod snapped a stillshot for the language file.

He listened intently before jogging to the next pair of towers. Again the inner facings were inlaid with marble slabs that were incised with lines of ancient script. Again the compartments were empty. Tod recorded everything for posterity.

One of the towers on the fifth bridge pier provided an item of interest. The floor of the compartment was filled with twigs and branches to a depth of four feet. In the middle of the pile lay inch-thick chalky slabs with jagged edges. The odd-shaped chunks bore no inscriptions. Tod hefted several pieces. Both sides were smooth to the touch, but not sheer.

According to the transcriber, the slabs consisted primarily of calcium carbonate, with the addition of complex molecules of polymerized amino acid. These chemical constituents conformed to those that were found in the eggshells of birds.

This was a roc nest!

Tod's heart pounded. He backed quickly from the doorway. He looked upward, then spun around and studied the opposite tower. The sky was devoid of flying

predators, and the other compartment was untenant-
ed. He eventually concluded that the nest had been
abandoned after the fledglings had learned to fly.
Nonetheless, he didn't think it was a good idea to hang
around. He ran to the next pier and pair of towers. The
compartments were vacant.

After passing several more piers and uninhabited
towers, he reached the abutment that denoted the end
of the bridge. The two towers that straddled the ramp
were likewise empty. Tod clung to the granite blocks as
he surveyed the lay of the land. The mist prevented him
from seeing more than a couple of hundred feet. All was
still.

He examined the overhead, and saw no rocs in the
air. Without looking for a closure, he climbed over the
wooden fence that separated the ramp from a basalt
roadway. Grassland extended to either side. Short trees
and bushes dotted the landscape. There were no signs
of grazing ungulates.

Tod may have appeared somewhat carefree as he
ambled through the haze, but he was ever alert for danger that might erupt from unexpected quarters – not
only from rocs swooping down from above, but from
Persian marines on patrol and anything else that was
out of the ordinary.

He could not help but smirk at his mental phrase
"out of the ordinary," for this very cavern was anything
but ordinary. Taken in context, "out of the ordinary"
meant anything that was more out of the ordinary than
the artificial construct that occupied this impossible
cavern.

He walked for nearly a mile without seeing or hearing anything "out of the ordinary." Then he encountered another wall. This one rose five feet above the
ground. He did not have to climb it because the roadway sloped up an embankment and then passed
through a broad notch in the wall to continue as a
roadway on a higher level. Paving blocks were laid to
either side as far as he could see through the mist.

Tod didn't care for the wide open spaces – not

because he was phobic like Lisa, but because he saw no place to hide in the event of an attack. He hurried ahead.

A building loomed out of the fog. Tod approached it cautiously, peered through the doorway, saw that the interior was vacant, then slipped inside and breathed a sigh of relief. He was hungry and thirsty. He sat down on the granite floor, leaned against the smooth lime-stone wall, and quickly consumed a meal. He took no additional time to rest, but proceeded onward as soon as he determined that the coast was clear.

Only a few minutes passed before he discovered another body – actually, widely scattered bones and body parts. He couldn't tell if the cadaver was that of a Persian marine because no uniform material was in evidence. He surveyed the gruesome scene with harsh distaste. The bones were too large to be Lisa's, but he couldn't help imagining that she had suffered a similar fate.

When he panned the area with the transcriber, it detected three femurs as well as triplicates and quadruplicates of several smaller bones. Only one human skull and one pelvis lay on the roadbed, but obviously the bones constituted the remains of more than a single individual.

Tod shuddered at the thought that the rocs had managed to massacre part of a squad of armed and well-trained Persian marines, while he was passing through their territory utterly defenseless.

His fear mounted several minutes later when he peered into another basalt block building and found a feather-lined nest that housed three unhatched eggs. Each egg measured more than a yard in length and a foot and a half across the widest part. There was enough yolk and albumen to feed eighty people – if they had sledge hammers to crack the shell, and a microwave oven the size of a bunk bed.

From the adjacent building he heard an ear-piercing sound that he took for the squeal that a loose fan belt made when a motor was initially started. He stepped through the doorway, his rattled mind expecting to see a compartment full of machinery. Instead he beheld two downy chicks. They were chirping for food with wide open beaks.

Tod was terrified by his next intellectual exercise: Where there were eggs and chicks, there were bound to be adults not far away. At the speed of thought there came a screech in the air.

He vaulted away from the building and searched frantically for cover. Another block building lay fifty feet away. He zoomed across the basalt roadbed to a yawning doorway. He stopped at the threshold, peered around the jamb, saw an empty compartment, inhaled deeply in relief, and jumped inside.

The building was not much of a refuge. An Arabian roc could easily fit through the doorway, just as it must fit through the doorways in which it had built its nests. All the openings were the same size. Tod's only protection lay in keeping his presence concealed.

The flapping of wings bespoke the approach of several rocs. The chicks chirped louder in synchrony with the adults.

Tod retreated to a corner in the rear of the compartment. Then he heard a scream.

A distinctly human scream.

A female scream!

Chapter 18

Tod had never heard Lisa scream, but there was no doubt in his mind that the scream had emanated from her slender throat.

Tod charged out of the building without thinking about what he was doing or where he was going – or what he was going to do when he got there. After several seconds he spotted a shape out of the corner of his eye, but not in time to avoid the talon that struck his head. He ducked and reached up at the same time, in order to avoid the blow or to diminish its impact. The leading curve of the talon struck his scalp and forearm. Instinctively he grabbed the claw with his other hand.

For several seconds he was buffeted by a tremendous wing. The quills were as stiff as lengths of copper pipe. Tod ignored the beating feathers, lunged forward before he lost his balance, and swung around with a firm grip on the talon. He was lifted off his feet, but only for a moment. Then his weight was added to the strength of his arms. Although the giant bird weighed three times as much as Tod, it was caught off guard by his aggressive action. It slammed hard onto the roadway on its port side.

Tod lost his grip. He staggered for half a dozen paces before he stumbled. He lowered his shoulder and hit the roadbed on a roll. He was unhurt.

The roc was beautifully graceful in the air, but not very nimble on the ground. Its attempts to gain a vertical stance would have been hilarious under less threatening circumstances. It utilized the lift of flapping wings to obtain sufficient height to rise onto its crumpled leg. It screeched from a standing position, preened the feathers on its rumpled wing, then flew into the air as if nothing had happened.

Tod didn't wait for another attack. He jumped to his feet and lurched away unsteadily until he regained his equilibrium, then he ran as if the devil itself were after him. He headed toward the recurring scream.

Multistory buildings now loomed into view on all sides. They were constructed of black basalt blocks whose joints appeared to be seamless. Glassless apertures pierced the upper levels. Tod noticed a pile of sticks protruding from a third story opening, and the beak of a sitting roc peering down at him with apparent lack of concern. Another adult roc was perched on the roof, and several fledglings were roosting on architectural projections.

He realized that he had stumbled onto more than a couple of isolated nests, but into a colony.

He passed tall buildings that reminded him of pagodas, then saw a roc backing out of the doorway of a squat structure whose roof was adorned with a minaret. He dashed into a side door.

"Squirt!"

Lisa stopped poking at the roc with a makeshift prod, and turned her head in astonishment. "Hunk! I thought you'd never get here. Help me with this overgrown pigeon."

Tod was startled into immobility.

"On the floor." She pointed with her chin. "Grab one of those tree limbs."

Tod grabbed. A moment later he was following Lisa's example, and prodding the roc with a blunt length of wood.

"Watch out for the beak! The neck extends like a telescoping tube, and is as flexible as rope."

The roc backed all the way out of the compartment, screeching all the while, and jerking its head from side to side on its sinuous neck, snapping with its black beak at the long sticks that were poking its gray feathered breast.

"Take that, you lousy scavenger." She stabbed the roc in the throat and ruffled some feathers, but did not do an appreciable amount of harm. She glanced at Tod. "That's good enough. I'll hold it off. You jump down that hole back there."

"Wha – what?"

Lisa pointed again with her chin. "In the back. In the corner. There's a square hole. Use the protruding blocks like a ladder. I'll follow you."

The roc screeched. Lisa screamed at it. The roc stood motionless, seemingly befuddled. It eyed her silently.

"Are you sure?"

"Just do it! I can't hold this biddy off forever. Now go!"

Hesitantly, Tod dropped his stick and went. He peered down a long square trunk that measured two feet across – barely wide enough to admit his broad shoulders. He looked back at Lisa. "Are you – "

"*Go!*"

It was with great trepidation that Tod squatted facing the trunk, sat on its edge, dangled his feet into the opening, and found firm purchase on a projecting block of basalt. He laid his hands flat on either side of the opening, eased himself down, and felt for the next lower block. The blocks were offset in such a manner that each one on the left was succeeded by one lower down on the right. A faint but noticeable effluvium assailed his nostrils.

Tod heard a stick clatter on the deck above him. He glanced up to see Lisa clambering nimbly down the trunk. After he touched the bottom, he saw that a low horizontal passageway extended in either direction.

Lisa stopped above his head. "Step aside."

"But it's too short – "

"Make like a bird and duck."

Tod grimaced. He hunched over and stepped into the passageway.

"Not that way. The other way."

Tod stood up in the trunk. He pointed with his finger. "That way."

"Yes, that way."

Tod hunched over again and entered the passageway on the opposite side.

Lisa climbed down beside him. "We want to go that way." She indicated the other direction. "But I want to be in front so I can lead. We're safe down here, but let's get away from this shaft."

She took off without another word. Because of her short stature, Lisa could walk normally in an upright posture. Tod not only had to hunch way down, but he had to twist his body so his broad chest would fit between the bulkheads.

The passageway was as dark as a pocket. Once they were out of the light zone, Lisa pulled her handlight from her knapsack, switched it on, and illuminated the passageway in front of her. She stopped and turned around, the light beam aimed at Tod's feet so as not to blind him.

"Do you have any water? I'm dying of thirst."

"Yes, sure." He handed his canteen to her. "I refilled it from a pond."

Lisa guzzled it down as if she hadn't drunk for a dozen shifts.

"It's got a slight metallic flavor."

"It tastes like nectar to me." She took another large gulp, then gave the half-filled canteen back to Tod. "I know where we can get more."

"I crossed a moat that was filled to the brim."

"Yes, I spotted it from the air when we flew over it. I also had an aerial view of the city. It's huge. Wait until you see . . . Let's get going. I've got some things to show you."

"Where – where are we headed?"

"Just follow me." Lisa turned and proceeded along the passageway. "The way is clear. There's nothing to trip over."

"But, what is this – this – "

"It's a sewer," Lisa said with confidence.

"A sewer!"

"Those buildings used to be divided into rooms by partitions, and the rooms used to be furnished. The wooden furniture has fallen apart – maybe thousands of years ago – or maybe the rocs tore it apart and used it for nesting material. Anyway, there used to be a lavatory at the top of that shaft. It's like a warren down here, with all the shafts connected to this discharge conduit. For sanitary purposes, it must have been flooded with water when the city was occupied."

"How do you know so much about this place?"

"I've been exploring. Now save your breath until we get out of here."

They proceeded silently for several minutes, with Lisa striding and Tod shambling. Finally they came to an intersection with a perpendicular passageway. Lisa did not hesitate, but turned right and kept on walking as if she knew the route. Tod followed meekly.

Eventually they reached another intersection. Lisa turned left. "It's not far now."

A couple of minutes later, Tod was able to discern a faint glow of light in the distance in front of Lisa. The light shone down a trunk like the one they had used to reach the horizontal passage.

"This is the way out." Lisa switched off her hand-light and stowed it in her knapsack. She climbed up projecting basalt blocks to the top of the shaft. "It's safe up here."

Tod waited until she stepped aside before following her up the trunk. He climbed into a compartment that was not dissimilar from the one they had recently vacated. Doorways pierced all four sides, and each doorway was flanked by two window openings. A spiral staircase occupied one corner.

"This way." Lisa ascended the staircase to an upper level, then continued up another staircase to yet another level. She flung down her knapsack. "The ports in this compartment are too small for the birds to fit through."

The deck was littered with debris from ages past: bits of cloth, shreds of parchment, ceramic shards, and carved sections of wood.

"Listen sharply before you get near a port. These wild fowl can hover, and their eyesight is keen. They'll poke their heads through the port and snap at you if you're not careful."

"Like that one in the other building?"

"No. That one wasn't attacking me. It was trying to feed me."

"Feed you! You don't look like a chick. I mean, like a bird chick."

Lisa squatted on the basalt deck and leaned back against an outer bulkhead. "I said they had keen eyesight. I didn't say they were smart. Whatever they are, they're half as dull-witted as a roasted chicken."

Tod tapped the transcriber with an index finger. "The databank identified them as Arabian rocs."

She laughed. "That's a good guess. They're about as bright as a bag of rocks. Rocks with a "k", that is. Maybe that's how they got their name. Anyway, I learned by accident that they were confused by screaming. I guess my high-pitched squeal reminds them of a rocling screeching for food – "

"Rocling?"

Lisa shrugged. "If a baby duck is a duckling, and a baby goose is a gosling, a baby roc must be a rocling. Anyway, what they see and what they hear muddles the birdbrain that keeps their skull from caving in."

Abruptly, Lisa burst into tears.

Chapter 19

Tod had never seen Lisa cry.

He didn't know what to say. He knelt by her side and engulfed her narrow shoulders with his powerful arms, yet hugged her gently as if she were a fragile kitten.

Lisa bawled inconsolably for five straight minutes. Gradually her sobs became intermittent. She wiped her eyes and her nose on her sleeves. She inhaled deeply for a couple of minutes. She wiped her eyes again.

"I was so scared." She started to cry all over again – not in an all-out caterwaul, but in disjointed whimpers. Finally she regained her normal composure, sniffled once or twice, pulled her knees to her chin, and wrapped her arms around her shins.

"How – How did you get away from the roc that – that carried you away?"

She didn't answer at once. "I was really scared. Not as much from being in its claws as from fear that it would drop me. I got sick when I looked down and saw how high I was. Above the trees. I felt dizzy. I threw up." She made brushing motions, as if she were wiping dry residue off the chest of her garment. "I grabbed its leg in case it let go, or found that I was too heavy to hold."

Tod kept quiet and let her talk at her own pace.

"It was having trouble keeping aloft. It kept losing altitude. Then it would flap its wings extra hard. I once read where sea gulls drop shellfish on the ground to crack their shell. I held on for dear life."

Tod ignored the disjointed nature of her narrative.

"One time it dipped into the treetops and dragged me through the branches. But it dived into a clearing, or a meadow, built up speed, and soared up into the mist. I had a bird's-eye view . . . " Lisa shut her mouth as soon as she realized what she had said.

Tod shrugged. "Well, you did say that you wanted to see a bird."

Lisa punched him playfully on the shoulder. "You." Then she burst into laughter.

Tod backed away. He sat cross-legged on the deck in front of her. Although he had the deep bass voice of a bullfrog, he did his best to imitate her soprano. "Oh, I'd love to see a bird."

She leaped at him as if she had been sitting on a spring. "*You!*"

Lisa did a full body thrust that caught him unexpectedly and bowled him over backward. She slammed down on top of him, then rolled off his massive chest and onto her back. She kicked her feet and howled with laughter. "I did say that, didn't I?"

Tod was laughing too hard to answer.

"I wish I had kept my mouth shut."

Tod sat up after he got control of himself. "I saw some small birds in the forest. None that I couldn't hold in the palm of my hand. You would have liked those."

"I would have *loved* them. Instead I had to go roc climbing." Lisa snickered at her own pun. "But seriously, Hunk, let me tell you what happened." She sat up and faced him. She put a sober mien on her face. "We flew over the outer walls of the city. Of course, I didn't know about the city at the time. Not until later. We crossed a waterway, which I guess is what you called a moat."

Tod nodded.

"Then we flew over a bunch of buildings to the rookery. I was scared breathless up to that point, but when the big bird, or roc, or whatever it is, spiraled down to what looked like a bone yard, I panicked. Two other birds were already there, tearing apart living animals like they were taking bites out of a sandwich. I screamed my bloody head off.

"The birds on the ground looked up. My bird hovered, then flew to a nest on a nearby rooftop. There were two hatchlings and an egg in the nest. The hatchlings started screeching as soon as we swooped over the nest. The big bird opened its claws and tried to drop me into the litter, or whatever they call a bunch of baby birds. Anyway, those nestlings looked like they wanted to eat me alive. Their beaks were snapping at my heels. I screamed and hung onto the claws. I yanked the food-kit knife out of my pack, and started stabbing the big bird in the thigh. I let go when it veered to the side of the nest."

Lisa paused to catch her breath.

"I fell ten to twelve feet, landed on my back, and had the wind knocked out of me. While I was lying there trying to get my breath back, the bird that dropped me circled the nest, and another one flew in to take its place. The parents, I guess. Anyway, I screamed again, and this other bird stood over top of me and dropped a chunk of raw meat smack on my face. I screamed and slithered away. I found a stairwell entrance in the corner. I crawled down partway then tumbled down the rest of the steps to the main deck – er, I guess if it's a building it would be a floor. Anyway, it was the ground level.

"One of the birds flew in through the open port – er, window. I think it wanted to put me in the nest with the other screechers. So I climbed back up the steps, retrieved my knife from where I dropped it, then limped down the steps to the bottom deck – er, ground floor. I ran out the back way to another building. I think the birds forgot about me once I was out of sight. They've got the intelligence of a sea slug."

Lisa looked at Tod with tear-filled eyes. "I knew you'd come after me. All I had to do was stay alive until you found me."

Tod shrugged. "The transcriber only gave me the general direction until you disappeared in the mist. Finding you was pure luck."

"Luck and guts."

Tod let the remark pass.

"Where were you when the lights went out?"

"In the forest."

"Out in the open? Alone?"

Tod shrugged again. "There wasn't anything dangerous in the woods. At least, nothing that *I* came across. There were huge elk and musk ox and aurochs, but they're all vegetarian. So I stayed put until the ceiling relighted."

Lisa nodded. "I spent the dark in an abandoned building. Abandoned by birds, I mean. They've all been abandoned by people – for centuries."

Tod nodded. "Did you see any Persians?"

"No. Why?"

Tod raised his eyebrows. "I found three dead bodies – at least three, maybe more. There was nothing left but bones, and some of them were mixed and scattered. I could tell by remnants of their uniforms that they were marines. My guess is that the rocs got them."

Lisa whistled. "I guess I was lucky to get away. Or lucky that I screamed at the right time. I'll bet those Persian marines didn't scream until they had their throats torn out."

"I've seen how the rocs attack. They hover high in the air, swoop straight down on their victim, and grab it before it knows what's happening. Who would ever think of looking *up* for an attacker?"

"Life in an air-filled cavern sure isn't the same as it is in an underwater base camp," Lisa allowed.

Tod nodded. "It takes getting used to. But the only danger I've encountered so far is from rocs." He shuddered as he remembered the climb down the cliff face. "And rocks." He told Lisa about the descent to the ground that preceded his trek through the redwood forest.

Lisa touched him tenderly on the cheek. "I knew you'd come after me. I knew it."

Tod kept nodding. "But we're not out of danger. There might be more Persians. Live ones, that is. The *Serendib* must have found an entrance to this cavern, and disembarked a marine reconnaissance patrol. If they haven't all been killed and eaten . . . "

"We've got to be careful. Real careful. We've got to keep our eyes open."

"You can hear their wings flapping when they get close." He pointed an index finger toward the ceiling.

"You've got to remember to look up as well as around."

"Yes, I found that out, too. That's why I keep a long stick handy. They're so stupid. All you have to do is stand still when they're swooping down on you, and plant a stick taller than you on the ground. They'll fly right into the upper end. And they're stupid enough to do it again. I sharpened one stick with my foodkit knife and made a spear point. The stupid bird impaled itself when it tried to grab me. Flew away with my spear stuck in its belly." Lisa swept her arm around her. "There are plenty of discarded tree limbs around, from old nesting sites."

"Then let's pick up a couple of sticks and sharpen the ends before we head back to the sub. We can follow the plotter track to the tunnel."

"What do you mean, head back? Have you forgotten that this is an exploratory mission? We've made the greatest discovery since the inception of the Benthic Resource Program. I'm wildly excited about this underground city, and I want to explore every corner of it before we go back."

"Well, I do, too. But what about Prof? And Denny?"

"They'll find us." Lisa pointed to the transcriber in Tod's belt loop. "They'll home in on the tracking chip."

"Well . . . "

"Denny can take care of himself *and* Prof."

"Well . . . "

"Besides, I've found some things that I've simply *got* to show you. And one of them is located at a source of water where we can refill our canteens."

"Well . . . "

"It's not a well. It's a fountain."

"You know what I mean."

"I know what you said." Lisa stood. "Come on. We can eat at the watering hole."

Reluctantly, Tod followed her through the doorway to a broad esplanade that stretched past a hodgepodge of buildings of various sizes, heights, and architectural styles. Some buildings were squat with dome-shaped roofs; others were tall and topped by towers; a few were sprawled out and pierced by numerous doors and windows. Some were constructed of black basalt, others of speckled granite. Many sported facades of limestone or pink marble.

"It'll take scores of shifts to examine every cubicle," Tod extemporized.

"And a gang of researchers. To say nothing of armed guards to prevent roc falls."

Tod groaned.

The paved walkway was monotonously black. The basalt had not been cut into blocks and laid side by side to produce the pavement. Rather, the bedrock had been honed and polished in place to produce a fine glossy finish. The entire city was built on a bed of solidified lava. Or was it magma, Tod wondered?

Both lava and magma were molten rock that consisted of the same basic elements: primarily aluminum, calcium, iron, manganese, oxygen, potassium, silicon, sodium, and titanium, along with traces of other elements. This molten rock was called magma when it was located beneath the surface of the Earth; it was called lava after it erupted from a volcano or seeped out of a volcanic vent. When this molten rock cooled and solidified, it formed igneous rock such as basalt and granite.

To Tod's way of thinking, basalt that was found inside a cavern had not yet reached the surface, and consequently had been formed from magma. But what about rock on the floor of a lava tube?

A lava tube was formed when the upper layer of flowing lava cooled enough to solidify. This surface rock then acted as insulation so that hot lava underneath remained liquid and continued to flow. If the still-molten rock flowed beyond the solidified roof, or flowed back into the throat of a volcano as the magma column receded, it created a hollow or cavity that was known as a lava tube. Some lava tubes extended horizontally for miles.

Did that mean that the floor of a lava tube was formed from magma or lava? It all depended upon what was defined as the surface: the surface of the Earth's crust, or the surface of the lava flow that solidified. Tod finally decided that the answer was more a matter of semantics than of vulcanological definition.

But Tod's methodical speculation did pose an interesting question: was this immense cavern, which the forest and city occupied, a lava tube or a product of erosion?

Lisa stopped in front of a rock-rimmed fountain of artificial construction. The circumference of the circular rim measured more than six hundred feet. As nearly as Tod could estimate, the fountain was approximately the size of the various ponds that he had encountered in the forest.

Water spouted more than thirty feet into the air from seven locations, arcing outward from a submerged perimeter that encircled the center of the fountain. Tod was stunned, for an active fountain implied pumps that were operated by electric motors or fossil fuel engines.

"Don't go away." Lisa placed her hand on Tod's broad chest. "Watch me."

She skipped along the pavement in a clockwise direction. Tod watched as her bouncing figure disappeared momentarily whenever she passed streams of water that lay between them. She stopped diametrically opposite from him. She stood still, then slowly raised and lowered her arms as if she were doing calisthenics. Her arms appeared to waver sinuously, like an optical illusion.

She continued to skip around the fountain until she reached his side. "Did you notice?"

Tod squinted his eyes in consternation. "Something – something was – I don't know, out of kilter – when you swung your arms." It came to him in a flash: the distorted musk ox calf. "What – what caused it? The refractive index of water?"

Lisa grinned like the Cheshire cat. "I'll show you." She climbed over the three-foot-tall rim of black basalt. The water rose midway to her thighs. She waved for him to follow. "Come on."

Tod stepped over the rim. The water barely reached his knees. The syntactic foam of his one-piece garment was waterproof, and insulated him from any temperature differential.

Lisa took him by the hand and led him between two spouts of water toward the middle of the fountain. The sound of colliding water was almost thunderous. She stopped inside the perimeter from which the water erupted. She extended her hand, palm outward. She seemed to be leaning against an invisible barrier. "You do it."

Tod held out his hand with his fingers foremost. He touched something that he could not see; or, if he stared fixedly, appeared to be more transparent than clear thermoplastic resin. He pressed hard against the unyielding surface. "What – what is it?"

Lisa pointed upward with the index finger of her other hand. "It's a roof support."

Chapter 20

Tod could hardly believe it. But if Lisa said it was a roof support, it must be so.

That singular fact provided the glue to mold the rest of the mysterious puzzle pieces into a recognizable pattern. Once he made the conceptual breakthrough, everything else made sense. Sort of.

"So this cavern isn't natural. It's artificial." Tod tried to string together the random clues. "That means that everything inside the cavern is artificial as well."

Lisa urged Tod to continue his train of thought. "Go on."

"No, that's not right. The forest isn't artificial. The plants and animals aren't artificial. They're all real plants and animals." He paused to think it through. "But, they were placed here artificially. They were gathered from around the world. Because in the real world a lot of those species didn't inhabit the same environment. Not that they *can't* live together; they just didn't. They evolved separately. At widely dispersed locations."

Lisa's eyes twinkled.

Tod thought of the rocs and the Irish Elk and the aurochs. They must not have been extinct when this cavern was created and the enclosed environment was stocked with living samples. "Not only from different continents but from different periods in Earth's geological history."

The implications were enormous.

"So what is this place? A conservatory? A zoo? The basis for the fable of Noah's *Ark*? And who built it?" Then an awful possibility crept into his mind. "Or *what* built it?"

Lisa shrugged.

"Aliens?"

She shrugged again.

He didn't have all the answers. Important evidence was missing. He filled in the logic gaps with speculation. Wild speculation. He chastised himself for such an unscientific approach.

"All right, let's enumerate what we know about this place – "

"Let's do it while we eat. I'm famished. And if my internal clock is keeping good time, it's due to get dark soon."

"Dark?"

Lisa cupped her hands and dipped them into the water. She brought a double handful to her mouth, slurped down the icy refreshing liquid, and repeated the process until her thirst was slaked. "I think the light and dark are cyclical, like shifts. Or rather, more like daytime and nighttime in the surface world. This cavern environment may be artificial, but the forest and its creatures are all products of natural evolution. Ergo, in order for them to live a normal life, the recurring appearance of the sun must be simulated. Make sense?"

Tod thought long and hard. "Yes, I guess it does make sense." He was less certain than his comment implied.

Lisa started wading between waterspouts toward the perimeter of the fountain. "Let's sit on the edge and eat. And remember to look up."

"Wait!" Tod pulled out the transcriber. He pointed the lens at the invisible column and took a stillshot for analysis. He frowned at the results that were displayed on the transcriber. "Silicon and oxygen in a crystalline matrix.

Silicon dioxide was the most common mineral found in the crust of the Earth. Small grains were known as sand; large chunks were known as quartz. Melted silicon dioxide was commonly molded to form clear material for windows and food containers. Depending upon how the atoms were bonded to adjacent compounds, the solid crystalline structure could assume a number of configurations. Impurities added a variety of colors.

Silicon dioxide was a strong dielectric. Thin layers applied to silicon wafers formed the basis of solid state circuitry that was utilized in all computer technology.

"I figured it was glass." Lisa kept on the move. "In its purest form."

As Tod trod through the water, the transcriber scrolled through the different crystalline forms that silicon and oxygen could take: amorphous, cubic, hexagonal, monoclinic, orthorhombic, and tetragonal. In addition to silicon dioxide, which consisted of one atom of silicon and two atoms of oxygen, silicon and oxygen could combine in multiples of the constituent atoms. The transcriber was unable to identify the lattice structure of the roof support.

Tod shook his head at the transcriber readout. "It says 'Allotrope unknown.' That means advanced technology."

"Sure, like the technology it takes to manufacture a disruptor beam that can cut through steel." Lisa sat on the rim of the fountain, her legs dangling in the water. She glanced overhead for rocs. "I'm not surprised. What does surprise me is this prehistoric city. It's an anachronism. On one hand the buildings are put together from native stone, while on the other hand the builders used fitted blocks and mitered joints instead of mortar."

Tod perched next to Lisa and pulled food containers from his knapsack. "I checked that already. You can't fit a hair between the blocks. Each one was carved with such precision that I would not be surprised if they are held together by molecular cohesion between two flat surfaces. Then you've got machinery to operate these fountains – "

"That's what I thought at first, but I was wrong. There *is* no machinery."

Tod dunked his canteen in the fountain to refill it. "Water doesn't spurt thirty feet into the air on its own. That goes against the law of gravity."

"You're right, Hunk, but only partially. Let me tell you what I found. Yestershift, before lights out, I stumbled into a dry reservoir." In aside, "I was still running away from those pesky pigeons. Anyway, it was five times the diameter of this fountain, and about fifty feet deep, with steps running around the inside of the wall. My canteen was empty, and I spotted a puddle at the bottom of what looked to me like a Roman arena, except that there weren't any bleachers.

"Anyway, I didn't care what it was, as long as it had water. So I climbed down to the bottom and took a good long swig from the puddle. At first I figured the hole was a cistern. You know, a water catchment like they have on small islands where the water table is salty, and they have to catch and store rain? Anyway, there were conduits leading out at various heights, with stone steps leading to them. Some of the conduits led to sewers. That's how I discovered the one that we escaped through. Other conduits were blocked by stone sluice gates. That's what got me to thinking.

"Eventually I found the intake sluiceway. It was blocked by a gigantic slab of basalt that fitted into a track. A huge gear mechanism opened and closed the sluiceway by sliding the basalt slab up and down. The slab was resting on the bottom of the reservoir, preventing the reservoir from filling, and from feeding water to the outflow conduits. The puddle I drank from was formed by minor leakage.

"A conduit near the top of the slab was partially closed by a sluice gate so that the flow was restricted. I could see sloshing water through a sight hole. I figured the water was being channeled somewhere, so I walked in the direction of the conduit. It led to this fountain."

Tod was amazed. "And all the time, I thought you were in the clutches of the rocs. Maybe half devoured. Instead you were out exploring sewers and waterways."

Lisa grinned. "This *is* an exploratory mission. Once I was out of danger, I had nothing better to do but explore. You would have done the same, in my booties."

Tod didn't answer.

"Now picture this." Lisa proceeded with enthusiasm. "I can't prove anything but I can envision how the system must operate. We know that the *Benthic Explorer* was proceeding somewhere beneath the Ross Ice

Shelf – or, what's left of the ice shelf after it started to retreat as a result of global warming. Sometime during our transit through the submerged caves and lava tubes, we entered the continent proper – that is, that part of the landmass whose surface rises above sea level.

"Our depth decreased as we followed extinct volcanic vents upward. We surfaced at sea level, but underground. Then we walked up that lava tube for a couple of miles. That placed us at a high elevation but still under the surface in this hollowed-out cavity.

"Now here's the important part. Elevation rises toward the center of Antarctica. The ground is covered by hundreds or thousands of feet of prehistoric ice. The top layers of ice insulate the lower layers. Geothermal activity, which we witnessed at that hydrothermal vent, is prevalent in this area. Waste heat is transferred through overlying rock, melting the subglacial ice. The ice-melt forms rivers on the landmass surface beneath the glaciers. The water is channeled into culverts that feed the city reservoir. If the reservoir were filled to capacity, water would overflow into the conduits and flush the sewers on a continuing basis."

Lisa gestured with a sweep of her arm. "This fountain is an artesian well. Hydrostatic pressure is what causes the water to spout."

Tod was astonished at her vivid extrapolation, but in his mind he could envision how the system would operate. "That's – that's ingenious."

"My interpretation, or the water-feed system?"

"Well, both. I don't know how you figured it out."

"I didn't get the picture all at once. I had to piece it together from several observations. The tip-off came when I discovered the glass column, and realized that it was a roof support."

"I don't know how you saw it. I looked right through one in the forest, and never made the connection."

Lisa humphed. "It's more obvious in the dark. I was skulking around the fountain when the ceiling glow diminished to practically nothing. When I switched on my handlight, the beam reflected off the column and caught my attention. I investigated, saw that the column went all the way to the roof, and deduced that it must be a support. I remembered Prof explaining how the roof of that submerged cavern was supported by water, and how it would collapse if the water receded.

"I figure that the crystal has the same refractive index as air, or very close to it, thus rendering it practically invisible under all-around lighting conditions. The rocs must have superior eyesight because they never seem to fly into it."

Tod nodded in agreement. "And I'll bet that every pond I found in the forest has a crystal column in the middle of it."

"No doubt. And *I'll* bet the ponds are fed by conduits that were drilled through the bedrock under the forest floor."

"Wow! You think so?"

"Once you postulate that everything in this cavern, including the cavern itself, was constructed to a grand design, a lot of unexplained phenomena begin to make sense. The purpose of this fountain, for instance."

Tod dunked his canteen and took a long draft. "What about it?"

"Other than the moat, it's the only water in the city that is still running. And it's conveniently located near the rookery. The rocs come here to drink."

Instinctively, Tod looked upward and did a visual sweep of the air. "Shouldn't we – "

"There are none in the vicinity. Even before you suggested it, I attuned myself to listen for flapping wings." She glanced upward anyway. "Think about this: the city has been abandoned and the irrigation system has been inactivated – all except for the conduit that feeds this fountain, and probably the conduits that feed the moat and ponds. If we presume that everything in this cavern has a purpose, and the water was left running into this fountain . . . "

Tod grew anxious at Lisa's hesitation. "Yes."

"Then this water is being provided for the birds."

Chapter 21

"Now that's an original concept." Abstract notions ran rampant through Tod's mind. "Maybe past tense would be more accurate. The dwellers provided water for the rocs before they abandoned the city."

Lisa pursed her lips. "Okay, Hunk. I'll grant you that one. I haven't seen any signs of recent occupancy. And as far as I can tell, no one has lived her for quite a long time – centuries, maybe millennia. But there are other things that I've got to show you. The first is in a building not too far from here."

"Lead the way." Tod packed his knapsack. "But first admit that I was right."

"About what?"

"About this fountain being a well. An artesian well."

Lisa humphed. "Only by a technicality." She stood and shouldered her pack. She pointed with her chin. "This way, toward what I believe is the city center."

After checking for aerial predators, the twosome pattered along the black basalt esplanade with a new-found sense of splendor and awe. They passed several buildings whose architectural style was hauntingly familiar. Each one was square but the roof was inset and topped with a dome whose spiral lines terminated in a twisted point. The doorways were arched and sep-arated by slender columns that were decoratively carved in the manner of newel posts. The simplistic design was offset by balconies that wrapped around every story. One building reminded Tod of pictures he had seen of a mosque.

"It's getting dark," Lisa observed.

The dimming was so subtle that Tod failed notice it until Lisa called it to his attention. "The fading doesn't seem as pronounced as it did in the forest. I guess the shade of the redwoods must have accentuated the oncoming darkness."

"It's not like switching off the lights in our cubicle,

that's for sure."

The light that emanated from the ceiling continued to diminish with agonizing slowness.

"Will we make it before total darkness?" Tod wanted to know.

"It doesn't matter. I can navigate in the offshift glow, even without a handlight."

They walked in silence for several minutes. A basalt ramp led the way through another concentric wall: the fifth, if Tod counted both the inner and outer walls of the moat. Now the landscape changed from one of isolated buildings to solid façades on the left and right. The structure on either side was either a single long building that was compartmentalized, or a series of buildings that were connected by means of common walls or partitions.

The thoroughfare stretched illimitably through the mist and gathering darkness.

Lisa turned into the first doorway on the right. They passed through several empty rooms to a courtyard. She halted in front of an obelisk that occupied the precise center of the quad. The pointed top stood twenty feet above the floor.

She gestured with her arm. "Ta-*da*!"

Tod stepped close to inspect the smooth granite surface. Graven images were accompanied by text that could have been captions. The picture boxes depicted flowers, shrubs, and other small plants on all four sides. Carved near the top of each flat facing was an elongated, stylized, bigger-then-life-size outline of a cat that was sitting on its haunches, with its fat tail curled in front of its paws.

"This is probably a garden guide rather than a Rosetta Stone, but it sure can't hurt to transcribe the pictures and lettering, and put Sarah's decryption software to work."

Tod wasted no time in whipping the transcriber from its belt loop, and focusing the lens on the obelisk. "It's pretty dark . . . "

Lisa set her handlight to wide beam. She played

light over the surfaces as Tod directed. The four sides of the obelisk had different engravings. By the time Tod had recorded everything, it was nearly dark. He went through the laborious process of extracting the decryption chip from its self-destruct device, inserting it into the transcriber slot, and inputting the coding sequence.

"Did the program find any matches?"

Tod studied the transcriber. "There are several words that match some of those that were on the gold foils. It's looking for correlations with the pictorial engravings." He looked up in slight exasperation. "The program is going to have to run for a while to determine if anything is related to Farsi or Old Persian."

Lisa switched off her handlight.

The transcriber's backlit screen highlighted the image of the cat. Tod humphed. "The databank found bronze and alabaster statues that resemble the tabby at the top. It represents Bast, the feline goddess that was worshipped by the ancient Egyptians."

"That's just a software prejudice or default. Let's get some shuteye. There are more samples in other buildings – the few that I explored – and probably a lot more in the buildings that I didn't explore when I turned around to wait for you at the rookery. I'm much more eager to see this city now that we're together."

Tod returned the transcriber to its holder. "I was afraid that I'd never find you. Or that if I did, it would be too late . . . "

Lisa smiled. She placed her warm hands in Tod's. "There's one more thing that I've got to show you. Then we can sack out in one of the rooms."

They re-entered the building. She took him by the hand and led him through the semidarkness along a corridor that had doorways on either side. She passed empty rooms without a sideways glance. The corridor opened into a large room whose ceiling was decorated with square quartz crystals that admitted the last of the fading light. Water poured out of a pipe in one of the basalt walls, splashed into a pool about half the size of the *Reef Cruiser*, flowed over a low rim at the opposite end, and gurgled down a drain.

"Stick your hand in the water."

Tod did as he was instructed. "It's warm!"

Lisa's grin was hardly visible in the last dregs of light. "It's a communal bathtub."

"A bathtub? You mean, for taking baths?"

"Nice jump to the obvious. Of course for taking baths, you silly. That's how they keep clean on the surface. They don't sponge their skin with disinfectant solutions like we do."

"But – a bath."

"Try it. I did."

"You – you took a bath?"

Lisa maintained her grin. "And loved every minute of it. It was luxurious."

Tod dipped his hand again. They he scooped some water to his nose. It had a faint odor of sulfur. "That means that there must be heating equipment – "

"Negative, Hunk." She swept her arms wide. "The whole plateau around us is volcanic. Remember the hydrothermal vent with the giant tubeworms?" She pointed to the pool. "This water is heated geothermally, and has been for thousands of years. You know how reliable geothermal activity can be. Look at Old Faithful, a geyser that is still spouting faithfully, hundreds of years after its discovery."

Tod thought for a moment. "So you're saying that the builders of this city ducted bath water past volcanic vents?"

"That's what they do in Iceland. They even heat their houses with steam generated by volcanic activity. And it's not a new idea. The ancient Romans utilized geothermal energy for heating purposes. The first hot tubs were built by Paleolithic man, when he placed rocks around hot springs to create bathing pools."

Tod could visualize Lisa's thoughts. "It makes sense."

"Of course it does. So what are you waiting for? Jump in."

"You mean – in the pool?"

"Yes in the pool. You'll love it. In fact, I'll join you."
Lisa shrugged out of her one-piece garment. "That first
bath felt so good . . . " She dropped the garment on the
floor and stepped over the lip into the tepid water. She
sat down and leaned back against the wall until only
her head was exposed. "I wish we had soap. I'd love to
know what soap feels like on my skin."

Tod could see only her teeth and eyeballs in the
near darkness. "I've got some moist cleansing cloths – "

"That's not the same."

Tod shrugged, and stripped off his syntactic foam
suit. He tested the water with a toe, the way he had
seen people do it in kinetic recordings. Then he stepped
in, sat down, and let the wetness roll over his body. Lisa
was right: the feeling was luxurious. And relaxing.

They steeped in silence for many minutes. When
the darkness became absolute, they rose from the bath
and stepped naked onto the cold basalt floor. They had
no towels. They wiped water off their skin as best they
could with their hands. Tod started to shiver, and so
did Lisa. They slipped into their garments without waiting to air-dry. Warmth returned almost immediately.

They vacated the bathhouse. They found a cozy
cubicle that might have been a closet when the city was
inhabited. They lay down next to each other, barely
touching. It was comforting to have Lisa sleeping next
to him again – almost as if they were safe in their cubicle in Benthocity 3.

In the distance, Tod could hear the chortling of rocs
in their nests. They sounded a lot less ferocious than
they did when they were stalking prey – especially when
he was the prey. He used his knapsack as a pillow. Lisa
followed suit.

"Sweet dreams, Squirt."

"You too, Hunk."

"We never got our spears."

"Next shift."

The basalt walls offered a modicum of protection.
The quiescence made him drowsy. He drifted off to
dreamland . . .

Chapter 22

Tod was jarred out of his dream-filled slumber when something hard smacked against his shoulder. He opened his eyes. For a moment he was disoriented. Then he saw Lisa kneeling over him with a clenched fist.

"Hey, sleepyhead, it's been full brightness for at least ten minutes. Are you going to sleep through the entire shift?"

He squinted his eyes and shook his head to clear out the cobwebs. "Whew. I guess I was more tired than I thought I was."

"Yes, physical exertion will do that to you. I found that out yestershift. My legs are sore."

"I'm sore all over." Tod sat up and stretched his aching muscles. He yawned. "But the soreness feels kind of good. I don't know why, but it does."

Food concentrates were laid out for easy viewing. Lisa handed him a canteen. "Drink, eat, and let's get on the move. We've got a busy shift ahead of us."

Tod first took several gulps of water, then picked some packaged goods from the assortment.

"I know where we can get fresh eggs."

Tod had never eaten an egg that wasn't powdered. "I'll pass."

"It's just as well. We don't have a nuker."

"Or a long enough extension cord to reach the sub."

"We could start a fire."

"How? We don't have an igniter."

"Didn't American pioneers rub two sticks together?"

"No, that was Amerindians. Pioneers struck flint on steel. Flint is a hardened variety of quartz found in sedimentary rock; all the rock around here is igneous. And we don't have any steel . . . although a spark can be struck from iron pyrite, just not as easily." Tod examined his knapsack. "Except for minute amounts of silver in the transcriber and computer chips, everything else we have is a plastic derivative."

"All right, already. You don't have to go scientific on me. I'm just a dumb sub driver." Lisa cogitated. "I'll bet we could poach an egg in a thermal vent."

Tod mocked a scowl.

"I'm so hungry I could eat a roc."

"Igneous, metamorphic, or sedimentary?"

"Avian. I'll bet they taste like chicken paste." Lisa licked off the knife and restowed it in the foodkit. "I've finished all the peanut butter."

"That's okay." Tod was not particular about victuals, as long as he had enough to fill his stomach. "There's plenty of other stuff."

Lisa studied the transcriber data. "No luck with the lingo. The language program is as baffled as I am. It shows some correlations between the obelisk and the foils, but no definite translations."

Tod chewed thoughtfully. "A larger sampling might help, but an illustrated dictionary would be better."

"I'll check the library when we find it."

After breakfast, they spent several hours in wandering through buildings and ambling along intersecting thoroughfares that they now called streets. Many cornerstones were adorned with script above head height, much like emergency signs and instruction plaques in Benthocity 3.

Tod recorded every line of script that they found, but the translation program had only limited success in recognizing the ancient language. The transcriber presented high percentages of probability that individual characters and certain word groups might be analogues for the same in Old Persian, but tentative translations into English resulted in gibberish.

They stopped in front of a white limestone plaque that stood out harshly against a speckled granite partition in what could have been a farmyard had the wood not rotted out of notches and indentations that surrounded the broad open area. Half a dozen indecipherable words were inscribed on the plaque.

Tod duly recorded the script. "Hey! I've got a perfect

translation."

Lisa inhaled sharply. "What does it read?"

" 'No handball playing against this wall.' "

Lisa stood expression for five full seconds before she yelled, "You!" and punched Tod playfully on the shoulder.

He grinned from ear to ear.

Lighthearted banter ensued. They periodically looked upward for rocs, but they neither saw nor heard any signs of them, the presumption being that they foraged only where there was food to be found. There was no nesting material from which to fabricate spears; and no immediate need for any kind of protection.

They ascended a long ramp that arched over the sixth concentric wall. Now they entered an area that was occupied by what could best be described as stalls, or kiosks, which were scattered widely but with precise regularity. Occasional granite towers vaulted fifty feet into the air. Each tower had but a single doorway at ground level. Steps rose around the inside of the wall, which was pierced with openings that provided lookout vantages. Had it not been for the cloying mist, a panoramic view of the entire city would have been visible from the tops of these towers.

Most intriguing of all were the statues. A long line of them were oriented outward, peering over the misty city environs. The curvature of the line matched the curvature of the concentric circles. Each monument was carved from a single block of granite or basalt. A few were carved from limestone or marble. The plinths were inscribed, and each one was decorated with the outline of a cat.

"Well, at least they were human." Lisa ran her hand over the smooth marble surface of a life-sized representation of a fully garbed female. The ensemble consisted of a triple-lobed tiara, a garment that was a cross between a ceremonial kimono and an ancient Grecian robe, and dainty slippers. "Not bad looking, either. And graceful. Clearly not aliens or troglodytes."

Tod took high-resolution stillshots of the sculptures, and close-ups of the faces. The physiognomies were like none that he had ever seen before. He recognized facial characteristics and cranial dimensions of several races and ethnic groups, from widely dispersed geographical areas that encompassed most of the Old World, including populations of Nordic to Ethiopian descent, and every group in between. The visages resembled all of these, yet none of these. They were indefinable.

He canvassed the transcriber's databank for racial recognition suggestions. The computer scrolled indecisively, comparing current subspecies of *Homo sapiens* with reconstructions from the fossil record. Finally it selected the most likely match.

"Mesopotamia," Tod announced.

Lisa arched her eyebrows. "The Tigris-Euphrates Valley. The birthplace of civilization."

"And close to the cave of Ali Baba and his forty thieves," Tod quipped, half in earnest. "Where the Persians unearthed the gold foils that charted the way to this fabulous place."

The pregnant pause that followed this unexpected revelation seemed to last for all eternity. Neither Tod nor Lisa knew quite what the information implied. They stared at each other in silence, minds in turmoil.

Finally, Tod declared. "I want more samples."

The pair spent the next couple of hours in transcribing the rest of the statuary. The computer collated the additional images, but did not update its assessment of the situation.

The seventh concentric circle lay only one quarter mile from the sixth. Because this wall stood more than twenty feet in height, the ramp was long and gradual; the uplift started several hundred feet from the barrier of black basalt.

Tod and Lisa halted simultaneously at the top of the ramp, stunned at the spectacular edifice that lay before them.

"It's a – It's a . . . " Lisa was at a loss for the proper word.

"It's a ziggurat," Tod said with confidence. "A step pyramid."

The Aztecs and the Mayans built ziggurats that were similar to the one that confronted them. It stood one hundred feet in height, and stepped back from a base that measured two hundred feet across the front. It was different from most Egyptian pyramids in that it lacked the facing that gave their sides their distinctive smooth slope. The Mesopotamians also built ziggurats; several examples were still extant on the Persian plateau.

In actuality this was only half a ziggurat. It was built on the plan of a square base, but against the cavern wall, bisected as it were by a bluff of basalt. Thus the two retreating sides of the ziggurat measured half the length of the front. Adjoining the cavern wall on either side of the ziggurat were long ramps that led to the ground from a shrine that stood on the summit. On either side of the center staircase were seven tiers that formed flat terraces.

The oldest ziggurats in the known world were built from bricks of sun-baked clay. Egyptian pyramids were built from rectangular blocks of stone that weighed many tons.

Like the concentric walls and other structures in the subterranean city, this ziggurat was constructed from thick slabs of basalt that were fitted together with such precision that the spaces between them were discernible only upon microscopic inspection. The builders were master craftsmen.

Lisa looked at Tod. "What are we waiting for?"

Tod glanced into the air over his shoulder, then peered into her hazel eyes. "Ladies first?"

Lisa placed her hands on her hips, arms akimbo, and cocked her head sideways. "Don't be ridiculous."

Tod shrugged, and climbed onto the first step. The riser was twice as high as those on a standard staircase. His legs were long enough to step up easily, but Lisa's short stature made it difficult for her to climb because her upper leg was bent so far down that she could not get the leverage to push her body upward, even by shoving off with her toes. Tod grasped her hand and helped her by pulling. As they continued up the basalt steps, he held onto her hand and stayed one step ahead of her, pulling her up to each higher step.

Finally they reached the last riser. Tod stepped onto the smooth black basalt that comprised the floor of the shrine. He pulled Lisa up after him. Hand in hand, they took several steps forward – then halted and stared open-mouthed at the tall figure that was posed in the middle of the shrine.

The features were the same as those of the statues down below.

Only she was not a statue.

Part Three

So when they saw it as a cloud appearing in the sky advancing towards their valleys, they said: This is a cloud which will give us rain. Nay! It is what you sought to hasten on, a blast of wind in which is a painful punishment.

The *Koran*, The Sandhills

And you shall not escape in the earth nor in the heaven, and you have neither a protector nor a helper besides Allah.

Surely we will cause to come down upon the people of this town a punishment from heaven, because they transgressed.

The *Koran*, The Spider

If they could find a refuge or cave or a place to enter into, they would certainly have turned thereto, running away in all haste.

The *Koran*, The Immunity

Chapter 23

The stunned tableau that lasted for several seconds felt like hours to Tod.

The expression on the young woman's face was inscrutable. She stood tall and erect, as stately as a statue of an ancient goddess. She wore a thick-pile robe that was vividly patterned with red, white, and black swirls. The hemline reached to her ankles; the loose folds of the sleeves rested on her wrists. Her feet were encased in brown leather boots whose tops were hidden by folds of tri-colored cloth. Her attire was accented by a white silk scarf that lay loosely on her narrow shoulders; the scarf partially covered a pair of decorative leather straps that crisscrossed in the hollow between her breasts. Each strap came over one shoulder and went behind her back above the opposite hip.

Long black silky hair flowed well past her shoulders and over her breasts. Across her crown she wore a white tiara that was functional rather than decorative: in addition to sweeping her fine hair off her delicate face, the ends were affixed with black bulbous earmuffs that swaddled her ears. White downy feathers, angled backward, adorned the earmuffs. For jewelry she wore a gold bangle on her left arm, and a string of opalescent pearls around her slender neck.

The silence that ensued was deafening. Tod was reminded of the constant background noise in Benthocity 3: the humming of motors, the buzzing of transformers, the clicking of solenoids, the hissing of air circulating units. The redwood forest was equally as consistent in the multifarious production of sound: the chirping of birds, the stridulating of insects, the chattering of squirrels, the crackling of dry leaves and needles underfoot. Now, for an agonizingly long moment, the air was pregnant with a drawn-out hush.

Tod and Lisa stared in wonder at the young woman. The young woman's dark eyes danced back and forth between Tod and Lisa.

Suddenly Tod remembered the transcriber. He yanked it out of its belt loop and pointed it at the woman. He snapped a stillshot for posterity, and keyed the computer for a quick analysis. Instantly the transcriber filled with data: human female; height five feet nine inches; weight one hundred twenty to one hundred twenty-five pounds; hair black; complexion dark; eyes brown; sheep bone headband; roc downy feathers; cashmere caftan; Irish Elk-hide boots.

Possible identification: peri (a Persian angel or fairy).

Just as suddenly the air was rent with a high-pitched scream that nearly jolted Tod out of his booties. He looked up from the transcriber. The young woman was staring in horror at the transcriber lens.

"Put it down, Hunk." Lisa slapped the arm that held the transcriber. "You're scaring her."

Tod stopped goggling at the young woman. Now he gawked at Lisa. "I was only recording data."

"She doesn't know that." Lisa nodded to the horror-stricken young woman. "Look at her face. She's terrified."

"But – "

"Give me that." Lisa wrestled the transcriber out of Tod's grip. "She thinks the transcriber is a weapon."

Lisa pointed the lens downward. She rotated the transcriber until it was pointing at Tod. Slowly she sidestepped closer to the young woman, maintaining eye contact all the time. She held the transcriber in front of the young woman's face. Tod's image was prominently displayed.

The young woman stared at the transcriber for a moment, glanced at Lisa, returned her gaze to the transcriber, then looked at Tod.

Lisa grasped the transcriber by the head, and held out the handle toward the young woman. The young woman took a fearful step backward. Lisa stretched out her arm so that the transcriber handle was within the young woman's reach. She wagged the handle as an inducement for the young woman to take it.

The young woman looked at Lisa suspiciously. In a low, mellifluous voice, she uttered a few words in a language that neither Lisa nor Tod understood. Hesitantly, she reached out and grasped the transcriber by the handle.

Lisa turned to Tod. "The only way I could think of to get her to understand that the transcriber is nothing more than a recording device was to let her hold it and see it in operation."

Tod nodded. "Good idea, Squirt. I wish I'd thought of it."

"You would have."

The young woman panned the lens across Tod and Lisa. After a moment she looked satisfied that the transcriber was nothing to fear. She offered it to Tod. He held it loosely, but kept it trained on the woman for continued transcription of her appearance and actions.

"Now what?" Tod asked.

Lisa shrugged. "I don't know. She doesn't understand our language, and we don't understand hers. Did the transcriber catch her words?"

Tod studied the transcriber. He scrolled through several links. "It recorded them, but it couldn't translate them."

"I'm not surprised. My guess is that she's speaking the archaic language that preceded Old Persian."

"Mine too." Tod wanted to fiddle more with the transcriber but thought better of it until they could completely allay the young woman's fears. "So what do we do?"

"Let me talk with her. Woman to woman. She won't understand my words, but she'll – "

"No! I have an idea." Tod instinctively yanked the transcriber up toward his face. He stopped before the young woman entered its line of sight. He pointed the lens to the side. He turned to Lisa. "If I show her the image of the foil, she should be able to read it. Then she'll understand how we came to be here."

"Excellent idea, Hunk. But do it slowly."

In order not to frighten the young woman, Tod indicated the transcriber with a stiffened finger. He didn't know what to say, but figured that any words he spoke wouldn't help the situation. With exasperating slowness, he tapped the backscreen's links and scroll tabs until he retrieved the image of the seventh gold foil.

He pointed to the transcriber. He rotated the transcriber and held it high so that the young woman could see the image. She studied the archaic language. Her eyes pinched as they scanned the lines of text. She inhaled sharply. She glanced at Tod, then at Lisa. She spoke several unintelligible sentences with a singsong cadence.

"I think she was able to read it and understand it."

"I agree." Tod kept recording in order to add more words to the databank. "Now what?"

"Now I hope we've established friendly relations. But what we do next is anyone's guess."

Silence returned.

After a perceptible lapse of time, the young woman uttered a single word. "Amina."

Lisa shook her head. "I don't understand."

"Amina." The young woman placed her palm flat against her chest, beneath her throat. "Amina."

Lisa sucked in her breath. She turned to Tod. "I get it. She's giving us the 'Me Tarzan, you Jane' treatment." Lisa faced the young woman, waited a moment, then placed her hand against her small breastbone. Enunciating carefully, she said, "Lisa."

"Lee-sa?" The young woman's pronunciation was stilted.

"Lisa."

"Lisa."

" 'By Jove, she's got it.' " Lisa quoted *My Fair Lady.* " 'I think she's got it.' "

Tod tilted his head. "This is no time for wisecracks."

Lisa ignored him. She placed her hand on Tod's bulging chest. "Tod."

"Tod."

Tod placed his own hand on his chest. "Tod."

"Tod."

"She's definitely got it."

"Squirt! Cut it out. This is serious business."

"All right, already." Lisa smiled at Amina. "We're a couple of jokesters."

Amina did not smile, but she relaxed somewhat and her face brightened considerably after the exchange of names. She spouted a few sentences in her native language.

"Sorry, Amina. It's all Greek to me."

"It's not Greek, Squirt. It's archaic Persian."

"Whatever. I still don't understand it."

"Well, if we start transcribing it, we might get Sarah's decryption software to translate some of it."

"Let's gain more of her confidence before we frighten her any more with the transcriber."

"And how, exactly, do we do that?"

"I don't know, Hunk. I guess we'll just have to play it by ear."

"Your verbal expressions are almost as outdated as Amina's Persian."

"If we could only translate 'Take me to your leader.'"

Tod threw his hands into the air. "You're impossible."

"No, just improbable." Lisa gesticulated to Amina. "You see, we have this thing between us. A kind of rivalry. But it's all in good fun. I know you don't understand a word I'm saying, but I'll explain it to you after we're able to communicate properly. You know – woman to woman."

Amina's face remained blank.

Tod was stirred by Amina's strange beauty. He hoped that she could not read his mind. Although telepathy might remove the language barrier, it would reveal certain thoughts that he would rather not have made public. Casually, he checked the transcriber's audio circuit to ensure that he was recording Amina's words for later playback.

"What would make her assume that the transcriber was a weapon? She's never seen one before."

Lisa hmmnned. "There's only one reason I can think of."

"Persian marines?"

"Exactly. My guess is she's had a bad experience with them."

Tod cogitated furiously. "Okay, so the Persians have been here. We know that from the bodies – " He had an idea. He located a stillshot of one of the dead marines – most of whose uniform was evident – and showed it to Amina.

She inhaled sharply.

Lisa imitated a roc by flapping her arms and gnashing her teeth.

Amina voiced a single syllable.

"Well, now we know the archaic Persian word for roc."

"We're making progress, Hunk. In another thousand hours we'll be chatting about fashion lingerie."

"*I* won't."

Amina spoke volubly for half a minute. She pointed to the transcriber, then made popping sounds while poking Tod on the sternum with her middle finger.

Lisa humphed. "I don't need decryption software to interpret that."

"Yes. The Persian marines must have shot at her, or at her people. *Her people!* Squirt, she can't be alone in this cavern! She must be part of a group – an underground civilization."

"Honestly, Hunk, sometimes you're so slow."

"But, the city is abandoned."

"*This* city is abandoned."

Tod pondered the implication.

"It's been obvious to me all along that the Persians didn't build this city. Not modern Persians."

"Yes, you're right. I knew it, too, in the back of my mind. I just didn't process the information on a conscious level."

Amina interrupted the discussion by uttering a few words in archaic Persian. She indicated the ceiling outside the shrine. The overall glow was dimming and the cavern was growing dark. From a fold in her caftan she pulled a slender wand that measured more than a foot in length. She manipulated one end – Tod did not observe how. Except for the part that Amina held in her hand, the rest of the wand shimmered with a soft white luminescence. A focused beam of pure white light flared from the end opposite the handle. Amina manipulated the handle again. The spotlight expanded to a broad, cone-shaped beam of diminished brightness.

Darkness was descending in the cavern. To Tod it indicated the end of another shift.

Like an usher in an old-time movie theater, Amina waved the beam back and forth along the floor of the shrine.

"A magic wand," Lisa soliloquized. "I wonder what other tricks she has up her sleeve."

Amina wiggled her fingers at Tod and Lisa.

"I think she wants us to follow her." Tod took Lisa by the hand. "Maybe she's going to take us to her leader."

"I hope her leader has rations. My foodkit is just about empty."

Amina turned toward the rear of the shrine. As she did so, Tod saw that the leather straps across her chest were more than decoration. One supported a tubular sack and the other supported a T-shaped mechanical device the way Tod's strap and Lisa's strap supported their knapsacks. Tod did not recognize the device. He snapped a stillshot.

They sauntered after Amina, emulating her leisurely pace. She led them through the shrine to where the rock wall was pierced by an opening that was larger than an airdock hatch. Amina waved the wandlight at the ceiling and both sides, so that Tod and Lisa could envision the dimensions of the chamber. It was slightly larger than a submersible airdock.

The floor of the tunnel was polished to a high gloss, the same as the basalt pavements in the city, but the walls and ceiling were unfinished, seemingly cut from naked, rough-hewn rock and left that way. The floor sloped downward for nearly one hundred yards before doubling in width.

Parked to one side of the now enlarged tunnel was a strange-looking object that reminded Tod of a toboggan. The brick-shaped chassis measured eight feet in length, four feet in width, and two feet in height or thickness. Atop the platform stood an inset enclosure with sidewalls that rose three feet high. There was no overhead or roof. Tod snapped another stillshot for later processing.

Amina played her wandlight over the contrivance. What Tod took to be the rear looked like a cargo compartment. Forward of that was a bench seat. At the front were a pilot's seat and a full-width control panel.

Tod said, "I think it's a vehicle."

"But don't land vehicles have wheels, like forklifts?"

Tod shrugged.

"Maybe she really *is* taking us to her leader."

Amina pulled open a side panel, permitting entrance to the bench seat. She motioned with the wandlight for Tod and Lisa to enter. Tod lifted Lisa onto the platform. She alighted on the seat and slid to the other side. Tod sat next to her. Amina closed the panel with an audible click. Tod tested the latch by opening and closing the panel. The panel wasn't locked.

Amina spoke in her singsong cadence which Tod presumed was meant to impart reassurance. She then opened a side panel to the pilot's seat, stepped inside, and sat down. She activated the control panel by pressing a green luminescent crystal. The panel lit up with a number of circular lights; at the same time, dim floor lights and perimeter lights illuminated the rest of the vehicle.

What sounded like an induction motor whined into operation beneath the platform. Tod felt the hairs rise on his nape and the back of his hands.

The side panel was now locked; Tod couldn't push it open. He figured that an automatic latching mechanism had been actuated: a safety feature for when the vehicle was in motion. He could easily climb over top of the panels if he wanted to escape. He sat tight.

Delicate fingers moved across the lighted crystals on the upper surface of the control panel. Tod had the impression that Amina was inputting instructions on the equivalent of a keyboard.

The whining of the motor increased in pitch and volume. The vehicle levitated several inches off the ground, wobbled slightly for a moment, then stabilized. Both Tod and Lisa gripped the side panels.

Amina turned and offered the faintest and briefest of smiles. Then she looked ahead into the blackness of the tunnel. She switched on a searchlight that illuminated the foreground in front of the vehicle. Amina pushed a tall central lever forward. The vehicle moved ahead smoothly, silently, and effortlessly.

Tod wanted to say something but couldn't find the words.

Lisa was quite serious when she said, "I don't know if it has occurred to you, but I think we're going for a ride on a magic carpet."

Chapter 24

As astonished as Tod was about meeting a strange woman in an ancient city in the depths of a vast cavern under the Antarctic ice, he could not help but be overwhelmed by the scientific and engineering marvel of their mode of transportation: a fabled flying carpet.

Surreptitiously, he slipped his hand over the door panel and down to the side of the chassis. His fingertips tingled as he rubbed them over the smooth wall of the housing that concealed the propulsion unit. It felt as if he were touching the metal casing of a high-speed electrical motor, whose rapid rotation caused the outer shell to vibrate. He noticed the odd lack of heat that was usually generated by a motor, and that was dissipated through heat sinks which communicated with the air.

Tod gasped in astonishment as he experienced an epiphany. In mulling over the scientific principles that could account for his observations, and that could cause the phenomena of levitation and lateral movement, a detailed diagram appeared suddenly in his mind's eye.

The Earth was a huge magnet. Forces deep within the planetary core generated a magnetic field that spread far beyond the atmosphere. These external lines of force created the magnetosphere and the Van Allen belts. The lines of force were made visually apparent by spectacular auroral displays, when free protons and electrons that were emitted by the sun – the so-called solar wind – collided with the Earth and traveled along these lines of force to converge at the magnetic poles, where they interacted with atmospheric molecules and discharged energy whose byproduct was colored light.

Tod postulated that the lifting force of the magic carpet was an electromagnetic induction coil. Electromagnetism was one of the four known forces in the Universe: the strong nuclear force, the weak nuclear force, electromagnetism, and gravity. Electricity and magnetism were paired manifestations of the same force: the flow of electrons induced a magnetic field; an expanding or collapsing magnetic field induced an electric current. The changing magnetic field also induced eddy currents: an electromotive force which extended beyond the conductor that carried the current. This in turn created a static charge, which was responsible for raising Tod's hair.

The vehicle was not a magic carpet that defied the force of gravity; it was a magnetic car whose builders must have discovered a way to harness and channel the repulsive force of magnetism that was known as diamagnetism. Whereas two unlike poles of a magnet attract each other, two like poles repel each other. This magnetic car was repelling the Earth's magnetism with sufficient strength to lift it off the ground.

The car (or carpet) wobbled slightly upon initial levitation until a gyroscope was energized and spun fast enough to achieve stabilization.

He couldn't quite envisage the motive force, but it might have something to do with alterations in the angle of the magnetic field. The tall central lever that Amina pushed forward was obviously a control rod or joystick that governed acceleration and direction. If he could get his hands on it . . . Verification of his imaginative theories would have to wait until later. Nonetheless, he could not help but admire the simplicity of the power train. It was safer, quieter, and far more efficient than what nuclear energy could provide.

Tod leaned back to enjoy the magnetic car ride. Air whipped through his crew-cut hair and made whistling sounds as it passed his ears. He fancied that this must be what wind felt like. It was not much different from standing in front of a ventilation duct, as he used to do in his youth.

The ride was so smooth that he felt no sensation of speed. But he could see how fast the walls moved past the car – or rather, how fast the car moved past the walls. It was a curious and somewhat disorienting and disconcerting feeling. He had never traveled in a land vehicle before, and had never traveled at such velocity.

Lisa squeezed his knee with uncommon strength. "I don't like this supersonic flight. Give me a slow-moving sub any day."

Tod grinned silently. He placed his hand on top of hers.

Lisa's voice was barely audible. "What are those things hanging on Amina's back?"

"I don't know." He was lost in thought about the magnetic car.

"What did the transcriber call them?"

"I haven't looked."

"Give it to me."

Tod handed the transcriber to Lisa. She manipulated the controls and studied the transcriber. She squeezed his leg again. "It's a weapon!" She whispered, but the echo effect in the tunnel made her exclamation sound like a reverberating shout.

"A weapon?"

"According to this, the device is a crossbow and the tube is a quiver full of projectiles, like arrows, except that they're called bolts or quarrels. Look." She turned the transcriber so that Tod could see it.

The weapon had been prevalent in ancient China and in medieval Europe. It consisted of a wooden stock that was grooved for the placement of the projectile. A string was connected to a perpendicular torsion bar that was pulled back to create tension, and placed in a slot in the middle of the stock. A projectile was then fitted in the groove. A trigger forced a rod up through the stock. The rod pushed the string out of the slot and onto the base of the projectile, which was then propelled by the tension on the string. The quiver was a pouch that held extra bolts.

The transcriber demonstrated how the standard crossbow was loaded and fired. When fired, it was held to the shoulder like a rifle.

"Sarah input too much mythology in the databank."

Tod squinted. "What do you mean?"

"In collating data, the transcriber has associated Amina with her crossbow, and now postulates that she is either an Amazon or the huntress Diana."

She handed the transcriber to Tod so he could read the possible identifications on the transcriber. In Greek mythology, an Amazon was a female warrior who cut off her right breast so she could draw a bow string unimpeded. In Roman mythology, Diana was the goddess of hunting and childbirth.

Based on her looks and bearing, Tod was willing to grant Amina the status of a goddess. "It always does that when the databank can't make positive identification. It's only suggesting analogies that are based on history. Or in this case, on mythology."

Tod and Lisa had much to ponder.

The car traveled in a straight line on level ground for five minutes or more before Tod saw a light at the end of the tunnel. The magnetic car decelerated as Amina pulled back on the control rod. The draft decreased with the reduction of speed. As they approached the source of light, the white ball seemed to expand like a dilating iris. The light appeared bright only in comparison to the relative darkness of the tunnel.

The magnetic car turned and drifted to a stop in a large cubic chamber that was dimly lit by what Tod thought of as emergency lighting. A soft glow permeated the ceiling as it did in the cavern with the redwood forest and abandoned city, but it was nowhere near as bright. Tod could distinguish individual luminaries planted in the ceiling in parallel rows and columns, like fruit trees in an orchard.

The motor powered down. The car settled gently to the ground in one of the four corners of the chamber. Amina stepped out and signaled for Tod and Lisa to do the same.

At first blush, the chamber looked like either a garage or an ante room. Another magnetic car was parked in one of the other corners. Three other tunnels led away from the chamber. Tod realized that the chamber was in fact the intersection of four tunnels, each heading toward a cardinal point of the compass.

Amina led the way into a small dark grotto. Ceiling lights illuminated automatically as soon as she crossed the threshold. The grotto, or room, reminded Tod of a cubicle in Benthocity 3, except that it was the size of a submersible airdock. It was finely appointed with furniture: everything from tables and chairs to beds and workbenches.

Amina unslung the crossbow and quiver by pulling the straps over her head. She placed the weapon and ammunition pouch on a convenient bench.

"It looks like a combination cafeteria, bunkhouse, and workshop."

Amina turned around at Lisa's words. She could not possibly have understood the meaning of Lisa's proclamation, but nevertheless she made motions with her hands toward her mouth. Lisa nodded instinctively. A nod might be meaningless to an archaic Persian; or worse, it might mean something entirely different from what Lisa intended.

Tod simply smiled, and that seemed to get the message across.

Amina led them to a built-in wall unit which she operated by passing her fingers over inlaid crystalline discs. Tinkling sounds were accompanied by opening drawers filled with comestibles. Amina grabbed a double handful of items, placed them on a tray, and held the tray under a sunlamp that she activated by pressing a crystal disc. After a flash of light, she led the way to a nearby table that was constructed of red extruded resin. The chairs were identical in design and manufacture.

Lisa pursed her lips. "An automated food dispenser and a nuker."

"I wouldn't be surprised if there are laundry and bathing facilities. I think this place is a way station that caters to all needs." He took the proffered food from Amina, smiled at her, and pulled apart the plastic wrapping. "Looks like a prepackaged sandwich."

"Did you feel the cool air from the drawer? The dispenser is a refrigeration unit."

"This looks like real bread."

"And the processed meat tastes like chicken."

"Doesn't everything?"

"Just about." Lisa chewed a big bite, swallowed, and, taking a hint from Tod, smiled at Amina. "The grub is good. You're quite a chef, Amina."

Amina managed a weak smile. She did not eat. She observed Tod and Lisa as if they were her wards, or children. Yet she appeared to be no older than they were.

Tod and Lisa wolfed down the miniature sandwiches as if they hadn't eaten for a month of Sundays. Amina provided canisters of flavored water to quench their thirst. While they were drinking, she motioned them to a wallscreen. She pressed several crystal discs. Images appeared on the screen: lines of text in archaic Persian accompanied by graphic views of communities whose buildings represented exotic architectural designs.

Tod yanked the transcriber from its belt loop, but by the time he focused the lens on the screen, Amina had changed the screen to a different view. She changed it again, and again, and once again – all by pressing crystal discs on the desk pad.

"She's scrolling," said Tod. It was very much the same as he did with the transcriber. The only difference was in the mechanism.

Finally the face of a man appeared on the screen. Patriarchal was the word that Tod would have used to describe the mature masculine features. White hair topped a wrinkled forehead and aristocratic bearing. Brown eyes widened in momentary shock until Amina singsonged softly in her archaic language. A voluble interchange ensued.

Lisa whispered to Tod in aside, "It's a communicator."

Tod nodded absently.

Amina did not gesticulate, but kept her smooth-skinned hands unclenched at her sides.

Tod did his best to look innocent. It didn't take much acumen to deduce from what he had seen so far that the archaic Persians possessed technology that was sophisticated enough to produce the disruptor beam that drilled so many holes through the Persian submarine *Serendib*. He did not want to antagonize the patriarch who, he presumed, Amina was persuading that he and Lisa were not hostile. That was the reason he lowered the transcriber instead of making a visual record of the conversation. Surreptitiously, however, he activated the microphone pickup in order to record the spoken language for possible translation.

After several minutes of dialogue, Amina turned to Tod and pointed to the transcriber.

"I think she wants you to show the picture of the foil to the old man."

Tod nodded. He scrolled through screens until he located the relevant stillshot. Slowly he rotated the transcriber until the transcriber faced the image of the patriarch. His reaction to the chart and the archaic Persian text was nearly the same as Amina's. Another discussion followed, this one more effusive than the previous one. The conversation ended when Amina passed her fingers over the crystal discs, and the wallscreen went blank.

Amina carefully pronounced, "Lisa. Tod," followed by a string of words that were unintelligible to the pair. She reactivated the wallscreen, scrolled through lines of text that Tod presumed were either links or menus, and selected a kinetic recording of an ancient sunlit city that looked very much like the one they had just toured.

Tod aimed the transcriber so as to record the flowing imagery. Either the recording instrument was hovering in the air above the buildings, or the city was a cleverly reconstructed animation. As far as Tod could determine, everything looked real – including the pedestrians.

"They're not aliens, either," Lisa muttered, reaffirming her previous observation of the statues in the outer courtyard. Then she gasped.

Tod felt a sharp twinge of vertigo. His stomach lurched as if from sudden acceleration. He felt himself being propelled into the air – yet he could see that he was standing motionless in front of the wallscreen. He seemed to have split in two: the physical part of him stood stationary, while his consciousness, or means of perception, soared into the air above the city.

The feeling of being in two places at once was disturbing and disorienting. Gradually his corporeality, his physical being, faded from material existence. His psyche – that part of the mind that encapsulated the functions of conscious awareness, and that mediated between the brain and what it perceived as reality – assumed substantiality.

He no longer viewed the cityscape through an optical lens. He *was* the lens – or a tangible personification of the lens. As he settled into his new frame of reference, the disorientation passed, and reality became a relative concept. All his senses now operated from a newly created and sentient viewpoint. The disembodied perspective became ordinary, as if he had always been that way.

Close-up views of people in motion showed carefree citizens dressed in robes or togas, as one might envision a scene from ancient Athens or Sparta or Rome. The streets were thronged with vendors who were trading their wares with grocers, bakers, and butchers. Stalls were populated by potters, clothiers, metalworkers, basket weavers, and a variety of smiths.

These were merely the sights. Tod was also aware of sounds and smells: the voices of tradesfolk and shopkeepers; the aroma of baking bread and fresh vegetables; the peaning of hammers; the fragrance of recently cut flowers; the clatter of tools and utensils; the scent of rare herbs and spices.

The point of view panned to a pastoral scene in which the outer wall of the city showed in the background. Farmers worked their fields, shepherds tended their flocks, and women weeded their gardens as they watched their children. Huge meadows glowed with golden grain. Some livestock wandered freely through pastures while others were locked in pens.

Tod felt the heat of the sun. He sniffed the essence of grain. He heard baaing and mooing and braying.

Again the point of view panned, this time to a wharf that was lined with wooden-hulled sailing vessels that resembled Chinese junks. Sailors bustled along the decks or climbed the masts, either raising quadrilateral sails in preparation for departure, or lowering canvas as the vessels were warped to the quayside.

Brine held a tang that was new to Tod's nostrils. His skin felt moist from the splash of water. Hull planks creaked and groaned.

Stevedores rolled barrels along a lengthy mole that prevented waves from crashing into the harbor. Gangplanks creaked and groaned under the staves as some holds were filled while others were emptied. Barkers shouted at passersby. Peddlers hawked everything from souvenirs to foodstuffs. Commerce proceeded smoothly and equitably.

The blue-green sea stretched interminably to the distant curved horizon.

The point of view rose high into the sky. A distinct volcanic peak rose prominently in the background behind the ancient city.

The field of view broadened as the omniscient optical recorder – Tod's eyes and ears and nose – rose up and away from the land. Now he was looking straight down from an increasing height. The sprawling community was shown in perspective: the stone-worked city, the surrounding farmsteads and ranchlands, the deep blue ocean, the inactive volcano. From higher still he saw the settlement shrink until it occupied but a small area in a vast forest. The verdant woodland receded until it was only a green blot on the edge of a continent. The continent became an island in the middle of a limitless sea. Other continents came into view along the perimeter of the screen.

Then the entire planet was visible: a large globe set against a black background that was studded with white pinpoints of light that must have been stars. Patchy white clouds floated above oceans and land-masses. Tod recognized continental outlines. In a flash he understood that he was looking down on Antarctica before it was covered with snow and ice.

The globe shrank as the Moon swam into view. The sun peaked around the lunar sphere, appearing out of eclipse. The recorder moved away from the solar disk until it was little more than a yellow dot among a sea of silvery stars. Another orb became the focal point. This one did not have oceans or continental masses. It was a collage of pastel colors that streaked horizontally across the hemisphere. The disk occupied the center of the screen. Sidewise motion was made apparent by color variations that traveled from one edge to the other.

The vacuum of space was cold to the touch.

A tiny dot appeared on the perimeter of the globe. The diameter of the yellowish-red bulge increased until it became a barely perceptible bulge. The bulge moved across the varicolored circle. If the circle was a basket-ball, the bulge was a marble. When the marble reached the opposite side of the circle, it detached itself from the main mass. A writhing streamer of red smoke or gas connected the marble to the basketball – but only for a moment. Then the marble separated. As it moved away from the perimeter, the connecting linkage fell back to the large circle, spread outward, and was absorbed. Only a splotch of red remained to mark the area of sep-aration.

The marble was a fiery yellow globe that became the focal point on the wall screen. The marble moved across the backdrop of stars with painful languor. Eventually it approached the twin planets that represented Earth and its satellite. The yellow globe did not touch the Earth or the Moon. As the traveling globe passed the Earth-Moon orbit, a stream of gaseous material stretched from each of the equally-sized globes, touched like two fingers pointed at one another, and intermingled. The connection evaporated as the yellow globe continued on its path toward the sun.

The Earth was now covered by an impenetrable layer of swirling clouds. The optical recorder descended into the cyclonic mass, dropped beneath it, and showed the erstwhile thriving city in a state of gloom. The ground trembled. Volcanoes erupted. The air smelled of sulfur. A black pall filled the sky. Lava flowed across the land and into the sea. Vast volumes of steam expanded into the atmosphere. Heavy particulates fell like rain. Thick gas choked the air.

The temblors subsided, but the continent on which the great city was located *moved* in a direction that was inconsistent with the rotation of the Earth. *All* the continents moved in coordination. Lagging water caught up with the movement and created incredible floods that inundated shores around the world.

The continent vanished beneath a shroud of vapor, snow, and ice.

The wallscreen dimmed and went blank. Tod's psyche abruptly snapped back into his head. It was as if he had been stretched between two ends of a rubber band that had suddenly contracted. He now looked through eyes that were lodged in his own sockets. He inhaled as if he had been holding his breath for eternity.

Slowly he regained his physical awareness. He was still in a daze when he glanced at Lisa. Her glassy eyes were coming into focus. They made the transference – the transmogrification – from virtual viewpoint to mental faculty. Their minds returned to their bodies.

The transcriber recorded the visual imagery but not the intense spiritual essence of the experience. It was only a memory chip, not a conscious entity. It collated the information and dug into its databank for relevant historical accounts. The closest analogy that it could locate was called Ragnarok: an age-old Scandinavian legend of worldwide catastrophe, when a comet struck the Earth, when the Moon was blotted from the sky, when stars fell from heaven, when the earth shook, when trees toppled, when mountains sank, when the sea rushed over the land, when chaos reigned.

The deluge and destruction saga that was recounted in Ragnarok coincided with biblical accounts from Exodus, with the Mesopotamian epic of Gilgamesh, with the Sumerian tale of Ziusudra, with the Babylonian fable of Atra-Hasis, with stories in Sanskrit texts, with the Greek fable of Deucalion, with chapters in the Muslim *Koran*, with narratives on Akkadian tablets, with the legend of Khun Borom from Indochina, with the Aztec Nata, with traditional mythologies from every culture in the world, including Andaman islanders, Maoris, Australian aborigines, tribes in Malaysia, American Indians, the Mayans, the Polynesians, and the Chinese classic *Hihking*. All were variations of the visual production that Tod and Lisa had just witnessed on the wallscreen.

The transcriber noted every instance of global annihilation that it found in its databank. It correlated that information with the abandoned city in the giant cavern, and with the imagery that Amina had shown on the wallscreen. The lowest common denominator was a single word.

Tod stared at Lisa in astonishment. He was speechless.

"Hunk, what is it?"

"Atlantis."

Chapter 25

With a few singsong phrases, Amina broke the stunned silence that arced across the space between Tod and Lisa. They both looked at her in newfound wonder, then at each other.

"Could Antarctica really be the lost continent?" Lisa murmured. "Lost to the ancients when it was covered with snow and ice instead of submerged under the sea?"

"I don't know how close the kinetic recording fits the legendary story of destruction, but it's as good a name as any. . . . At least until we can translate enough of Amina's language to learn what she calls this place." Turning to Amina, "So what do we do now?"

Amina spoke in archaic Persian – or in Atlantean, if this truly was Atlantis and if there was such a tongue. So far, the only effective means of imparting information from Lisa and Tod to Amina, and vice versa, was visual, via images on the transcriber and wallscreen. Verbal exchange accomplished little more than to evince cooperation.

"Hunk, her wallscreen is equivalent to our transcriber. I don't know if it can record, but it certainly establishes long distance communication, and it retrieves information from some kind of storage bank. If we could connect the two . . . "

Tod shook his head. "The systems are too dissimilar to communicate directly. They don't even operate on the same principles. From what I've seen so far, their technology is completely different from ours. And theirs is far more advanced. The transcriber is so crude by comparison, it would be like trying to use the diamond needle of an old-fashioned record player to read a digital video disc. It can't be done."

Lisa nodded with understanding. "But you could play the music and record it with a microphone."

"That's what I just did with the transcriber. I

recorded the visual imagery that the wallscreen projected. But that kind of transference can be done only in
real time. It's not like downloading data from a mainframe to an individual computer at multimegabyte
speed. Plus there would be a loss of detail." Tod pointed to the wallscreen and its activation crystals. He was
careful not to touch anything. "Their systems operate
through a medium that's embedded in a three-dimensional crystal lattice that rivals the complexity of the
human brain. I can't even begin to comprehend how
they encode and transmit data the way we just saw it
done – the way our minds perceived and experienced
it."

"Different is not necessarily better."

"In this case it is." Tod shook his head again. "We've
got a lot to learn from them – the Atlanteans, if that's
who they really are."

"So we're back to square one. We still need a Rosetta dictionary, thesaurus, and grammar text."

Tod shrugged. "A first-grade learner or a picture
album with captions would be a good starting point."

Lisa's eyes brightened. "They must have something
like that in order to teach their children. Amina seems
pretty smart. I'll bet if – "

Amina reacted to mention of her name. "Lisa?"

Lisa said to Tod, "Watch this." She picked up a
water flask and showed it to Amina. Because Amina
was so much taller than Lisa, Lisa had to reach up to
put her hand on Amina's chest. "Amina." She touched
her own chest. "Lisa." She then pointed to the flask in
her hand.

Amina said a word.

Lisa smiled and turned to the wallscreen. She
placed her finger on the smooth surface, and imitated
archaic Persian cuneiform. She held the flask in front
of the screen.

Amina passed her fingers over crystal buttons to
activate the screen and scroll through links. She located a picture of a similar flask. She detached a scribe
from the right side of the control panel. She used the

scribe to write a word on a clear flat rectangle on the level surface of the control panel. The image of the word appeared on the screen as she wrote.

"Voila! There's the written word for flask."

Tod recorded the image and text for the language program and decryption software. "Another thousand hours and we'll be chatting about fashion lingerie." He rolled his eyes. "And who knows what we'll talk about next?"

"You leave the lingerie discussions to the women-folk – "

Lisa was interrupted by a commotion outside the grotto. Three pairs of eyes turned immediately toward the doorway. The shuffling of boots on rock was accompanied by the clatter of loose equipment. It sounded to Tod like more than one person, perhaps a small group. He looked forward to meeting more of Amina's people.

His eagerness was tempered by his first sight of the interlopers. The men were wearing the uniform of Persian marines. On their heads they wore cloth turbans instead of steel helmets.

Amina screamed.

A squad of six enlisted men was led by an officer who possessed the visage of the Grim Reaper. His black eyes and dark skin were accentuated by a sneering down-turned mouth and thickly bearded face. He drew an automatic pistol from his holster as he advanced. The men behind him spread across the room, cradling their rifles in their arms in a threatening attitude, but aiming slightly off-target in case of accidental discharge. One rearguard was posted as a sentinel in the doorway.

The officer shouted derisively as he waved his pistol at Amina.

She turned and slammed her hand down on the control panel, pressing one of the crystal disks in the process.

The officer raised his pistol as if it were a baton. He swung his arm to strike Amina across the face.

Tod didn't have time to think. He just reacted

instinctively. Without knowing what he was doing, he leaped between Amina and the attacking officer. The pistol barrel struck his left temple at the same time that he got his hand on the officer's forearm. The partial blow stunned Tod and knocked him sideways against the control panel, but he kept his grip on the arm. His shoulder rebounded from the wallscreen.

Tod's vision was impaired by blood that ran into his left eye. His knees buckled, but he never let go of the officer's arm. Even as he slipped down to the floor, he used his free hand to grab the wrist that held the pistol. He outweighed the officer by a good fifty pounds. By exerting pressure, he wrestled the officer down to the floor with him.

The discharge of the pistol was followed by a *snap* and a cry of pain. Tod twisted the officer's broken wrist and yanked the pistol out of his hand as if it were made of papier-mâché.

Two rifle bullets ricocheted off the base of the control panel. The Persian marines were trying to shoot Tod from across the room without hitting their squad leader. Tod rolled so that the officer was on top of him. He wrapped his legs around one of the officer's calves, effectively pinning the officer to Tod and employing him as a shield.

Like a freeze-frame, the trenchant tableau held still for several seconds as Tod struggled to clear his head.

Two marines dashed toward the grappling pair while three others dispersed in good order. The doorway sentinel turned and raised his automatic rifle in preparation for entering the fracas.

Tod absorbed the situation at a glance. Four guards held the women at gunpoint as two marines closed on Tod and the officer. Unseen by the approaching marines, Tod gripped the handgun the way he had seen it done in kinetic recordings. The two marines were converging from different angles. Their rifles were aimed for a quick shot as soon as they could be assured that they wouldn't hit their squad leader. They both shouted in Persian.

Tod didn't understand the words. If they were ordering him to surrender, he had no intention of doing so. He had no time to weigh his options. He lifted the heavy pistol off the floor, aimed as best he could, and pulled the trigger. One marine screamed in pain when the bullet penetrated his shoulder.

Recoil was something that wasn't shown in kinetic recordings. The loosely held gun flew out of Tod's hand at the moment of discharge. The wounded marine was spun around by the impact of the bullet. He dropped his rifle, lost his balance, stumbled sideways to one knee, and then fell flat.

Tod fumbled the retrieve the gun and get a grip on the trigger. He saw that the other marine had his rifle already aimed at Tod's exposed face and was about to shoot. There was no time . . .

The marine's head exploded into fragments at the same second that a loud blast erupted from the doorway. Blood and bone flew everywhere. The marine collapsed to the floor like a marionette whose strings had all been cut at once.

Everyone – Tod, the women, the officer, and the marines – diverted their attention to the figure that stood in doorway.

Denny Harker!

Never in his wildest dreams had Tod imagined that he would ever be glad to see the arrogant reprobate.

The new tableau lasted only a fraction of a second. Harker shifted the aim of his rifle – the rifle that Tod now perceived he had taken from the doorway sentinel who lay on the floor at Harker's feet – and fired at the closest of the three standing marines. His bullet struck the man full in the face. Then pandemonium reigned as the other two marines raised their rifles, fired, and ducked for cover – all at once – while Harker, withholding his fire, dropped to a crouch and scuttled sideways behind the cabinet structure of a workbench.

In violation of the Geneva Convention, explosive bullets flew across the room in wild abandon.

The officer took advantage of the distraction to

break away from Tod. He rolled over on his back and then onto his front, got his knees underneath him, and scuttled across the floor on hands and knees toward one of his fallen men. Just as he grabbed the dead marine's rifle, Tod crippled him by shooting him in the leg. Tod fired again and struck the arm that held the rifle. The officer rolled onto his back, writhing in agony.

Persian bullets zinged harmlessly passed Tod's head. He was not in the direct line of fire of the two surviving marines. Nonetheless, he scrambled for better cover behind a table. Now everyone was hidden from everyone else by furniture and cupboards.

Harker ricocheted two rounds off the ceiling, then stuck his rifle barrel over top of the workbench and waited for one of the Persians to show his head. As soon as he did, Harker fired a bullet directly into the man's nasal cavity. The head expanded like a balloon as the body was hurled backward by the impact. Brain tissue splattered as high as the ceiling, and clung there.

The other marine was not as brazen. He tossed a grenade through the air in Harker's direction. The grenade bounced on the top of the workbench that was Harker's bulwark, and landed on the floor between the workbench and the cabinet behind it. Harker scurried out of the aisle just as the grenade detonated.

The marine did not wait to see the effect of the blast, but used it as covering fire. He charged silently across the room. Harker lay sprawled on the floor, his back and one side bloody from shrapnel hits. The rifle was still in his hand. There was no time to raise it.

The marine grinned as he aimed at Harker's unprotected chest. Harker did not freeze, but redoubled his efforts to bring the rifle to bear. He wasn't fast enough . . .

Thwack!

Tod heard the unfamiliar sound, saw something protrude suddenly from the center of the marine's chest, watched as the grin turned to a grimace, and saw rich red blood gurgle past whiskered lips. The marine dropped to both knees, then pitched forward onto his face.

Lisa took two steps forward with the crossbow in her hands. "Take that, you bastard."

Chapter 26

Harker leaped to his feet. He paid no heed to his bloody wounds. He swept his rifle around the room full of dead and dying Persians.

"Looks like I got here in the nick of time."

Lisa glared with evident hatred at the Persian who had the end of the quarrel sticking out of his back. Her jaw worked from side to side as she ground her teeth, but she didn't say anything.

Amina ran to Tod's side. She helped him to a sitting position. The way she touched him and said "Tod" sent tingles along his spine.

Tod inhaled deeply. He alternately squinted and widened his eyes in order to shake off waves of vertigo.

A deep-throated voice called out from the doorway in archaic Persian.

All eyes turned toward the grim young man who was standing at the threshold. He was pointing some kind of device at Harker. He was not dressed like a Persian marine, but like Amina, except that he wore a brown leather blouse and a kilt over slacks instead of a caftan.

Amina screamed, drew the man's attention, then stood and ran to him. She threw her arms around his shoulders and kissed him on the cheek. During the short dialogue that ensued, the wounded marine who had first tried to shoot Tod pushed himself up to his elbow and raised his rifle toward Harker.

Now Lisa screamed.

In one smooth motion, Amina stepped aside to give the grim young man a clear shot, wiggled her fingers at the Persian marine, and uttered a single syllable. The young man drilled the marine through the chest with a disruptor beam. The body collapsed like a house of cards.

Tod should have been shocked by the episode, but all he could think about was how Harker had to thank two women for saving his life twice in the span of a single minute. The young man might very well have shot Harker out of hand had Amina not intervened.

Thanks were not forthcoming. But neither did Harker point his rifle in the young man's direction. Instead, he notched the butt against his elbow and aimed the barrel at the ceiling. The common enemy made them allies if not necessarily friends. The young man did not aim the disruptor device at anyone else.

Harker ignored the groaning officer on the floor; he had no weapons. "Would someone please explain to me what the hell is going on here?"

Tod managed to utter, "It's kind of confusing. . . . It all happened so fast. . . . "

He jerked his chin at Amina and the young man. "Who are these people?"

Tod put his hand to his temple. It was sticky with blood that was still flowing profusely. "The woman is Amina. I don't know who the man is."

"Are they Persians?"

Tod winced with pain. "Yes, but not modern Persians. They're archaic Persians. Or Atlanteans."

"What is an Atlantean?"

"A person from Atlantis." When Harker looked perplexed, Tod added, "You know, the lost continent?"

Harker humphed. "Now I've heard everything. You haven't by any chance found the golden fleece, have you?"

"I know it sounds crazy – "

"It *is* crazy." Harker surveyed the large room and its contents. "But then, this whole place is crazy."

Tod stood shakily. He put one arm around Lisa's shoulders and eased the crossbow out of her hands. Amina clung to the young man's arm. Tod now saw that the handheld disruptor was connected by a thick cable to a fat belt that girdled the man's slender waist. He suspected that the belt was a battery pack that provided power for the weapon.

"I need a sitrep. Can you talk their lingo?"

Lisa was still silent, with a far-away look in her

eyes. She was in no condition to give a situation report.

Tod shrugged. "Only one word – for water flask."

"That'll get us a drink but not much more." He transferred the rifle to his left hand. He approached the young man and stretched out his right hand.

The young man returned Harker's gaze, but did nothing else. He stood stoically while Amina clung to his left arm.

"Do these people greet each other by shaking hands?"

"I don't know. We haven't got that far in communicating."

Lisa came back from wherever her mind had taken her. "Try putting your hand on your chest and saying your name."

Harker made the facial expression that was his most common: a scowl.

"No, really. Try it."

Harker wiped the scowl off his face as he looked at the young man. He placed his outstretched hand over his heart as if he were pledging allegiance to the flag. "Denny Harker."

Amina caught on right away. She placed one hand on her chest. "Amina." Next she placed her hand on the young man's chest. "Assad."

Harker sighed. "Assad."

Assad said, "Dennyharker."

Harker scowled again. "Okay, so we've been introduced. Now let's get this Persian to talk. The modern Persian, I mean. That I know how to do." He turned his attention to the officer who was lying supine on the floor. Glancing at Tod, "Good thing you're such a bad shot that you only wounded him."

Tod refrained from replying that he had wounded the man on purpose – not so he could be interrogated but because Tod felt appalled at taking human life.

In aside, "Tod. Lisa. You check the rest of the squad to make sure they're dead. I don't want anyone else pulling a gun behind me."

The officer stopped writhing and groaning. Now he

lay partially in shock from trauma and the loss of blood. Harker frisked him. He found two full clips for the pistol and a plastic identification card; nothing else.

"Habib Bistami," Harker intoned. "Well, Mister Bistami, what can you tell us about the Persian invasion of Antarctica? A place where you're not supposed to be? Talk."

Bistami rolled and uttered a moan of pain, but pronounced no words.

Harker slammed his rifle butt against the wound on the Persian officer's leg. "Talk."

The officer howled in agony, then mumbled a couple of words in Farsi.

"In English, you stupid Yuper, not that Neanderthal polyglot that you call language. Unless you want another broken leg."

Harker struck him again. The officer's initial shriek faded to a drawn-out caterwaul.

"I can do this all shift if you want to make it hard on yourself."

The officer spluttered a few more words.

Harker was about to hit him again when Lisa intervened. "I think he said he does not speak English."

"A likely story."

"You don't speak Farsi. Why would you expect him to speak English?"

Harker scowled. "Stupid Yuper. Not to worry, though. I've got the answer to that." He pulled a backup transcriber from his belt loop. It was identical to the transcriber that Tod possessed, but did not contain all the extra data files and decryption software. He switched on the audio circuit. "Now you can understand me."

The words that Harker spoke were picked up by the receiver, translated into Farsi by a standard language program, fed to an amplifier, then read aloud by the transmitter. It worked in reverse as well.

"I tell you nothing, you infidel scum."

"We'll see about that." Harker slammed the rifle butt against the broken leg. "Talk!"

The officer shrieked, but not as loud as before.

"Make it easy on yourself, Bistami."

"I die for my faith. Allah will be my guide."

"You're right, but not until I'm done with you."

Harker was about to hit the officer again when Tod called out, "This one is still alive."

Amina and Assad observed the proceedings mutely. Harker stepped past them without a glance in their direction. He knelt next to the sentinel who lay limp on the floor like a broken rag doll.

"He should be dead after that karate chop I gave him on the neck. I must be out of practice."

The sentinel's eyes were open and his lips were moving, but only a whisper emerged from his parched throat.

"Can you hear me okay?" Harker held the transcriber close to the sentinel's mouth, so the microphone could pick up the reply.

The transcriber translated his Farsi. "I – I cannot – feel – "

"His neck must be broken." Harker slammed the rifle butt hard on the sentinel's curled fingers.

The sentinel didn't even wince.

"He's paralyzed. From the neck down." Harker scowled. "Doesn't mean that he won't talk, though." He turned his head toward the officer, who was watching quietly. "Right Bistami?"

"I curse you. Allah curses you. A thousand curses – "

"Save your religious mumbo-jumbo for believers, Bistami." In aside, to no one in particular, "These fanatics are all alike. They can't tolerate a difference of opinion." To the sentinel, "Do *you* want to go to heaven, or paradise, or never-never land?"

"The word – of Allah – is great."

"Maybe so, but right now my word is greater. So listen up. If you want to go to Allah, I'll be glad to send you on your way – right away. The one who talks gets a furlough."

The transcriber translated and broadcast Harker's words literally, but without the emphasis or intonation.

"I go – with Allah."

"It's your choice." Harker stood and aimed his rifle at the sentinel's chest. He squeezed the trigger. The body bounced. The report sounded exceptionally loud in the pervading silence. "That put him out of his misery."

Chapter 27

"You – you shot him in cold blood." Tod's voice was barely a squeak.

Harker scowled. "So? Is hot blood in the heat of battle a better way to die? Dead is dead no matter how it comes about." Harker jerked his chin at the body on the floor. "He knew the job description when he signed up. He got what he deserved for enlisting in the Persian armed forces. And he would have done the same to you if he had the opportunity. So don't fret about it. He's happy now – he's in the Promised Land that he believed in. And in case you've forgotten, fanatical Yupers killed your folks in cold blood, and didn't think twice about it. An eye for an eye, as they say. Right, Lisa?"

Lisa was shocked but not aghast. Amina and Assad were emotionless.

"Now what have *you* got to say, Mister Bistami?" Harker strode to the officer and knelt by his side. "Are you ready to talk, or do you want to meet your maker, too?"

The transcriber translated the dialogue.

"I would rather die than submit to the will of an infidel."

"I can arrange that, but it will be slow going."

"Torture is against the Geneva Convention."

"Why do you towelheads fall back on humanitarian principles when it's to your advantage, but conveniently forget them when it suits you?"

"*We* are the faithful. *We* are the true believers."

"And why do you cite irrelevant platitudes when you don't want to answer a question with logic?"

"*You* will see. *We* will put an end to your kind."

"*If* that ever happens, *you* won't be one of the *we*."

"My life in this world is unimportant. The great Allah will save my soul."

"The only sole you've got is on the bottom of your boot. You use it to step on people who choose to differ with your way of thinking."

"You speak blasphemy."

"I speak truth."

"You speak lies."

Harker bludgeoned the officer with the butt of his rifle. "Can you speak with a broken jaw?"

Bistami's head was knocked aside by the blow. He spit blood and two broken teeth.

"I want answers, not self-serving dogma."

"I curse you. Allah curses – "

Harker struck him again. "You tried that already. Your great Allah must be napping because I haven't been cursed yet. Now give me some answers."

"I may – have some – answers." The voice did not emanate from the transcriber, but from the doorway. Prof stood on the threshold with an olive green pouch held aloft in his hand. He was breathing hard – one might even say gasping. "I found – these dispatches – in that – horseless – carriage."

"Prof!" Lisa ran to the professor and flung her arms around his slight paunch. Her head barely reached his sternum. "I'm so glad to see you."

"Careful." Prof pushed her away and held her at arm's length. "I am still – out of breath. I am not as young – as I used to be."

"Neither is anyone else." Tod shook Prof's hand.

"It has been decades since I proceeded on my feet at a pace that is faster than a walk. Is that blood on your head?"

Tod self-consciously touched the congealing clot. "I got in the way of a gun barrel . . . "

Prof surveyed the uniformed bodies, then turned toward Amina and Assad. "And who might these folks be?"

"Friends. They live here."

Assad did not look friendly. He held the disruptor device aimed at Prof's belly.

Lisa placed her hand on Prof's chest. "Prof." Next she placed her hand on Assad's chest. "Assad." Then she placed her hand on Amina's chest. "Amina."

Assad glanced at her, then at Prof, then at Harker, then at Prof again. His right hand maintained its grip on the disruptor device, but turned it away. He held out his left hand. "Prof."

"He's pretty sharp. He's picked up the handshake greeting already, even if he did get the wrong hand."

Prof shook Assad's outstretched hand with his own left hand. "My pleasure, Assad." He kept his right hand by his side and used the index finger to point to the device in Assad's other hand. "Would that be a weapon?"

Assad lowered the device.

Harker interrupted any additional exchange of pleasantries. "Now that we've all be introduced, what's in the pouch?"

"Those are sacred documents," Bistami screamed. "You are forbidden to see them."

Harker kicked him in the head. "Shut up, Yuper." To Prof, "Open it. Let's take a gander."

Prof glanced around the room once more. "Is the area secure?"

Tod hoisted his pistol. "I'll keep an eye on the doorway."

Prof nodded. "I suppose I must curb my curiosity about these interesting newcomers until we deal with more immediate matters, such as what these Persians are doing in this, uh, place." He looked at Amina and Assad, and at the bodies on the floor. "It does not appear that they are on a mission of diplomacy or the establishment of friendly relations." He removed a sheaf of paper from the pouch.

Bistami did not protest. He was unconscious.

"The dispatches appear to be in code."

"I've got the decoder chip already installed in my transcriber."

"Excellent. If we transcribe the documents, we should be able to decrypt them."

Before they commenced the operation, the wallscreen flashed and emitted a mild tone. The worried face of the patriarch appeared on the screen. Amina ran to the control panel, touched some of the crystals, and spoke hurriedly. Tod could follow none of the interlocution, but he knew by the facial expressions and the harsh sound of the voices that the news was not good. Assad joined in the conversation with equal excitement.

Prof was breathing easier now. "I feel as if I have arrived in the middle of something extraordinary."

"*That's* an understatement," Lisa said.

"I got here in time for a firefight and I *still* don't know what's going on." Harker gestured toward the pair of archaic Persians who were jabbering at the wallscreen simultaneously. "I gather that we're on the same side. Against the Yupers. But who *are* they? And where did they come from." He looked sharply at Tod. "And don't give me any of that Atlantis crap. The next thing you know, you'll be spouting about flying saucers or alien abduction or some other out-of-date craze."

Lisa humphed. "I wish the explanation was that simple."

"We don't know much more than you do," Tod declared. "We met Amina only a few minutes before the gun battle. In the shrine on top of the ziggurat." To Prof, "How did you find us, anyway?" To Harker, "And show up so fortuitously?"

Harker provided the answers. "We had intermittent contact with your transcriber in the forest. When there wasn't too much interference from the trees. We followed the broken track to that temple. You went out the back way before I could activate the voice comm. I had line-of-sight along the tunnel, but couldn't figure how you got so far ahead of me. Then the comm signal disconnected – you must have gone into this compartment. I ran all the way. Good thing I work out regularly in the gym. I chopped the Yuper standing closest to the doorway and took his rifle."

Prof took over. "I hustled as fast as I could. I spotted Denny's knapsack on the ground outside, near that contrivance with the rucksacks and equipment that the marines left behind. I peeked in and saw that Denny had the situation under control, so I went through the belongings and found the pouch with the dispatches." Prof paused for a moment. "So what is this about Atlantis?"

Tod shrugged. "It's just something that the transcriber dug up from the databank. We're not sure that it means anything."

"Are Amina and Assad residents of the city of stone?"

Lisa shrugged. "No. They live somewhere else. Some place we haven't been to yet."

"How interesting."

"Unbelievable is the word I'd use." Harker took a good look around the grotto. "This place is – unbelievable. I *wouldn't* believe it if I didn't see it with my own eyes." To Prof. "And that Assad, he has a handheld ray gun, or laser beam, like the kind that must have drilled holes through that Yuper sub. He almost drilled *you* with it."

Prof placed his hands on his paunch. "That would have been unfortunate."

"He drilled one of the Yupers. The beam went clean through him and the rock underneath, like a hot needle through soft butter." He jerked his chin toward Amina and Assad. "I'm glad we're on the same side. Even if we can't understand their language, we've got to work with them and rid this place of Yupers. According to the number that were missing from the sub, there must be others lurking somewhere in these caverns, maybe laying siege to these people, whoever they are."

"They're archaic Persians," Lisa explained. "These people write in cuneiform like the writing on the gold foils."

"How interesting." To Harker, "You are correct, Denny. We must put our curiosity in abeyance, and cooperate with the local inhabitants until the present adversity is resolved. If the Persians – the modern Persians, that is – get their hands on these disruptor devices . . . "

Harker was emphatic. "Exactly my point. And judging by what I see here, these people have other technology that the enemy could turn against us."

"And maybe they have technology that can help to solve some of the world's problems," Tod added.

"They would have to be gods to do that," Prof rejoined. "And goddesses."

Tod and Lisa exchanged knowing looks.

Tod was about to comment when he saw Amina wiggling the fingers of one hand at him while she pointed to the wallscreen with the outstretched fingers of her other hand. "We better see what she wants."

All four of them approached the wallscreen. Amina and Assad stepped aside so that the others could have an unobstructed view of the images. The picture of the patriarch faded and was replaced by a panorama of a sprawling and splendorous metropolis. The architecture was as modern as the architecture of the city of rocs was ancient. There were no tall spires or rounded bulges, no useless or impractical structural conceits, no fountains or statues or pointless decoration. The landscape was one of utilitarian simplicity, with expansive buildings nestled among groves of redwoods and interconnected by paved pathways that curved and convoluted. Facades of gleaming gold reflected the bright luminescence that glowed from the ceiling above.

The viewpoint moved magically to ground level, and focused on a squad of advancing Persian marines.

"There's our call to arms," Harker said with glee.

Lisa glowered. "You're enjoying this, aren't you."

Harker's perpetual scowl turned into a grin. "I'm just doing what has to be done." He clutched the rifle, and swept his free arm toward the doorway. "Lead on, Assad."

Assad interpreted the gesture correctly. He turned and trotted out of the room and into the garage. Amina blanked the wall screen.

"Go ahead, people. I've got to eradicate a cancer."

Tod followed Assad haltingly until Amina took his hand in hers and pulled him into the garage. He kept looking over his shoulder at Harker, and wondering . . .

Prof and Lisa did the same.

"I'll catch up in a second," Harker called.

Then they were in the garage and out of Harker's sight. Assad had already activated a magnetic car – not the one in which he had arrived, but the one that the marines had driven, and which held their supplies and paraphernalia. Amina sat next to Assad. Tod, Lisa, and Prof squeezed onto the bench seat behind them.

Tod heard clattering sounds from inside the room. A moment later, Harker appeared with an armful of rifles and a couple of satchels of ammunition and hand grenades. He tossed everything into the cargo compartment, donned his knapsack, then jumped into the compartment and crouched, his hands gripping the forward bulkhead as if he had done this all his life.

"Let's go!"

The magnetic car levitated off the ground. Assad eased the control rod forward. The car commenced to move.

"What about the Persian?" Lisa wanted to know.

"Military expedience." Harker was grim as he flexed the fingers of his right hand. "No sense in wasting ammo."

Chapter 28

The magnetic car zoomed smoothly and effortlessly along the tunnel through black basalt.

Amina and Lisa treated Tod's head wound with chemical ointments from a first aid kit that Amina produced from a compartment under the control panel. Lisa held her handlight in position while Amina did the ministrations. Despite the initial pain of dabbing the gouge, Tod tingled all over at Amina's tender touch. Within seconds, the ointment anesthetized the side of his forehead around the affected area. He felt not a twinge as the woman cleansed and bandaged the wound.

Tod pointed to the tube of ointment. "That's great stuff, whatever it is. I didn't feel a thing." He knew that Amina could not understand his words, so he smiled.

For the first time, Amina smiled in return.

Lisa sniffed the open end of the tube. "It must be some kind of miracle drug." She twisted in the seat. "Denny, turn around and pull down your top so I can put some of this stuff on those cuts."

"Forget it. I'm okay."

"But it will stop the pain."

Harker scowled. "They're only flesh wounds."

Prof said, "These archaic Persians might have more in that ointment than an analgesic. It probably contains ingredients that combat infection and promote healing."

Harker scowled again, but doffed his knapsack, yanked open the front of the syntactic suit, and pulled down the top to expose his muscular back. He turned so that Lisa could doctor the lacerations.

"Hold the light, Prof." Lisa applied the ointment to each of the half a dozen shrapnel wounds. "Amina."

When she acknowledged Lisa's call with a soft touch on her shoulder, Lisa moved aside and pointed to several places where jagged bits of metal protruded from nasty wounds.

Amina handed her an instrument that was a cross between tweezers and forceps. Deftly, Lisa removed each piece of shrapnel. "Does that hurt, Denny?"

"I don't feel a thing. Just a little stretching of the skin."

Lisa completed her clinical treatment by spreading more ointment on the wounds now that the shrapnel had been removed. "All done, Denny."

Harker redressed. He rolled his shoulders to test the effectiveness of the treatment. "It feels like nothing ever happened." The statement was the closest that Harker would ever get to giving thanks for a job well done.

Neither Amina nor Assad spoke. It was as if they knew that vociferations were a waste of time and energy, so they didn't bother.

"We have much to learn from these people," Prof prophesied to no one in particular.

Agreement was silent but no less explicit.

The car arrived at an illuminated intersection. Assad reduced speed, turned the vehicle left, and proceeded into another tunnel that was carved through black basalt. This tunnel led to another intersection, at which point Assad turned right. A minute later Tod spotted a bright light ahead. The car emerged from darkness into a brilliantly lighted cavern that must have rivaled in size the one that held the abandoned city of rocs, except that ultrafine mist obscured its farthest reaches.

A rifle barked in the distance.

Assad drove across an immense field of crops. Tod saw wheat, corn, and cotton in various stages of growth. Subaqueous installations relied on hydroponics for growing grain and vegetables. He had never seen crops grown in soil.

Assad brought the car to a halt in front of a rectangular building that gleamed with gold. The patriarch stood in the doorway. He wore leather sandals and a cloth toga that was dyed in red, white, and black swirls, similar in design to Amina's caftan. His white wispy hair was uncovered. A dozen men and women stood on either side of him. They wore garments like those of Amina and Assad. They were armed with pitchforks and adzes.

"Farmers," Harker said derisively. "This should be interesting."

The building stood on the outskirts of a city that reminded Tod of the one that he had seen on the wallscreen in the grotto where the firefight had taken place.

The patriarch engaged in a voluble conversation with Amina and Assad. The other archaic Persians looked at the Benthocity foursome with a mixture of wonder and trepidation.

Automatic weapons fire made everyone look in the direction of conflict. The patriarch wriggled his fingers for the foursome to go inside. Harker carried a rifle in each hand, and held a satchel of grenades and ammunition over his shoulder. A huge wallscreen dominated the back of the room. Without resorting to dialogue, the patriarch passed his fingers over clear crystals that were embedded in the control panel. What appeared to be a diagram flashed onto the screen.

Geometric figures were spread across the screen in a seemingly haphazard array. Most were perfectly rectangular, but some had rounded corners or L-shaped extensions; a few were T-shaped. Each plane figure projected a three-dimensional picture of a city that was similar to the one that lay outside the building. The figures were interconnected by a maze of straight lines.

"It is a map," Prof breathed. "A map of this marvelous civilization. Underground cities and a network of tunnels."

Additional revelation would have to wait. The patriarch touched an oblong figure in the lower left corner of the screen. Instantly the image expanded and filled the entire screen. The city was laid out like a satellite photomosaic. He touched one edge. That section of the city expanded to full screen size.

The patriarch pointed to the floor, then to a spot on the expanded view. He then imitated a marine holding a rifle to his cheek, and pointed to another spot. He touched this latter spot, and the section expanded to show two squads of Persian marines: one was advancing under covering fire from the other that was holed up in a corral that held several dead horses. Scattered archaic Persians hid behind walls of basalt, occasionally firing quarrels toward the advancing squad. Their offensive was erratic and uncoordinated.

"I get it." Harker leaned one of the rifles against the wall. "He wants me to take charge."

He ran a finger across the screen without touching it. With a complicated series of gestures and gesticulations, he conveyed to the archaic Persians where he wanted them positioned. For the benefit of his companions, he explained, "These people don't know how to plan a military campaign. I doubt if they even know how to fight a real enemy. Except for Assad."

Assad reacted to mention of his name.

"Here's what we're going to do." Again Harker resorted to complicated hand signals to explain flanking maneuvers that would catch the Persian marines in a pincer movement. "We'll pass out what weapons we have and split into two teams. One team will approach the enemy position from the top of the screen; the other will approach from the bottom. We'll attack the stronghold first. That will leave the roving patrol unprotected. Then we'll pick them off with sniper fire and guerrilla tactics. Casualties should be light."

"You seem to know what you are doing," Prof said.

"I wasn't always a submersible dispatcher. And security detail is the least of my background."

"So I am given to understand." After a pause, "Rather than take part in the fighting, I think I can render better service by opening a form of dialogue with the erstwhile general." He indicated the patriarch.

"He seems like a no-nonsense kind of guy. You two should get along well together."

"Tod, if you will let me have your transcriber with

the decoding chip, I can get started on the communication process."

Tod handed the transcriber to Prof. "Does that mean that I'm in the fight?"

Harker scowled. "You stick with me, kid, but keep in the background."

"I'm going with Assad." Lisa scooped up the rifle that was leaning against the wall. "Give me some extra magazines and a couple of grenades."

The patriarch explained the plan to the group of farmers. As one person, they laid down their farm implements, entered a room that was located adjacent to the wallscreen, and emerged a moment later with crossbows and quivers.

"I *like* these people," Harker announced with admiration. "They're not shy about fighting. All they need is a good leader to show them how." After a pause, "I wonder how they maintain their skills."

"We'll figure that out later. Right now, I've got an itchy trigger finger that I want to start scratching." Lisa wielded the rifle as if she had used one all her life, instead of only having seen them in operation on kinetic recordings of historic battle scenes. "Let's send some of these illegal explosive bullets back to their owners."

Harker grinned like the Cheshire cat. "Okay. You and Assad and half of this platoon circle to the top – " He pointed to individuals and indicated on the wallscreen where they should go. " – and Tod and I will head for the bottom with the other half. We'll swing around to the left, using this building for cover. Commence firing on my signal – three rapid shots, then two more. We'll hit the corral from two sides at once, and work our way to hand grenade range. Once the corral is secure, we'll engage the roving patrol from perpendicular directions. – that way we won't shoot any of our own people, but we'll still have those Yupers in a crossfire."

While Harker was dividing the erstwhile troops into squads, Amina approached Tod with a look of evident concern. Tod stared deep into dark, fathomless eyes that made his insides churn. She did not speak, but took both of his hands in hers and squeezed twice with her fingers. Tod did not know what to do or say, so he did and said nothing. She let go of his hands so she could swing the crossbow off her back.

"Grab a rifle, Lover Boy," Harker commanded.

Tod broke his heartfelt gaze from Amina's eyes. He followed Harker out the door, picked up a rifle and an ammo satchel from the rear compartment of the magnetic car, and slung the straps over one shoulder. Amina stood by his side with her crossbow cocked. Now Tod understood that she was going to fight by his side.

"Okay, people. Fall out." Harker marched merrily off to war.

Tod, Amina, and half a dozen armed farmers followed in his wake. Assad and Lisa led the other party. Lisa blew a kiss at Tod. He returned it with trepidation. Then he turned his full attention to the perilous matter at hand.

"In addition to surprise, our biggest advantage is that the Yupers won't be expecting the sheep to retaliate with tough tactical maneuvers. The way I figure it, they've been here for more than a week – ever since Assad or somebody drove off their submarine – and they've been pushing their way from city to city through the tunnel system. I think the red lines on the wallscreen marked their progress. Now that I see the kind of gumption the locals have, I suspect they've been doing the best they could with the weapons and background they have: shoot and run, or run and shoot back. If all the cities are part of a single community, and they are as old as you say they are, then they haven't engaged in war for thousands of years. Maybe since the time of recorded history."

Tod didn't know how to interrupt Harker's monologue, so he kept quiet.

"So the Yupers have been getting away with wholesale murder, while the defenders have been leading them around in circles, nipping at their heels but avoiding full-scale shoot-outs that they're bound to lose. Look at them. They have the strength of will. They dropped their tools and picked up weapons without any kind of argument. These are my kind of people."

Before long they reached the vicinity of the corral. Tod took a moment to wonder if the archaic Persians had domesticated the eohippus, or perhaps possessed the last remaining stock of unicorns. The preservation of extinct species seemed to be their forte.

"Let's hit 'em, and hit 'em hard!"

Harker's battle cry brought Tod out of his reverie.

"Slight change of plans now that I see the lay of the land. You and the others stay here while I sneak up on the corral. I'll give the signal when to fire the rifle shots. Remember: three rounds, then two. While the Yupers are distracted, I'm going to toss some grenades into the corral from the adjacent side. Then I want everyone to converge at once, shooting all the time in order to keep their heads down and gain fire superiority. Got it?"

Tod nodded mutely.

"Good." Harker ducked under a low wall and scuttled to the side of a nearby building. "Watch for my signal."

Tod paid heed as Harker sidled along the broad front of a two-story structure whose smooth walls shimmered like burnished gold. Harker reached the corner, peeked around it, then raised his fist and dropped it quickly. When Tod aimed his rifle toward the side of the corral, and fired, Harker disappeared from sight as he dashed into the alley that separated two buildings.

Heads and rifles popped above the corral's bulwark. The marines were close enough for Tod to see the shock and surprise in their eyes. Amina and the archaic Persians were spread out behind him, ready to go into action. Tod fired his rifle for effect just as automatic weapons fire erupted from the opposite side of the corral. Almost simultaneously, a grenade exploded inside the corral. The blast was followed closely by another, and another, and another.

"Let's go." Tod waved his arm at the archaic Persians in his squad.

As he stepped into the open in order to lead the way, the archaic Persians dashed past him and Amina as if they were standing still. Tod was all but bowled over in their mad rush to take part in the fracas. The archaic Persians on the other side of the corral did the same, with Assad and Lisa maintaining only a slender lead. Rifle shots filled the air with a cacophony that sounded like an endless string of fire crackers. Quarrels thwacked as they were released from their crossbows. Assad's disruptor beam was silent but deadly.

Most of the archaic Persians from both squads followed Harker's example as he leaped to the top of the wall with his rifle in hand, and fired down onto the marines who were huddled inside the corral, bleeding from scores of shrapnel wounds. The thick walls of basalt had acted like pool-table bumpers, ricocheting jagged iron pellets like superfast billiard balls.

Several archaic Persians from both attacking sides joined forces at the gate. They forced open the entrance to the compound, and unleashed their quarrels at the marines who now found themselves taking fire from three sides by overzealous combatants. They didn't have a chance to call for quarter, and none was given to them. The marines met death swiftly and completely. The attack was over in seconds. The smell of gunpowder reeked in the ensuing silence.

The battle was won but not the war. The eruption of rifle fire alerted the roving patrol that something was amiss to their rear. The marine squad double-timed toward the corral.

The archaic Persian defenders exhibited no elation over their easy victory. They turned to Harker for direction. Harker used his hands as semaphores. He waved individuals to the left and right of the corral, behind structures that offered protection from exploding bullets. He stood defiantly in the middle of the open gateway, encouraging the approaching marines to focus their attention on him.

The strategy worked perfectly. As the Persian

marines lifted their rifles to fire, Harker dropped to one knee and raised his weapon to his shoulder. He took quick aim on the patrol leader, squeezed off two rounds, and yelled for his newfound soldiers to open fire.

The Persian marines found themselves in the middle of an ambush. Resistance was sporadic against snipers from the sidelines. There might have been a rout and an attempt to retreat if the shooting against them had been less furious. They were scythed down by a withering fire from rifles, crossbows, and the disruptor beam. Soon the road surface was littered with bodies. Those marines who groaned from their wounds were quickly dispatched.

There were no survivors.

Only two archaic Persians were slightly wounded.

Harker grinned broadly as he clutched at a terrible wound in his side. Through gritted teeth, he croaked, "The Yupers are great at killing untrained civilians, but not worth a damn against organized resistance."

Then he fainted.

Chapter 29

Tod expected that an uproar of exhilaration would overwhelm the Atlanteans, if that was who they were, as a result of their deliverance. Instead, tension in the sub-Antarctic civilization merely relaxed with the passing of the Persian marines. The inhabitants returned to their normal routine of placidity, almost as if the invasion had never occurred.

There was no cheering, no feting, no pandemic emotional outbreak. Farmers exchanged their crossbows for plowshares and cultivated their crops. Ranchers tended their sheep and goats. Smiths labored at their trades. Vendors hawked their wares. Mechanics maintained machines. Technicians supported the technological infrastructure. Whatever their occupations, the underground dwellers returned to their work with seeming equanimity.

Yet there was a subtle undercurrent of acceptance that their lives were about to change.

Once discovered by the outside world, the archaic Persians could never again be undiscovered. Ten thousand years of isolation was on the verge of termination. The age-old tradition of containment and self-involvement was about to be demolished, or at least greatly modified. The status quo must yield to a newborn practice of worldwide intercourse. Insularity was soon to become a thing of the past.

Thanks to a generous application of the wonder salve, Harker made a remarkable recovery from the wounds he received in battle. "I don't care what anyone says, I'm for staying on with these blokes. They need me."

The Benthocity foursome reclined on blue foam cushions in one of many of the capital city's communal lounges. The spacious room was illuminated by the soft glow of concealed lights. Snacks and flavored drinks had been provided by automated dispensers that were integrated in multi-use tables that separated the cushions.

Professor Pembroke sipped green liquid from a clear plastic container. "I cannot disagree with you, Denny, but I think it would be prudent to await an invitation instead of forcing ourselves upon them. We have a delicate diplomatic situation to resolve before we can hope to gain their trust."

"Don't you think they should be grateful to us for getting rid of the Yupers for them?"

"I do, but that does not mean that they think the same way that we think. Their cultural heritage is older than the civilized world – the surface world, that is – and their civilization has been perfectly stable for all those millennia, while surface cultures have risen and fallen time and time again. If I were they, I would think long and hard about establishing relations with people whose history is dominated by warfare."

"There's only one reason for human warfare. Some individuals want to dominate others, and those others don't want to be dominated, so they fight back."

"That's two reasons," Lisa inserted.

Harker scowled.

"Those *are* two reasons." Tod winked at Lisa. He was feeling gracious toward Harker since his life-saving actions. "But the sentence can be reworded to a single reason: some individuals want to dominate others who don't want to be dominated." As an afterthought, "And who are willing to defend themselves against domination, no matter what the cost."

Harker's scowl morphed to a look of ambiguity, then to one of uncertain cogitation.

Lisa humphed at Tod. "The round goes to you."

Prof resumed. "My point is that these archaic Persians were forced to go underground in order to maintain their culture, and they might need some coaxing before they are willing to reintegrate with the rest of the human species."

"That's two points, Prof." Lisa quickly realized her grammatical error. "Oops. Those *are* two points."

Prof smiled. "You are correct, my dear. I have more points to make, but I would rather wait for Marzavan to join us before I make them."

Sarah's language and decryption package was being put to good use. Only one day after the gunfight at the archaic Persian corral, and a large number of facts had been ascertained by each civilization about the other – although with some reservation concerning literal translation versus allegorical allusion.

The so-called archaic Persians referred to the south continental landmass as Parrallah. Less certain was the meaning of the name. It could be translated literally as "The Domain of Allah," or "The Land of God," or "Godland," or "Heaven" – depending upon which religious associations were used as background criteria. By incorporating Biblical references instead of those from the Koran, Parrallah could be translated loosely as "The Garden of Eden." A scientific connotation yielded "The Birthplace of Civilization."

Parrallah consisted of forty-seven cities with an aggregate population of approximately 100,000 people. The administrative capital of Parrallah was Bussorah. "Mecca by any other name," Lisa had quipped.

Other cities were specialized as pastoral, mechanical, or technological in purpose. Each city was officiated by elected officials who maintained offices in their own city and in the capital, much like congressional representatives of the USAC, except that Bussorah was a city in its own right with its own elected official, and its inhabitants performed duties other than governmental. There was no president.

Marzavan was the chief elected official of Cassorah, the city in which the Persian marines were defeated. Because of the Persian bias in the translation software, his title could be translated approximately as "sultan" or "vizier," or possibly in more modern terms as "caliph" or "emir."

Tod shuffled his feet uncomfortably. "For what it's worth, on Sinbad's sixth voyage, he floated down a great river that entered a cave at the base of a mountain. The mountain was covered with colored crystals. The underground river carried him to a vast plain and a grand city whose people spoke a language that was foreign to him. The city was in a valley that was surrounded by tall mountains. Near the city was the place where Adam was confined after his banishment from Paradise." Tod paused for effect. "The name of the city was Serendib."

Tod didn't state the obvious: that *Serendib* was the name of the captured Persian submarine.

Harker scowled. "Coincidental nonsense."

"It isn't nonsense," Lisa spouted vehemently. "It's oral history that's been warped over time by constant retelling and distortion in translation.

"It's a fairytale, like Humpty Dumpty."

"It is not." Lisa challenged Harker was a glare that would have turned Medusa to stone.

Harker scowled –

Prof interrupted before the argument escalated. "It has often been said that the early works of literature have some basis in fact. The *Bible* can be construed as a history of religious movements and catastrophic events. The gods of ancient civilizations may have referred to aliens who visited Earth in prehistoric times. These stories may sound quaint or preposterous by the standards of today, but who can say how much truth is to be found in the legends and myths of yesteryear, and how much falsehood and exaggeration?"

Prof shrugged. "It is impossible to know. Were there ever such creatures as elves, trolls, pixies, hobgoblins, and leprechauns? Probably not, despite the fact that people used to take their existence for granted. Mankind once believed in all kinds of things that nowadays are looked upon as juvenile. Perhaps these beliefs started as fantastic stories to capture the imagination of innocent children, and became tradition in the manner of Santa Claus. Perhaps these traditions assumed some sort of quasi-reality because naive adults found greater satisfaction in them than they found in the true reality that they were forced to face.

"One thing I *do* know: The persistence of beliefs derives from the comfort they bring. Cro-Magnon's cultural immaturity persists today on a subconscious level – what we might call racial memory. The fables of the past are firmly ingrained in modern-day society, whether or not they depict actual events. Were the existence and fate of Parrallah, and other such disasters, recounted truthfully in Plato's *Republic*, in the *Bible*, and in *Arabian Nights*? Perhaps. And perhaps, as Denny suggested, the stories are nothing more than puzzling coincidences, like the predictions of Nostradamus."

No one had an answer to Prof's philosophical conundrum. Tod hoped for elucidation when Marzavan made his appearance, which occurred several minutes later. Amina and Assad followed him into the lounge, along with three patriarchs and three matriarchs. Everyone sat on a blue foam cushion.

The patriarch held two transcribers in his hands: Tod's and Harker's. He handed Tod's transcriber to Prof, and kept the other one for himself. He activated the audio circuit, placed the transcriber to his lips, and talked into the microphone. He spoke in his own language, but the words that the transcriber broadcast were in English.

Marzavan held out his left hand and wiggled his fingers. "Welcome, strangers from the convex globe."

There was a collective gasp of astonishment from the Benthocity foursome. Even Harker was nonplussed.

"Do you comprehend my words?" Marzavan indicated for Prof to speak into the transcriber.

Prof fumbled with the device as he activated the audio circuit. "Yes – yes, we understand your words."

Marzavan reclined on a foam cushion. Amina, Assad, and the others did the same. Formality was not practiced in Parrallah.

"Have your people had sufficient refreshment?"

"Yes – yes we have."

"That is good." Marzavan ran his fingers over crystals that were inlaid in the table that was positioned nearest to him. An inlaid spigot slid upward on a silvery shaft, as if it were a periscope. He produced a red plastic container from a tray under the tabletop, filled it with blue liquid, and took a deep draft. "Now we are able to communicate."

Although Marzavan articulated his speech clearly in a smooth and flowing manner, the words that the transcriber broadcast were somewhat stilted, each one enunciated individually and with a perceptible gap between each word.

"Our technicians transported language learners for your computationer to absorb and rehash. This has made it performable for our computationers to communicate together for mutual intellection. The system is not perfection but it should qualify for now. Do you comprehend my words?"

"I comprehend your words."

"That is good." Marzavan paused to take another drink. "The people of Parrallah credit your aid. The bad hunters from the convex globe destroyed the city of Kannallah with a jumbo explosive device – "

This statement elicited loud murmurs from the Benthocity foursome.

For once Harker did not scowl. "That explains the missing nuke. They detonated the warhead as their first act of terrorism." His words were not detected by the transcriber.

"Many of our citizens perished. The cavity is uninhabitable due to inflammable infection."

Harker whispered, "Radioactive contamination."

Prof spoke into the microphone. "I am very sorry for such an act of aggression. We of the surface world have also suffered at the hands of the same enemy." After a slight pause, "Please do not, uh . . . " He moved the transcriber out of range of his voice, and covered the microphone with his hand. To his companions, "I want to say something like 'do not tar us with the same brush,' or 'do not put us in the same basket with the Persian marines.' But those idioms will not translate properly."

Lisa suggested, "How about 'don't put us in the same category with them.' That's fairly generic."

"Thank you." Into the microphone, "We come from a land of peace. Do not categorize us with the bad hunters from the surface world."

"I comprehend your words. We have observed sufficient of your land from your computationer to have knowledge that you are peaceful, and fight only in self-defense." After a pause, "And in the defense of others."

Despite the coolness of the air-conditioned lounge, Prof had to wipe sweat off his brow with his sleeve. "We can help – we are willing to provide additional military support for your defense."

"That is good. Perchance we are able to conduct barter. Because the bad hunters from the convex globe know our position, they may return with more jumbo explosive devices. Even now our technicians are converting diggers to transportable weapons like the transportable weapon that Assad converted."

"Diggers?" The transcriber could not translate vocal inflection. "I mean, what is a digger?"

"A digger is a tool that is managed to create cavities through rock. That is how we expand our territory and collect minerals for manufacture. After the bad hunters from the convex globe invaded our land, Assad converted a digger to a transportable weapon to attack the through-the-water machine that brought the bad hunters from the convex globe to our midst."

Harker whispered, "He means a laser gun or disruptor beam. That's how they hollowed out these immense caverns. Boy would I like to get my hands on one of those converted guns."

Prof held up his hand in Harker's direction. "Let us not bring up the subject of weapons just yet. I would rather – "

Because he forgot to move the transcriber away from his lips, Marzavan overheard Prof's part of the aside.

"We are able to conduct barter for transportable weapons that are converted from diggers. We have many diggers in our storage facilities. We dig mines ceaselessly for raw materials for our made-by-hand products. We have many electricity charge holders – "

Tod whispered, "Batteries or capacitors."

" – that can be motivated by energy from the sun."

"How can they have solar power underground?" Lisa said a bit too loud. The microphone picked up Lisa's voice and broadcast it.

Marzavan said, "Energy from the sun is the sole fountain of energy for our land. We have managed energy from the sun since before the Big Water."

Prof cleared his throat. "We – we of the outer world have legends, myths, that have been handed down from generation to generation, by word of mouth. These legends tell of an ancient but advanced civilization whose people worshipped the sun. These people lived on an island, or perhaps on a continent, that was separated from the rest of the world. They built their capitol city in the form of concentric circles. They were great crafters and mariners. They traded with people all over the globe – until one day the land which these sun-worshippers occupied was sunk beneath the sea because, it was said, the inhabitants fell upon evil ways. It was said that they caused their own demise, that they destroyed themselves by misuse of their scientific knowledge, that they had only themselves to blame for their destruction."

"I comprehend your words." Marzavan manipulated crystals on the tabletop next to him. All four wallscreens switched on, so that no one had to move or change position in order to see the kinetic recording that was displayed on each. "It may be true that the not-civilized people of the convex globe blamed the people of Parrallah for inviting the Big Water. They had not the knowledge to observe beyond the atmosphere."

Tod recognized the replay of images of destruction that Amina had shown to him and Lisa. This time the kinetic recording was projected flat on the wallscreens, without the perceptual transference that he had found so enlightening – and disturbing.

Marzavan narrated. "Observe the planet Jupiter.

The planet Jupiter is so big that it is almost a star. Despite its big bigness, it rotates fast upon its axis – more than twice as fast as the planet Earth rotates upon its axis. The big bigness and the speed of rotation make the planet Jupiter unstable. Its gravitational influences are unbalanced by the sun and by the other big planets that are positioned farther from the sun than the planet Jupiter. At big displacements in time, the planet Jupiter balances itself again by exhaling concentrations of mass. In this manner were exhaled the satellites of the planet Jupiter and the planets that occupy the space between the planet Jupiter and the sun, these small planets inhaled by the gravitational attraction of the sun.

"Observe this bulge on the convex globe of the planet Jupiter. In one half the displacement in time of the spin of the planet Jupiter upon its axis, a concentration of mass was exhaled. The point of exhalation is marked by disturbance in the atmosphere of the planet Jupiter." Marzavan indicated the feature that modern astronomers referred to as the Great Red Spot. "We call this disturbance the Birth Scar."

Every one of the Benthocity foursome reacted: by gasping, by scowling, by enlarging the eyes. No one interrupted Marzavan's explanation by speaking.

"The concentration of mass was inhaled by the gravitational attraction of the sun. The concentration of mass passed close to the planet Earth. The gravitational attraction between the concentration of mass and the planet Earth caused many changes in the planet Earth. The convex globe was moved briskly in relation to the dense metal core, shifting the position of the lands with respect to the axis of rotation.

"The shift of the position of the lands caused the Big Water. The oceans washed over the lands on many shores. The lands were cracked. Liquid rock flowed out of the cracks. The atmosphere of the concentration of mass blended with the atmosphere of the planet Earth. The wild flow of electrons caused badness in the high atmosphere of the planet Earth. Chemicals rained upon the lands. The rays of the sun were blotted from sight.

"Whereas Parrallah had previously enjoyed a climate of warmth near the equator, its new position placed it above the pole of rotation. The blotting of the rays of the sun reduced the fountain of energy that could be gathered from the sun. Cold plagued Parrallah. The planet Earth made many revolutions around the sun before the rays of the sun were no longer blotted and the fountain of energy could again be gathered.

"The people of Parrallah observed that the concentration of mass moved to a position that was closer to the sun than the planet Earth.

"Some people of Parrallah chose to escape the cold by going to live with the non-civilized people with whom we conducted barter. These people of Parrallah carried the Parrallah culture with them. Other people of Parrallah chose to struggle with the cold, to adapt to the new conditions. They dug into the rock to create cavities in which to avoid the snow that was concealing the cities, and to build new settlements for their children.

"The crystals that gathered the fountain of energy from the sun were grown in big quantities. The energy was focused for many purposes: to provide energy for the diggers, to illuminate the cavities, to energize machinery, to stimulate the growth of vegetation. Other crystals were grown to create a ceiling and ceiling supports over the original port city of Attallah, which you have explored, although you entered from a cavity in the rock instead of from the frozen sea. Because frozen water is crystal, the people of Parrallah were able to gather the fountain of energy from the sun by absorbing the energy that was reflected through crystals of ice. Thus the people of Parrallah have maintained their survival for many thousands of revolutions of the planet Earth.

"So you see, strangers from the convex globe, the people of Parrallah were innocent of any wrong-doing. The people of Parrallah were not to blame for the exhalation of the concentration of mass that became the planet Venus."

Chapter 30

"Ice crystals for solar panels," Lisa breathed. "Amazing."

"And I'll bet that's only the tip of their technological iceberg," Tod responded.

"Very funny."

Tod ruminated. "They seem to be experts in crystallography. That explains a lot about what we've seen."

Prof added, "Ice is only one of hundreds of common crystals that are found in everyday use, although ice is applied more for cooling drinks than for transmitting electromagnetic waves. The medium is too fragile because it melts at room temperature. But in the Antarctic – " He paused at the implication. "In grade school I made radio receivers by growing crystals of galena that could be tuned to specific frequencies – "

"I built a laser at the age of twelve," Harker interrupted. "Used it to fry ants."

"I am not surprised."

Harker scowled. "Their expertise in crystal studies must account for their invention of the disruptor beam. My guess now is that it's a maser instead of a laser – microwave amplification by the stimulated emission of radiation. They've got some kind of crystal that stimulates and amplifies coherent microwaves without the production of heat as a byproduct. That's why there weren't any singe marks on the Yupers and their sub."

Harker might have elaborated but the short respite was ended when Marzavan stopped conferring with his compatriots, and signaled for the colloquy to recommence by wiggling his fingers in Prof's direction.

"The people of Parrallah possess another hazard that is aggravating for many revolutions of the planet Earth around the sun. In the spirit of conducting barter, perhaps the people of the convex globe can suggest a solution to this hazard."

Prof spoke with solemnity. "We will do all we can to

help our brothers in distress."

"I comprehend your words. You have seen the vapor of water in the atmosphere of Attallah and in the atmosphere of the inhabited cities. Comprehend that this vapor of water is a recent action. For thousands of revolutions of the planet Earth around the sun, since the time of the Big Water, the atmosphere in the cavities of Parrallah was without vapor of water. Only in recent revolutions of the planet Earth around the sun has the vapor of water appeared. The reason for the vapor of water is the rising of the ocean that surrounds Parrallah. The rising of the ocean has flowed big water through cavities in the solid rock and to engage liquid rock, which exists beneath Parrallah. The sea converts to vapor of water which seeps through small cavities into big cavities, and rises above the cities.

"The engagement of the ocean with liquid rock makes the liquid rock violent. The liquid rock explodes big and flows into cavities. Already three of the lowest cavities of Parrallah were forced to abandon. If the ocean continues to rise, if the liquid rock continues to explode big, the liquid rock will flow into many cavities of Parrallah. The people of Parrallah have been unable to cease the flow of liquid rock or vapor of water."

Tod gulped. "He's saying that the rise in sea level is causing eruptions by flooding volcanic vents, and turning water to steam."

"My interpretation, too." Using his sleeve, Prof wiped beads of perspiration off his forehead.

Lisa grinned. "Is becoming a diplomat like becoming an administrator? There are no courses to take, you just pick it up as you go along?"

Prof was not amused by her sardonic sense of humor. To Marzavan, "The people of the convex globe are experiencing similar hazards. It is said by many of our people that mankind's evil science and industry are the root of the afflictions that plague the environment of the convex globe." Prof rolled his eyes and held the transcriber away from his lips. "I'm so nervous that I'm beginning to talk like Marzavan."

For once Tod knew exactly what to say. "You're not talking like Marzavan. You're talking like his translation. Just talk naturally and let the translation software do its job."

"Yes, of course, my lad. You are correct." Prof wiped sweat off his brow. To Marzavan, "It has long been believed that manmade air pollution, deforestation, and over-industrialization have conspired to cause ozone depletion, global warming, the melting of the polar ice caps, and other harmful phenomena. The burning of fossil fuels and the emission of chlorofluorocarbon compounds – "

"Try not to use big words or technical terms without defining them."

"Yes, of course." To Marzavan, "It has been proven scientifically that man's interference with the global environment has had no effect on the natural processes that are at work in the planetary atmosphere. Even after the discharge of harmful gases was almost completely stopped, the world still suffered in the throes of a runaway Greenhouse effect and – "

Marzavan wiggled his fingers at the professor. "I do not comprehend all your words."

Prof took a moment to dry his glistening scalp. "The Greenhouse effect is responsible for the increase in temperature that is causing the polar ice caps to melt, and sea levels to rise. It is correlated with ultraviolet radiation, excess carbon dioxide, the reduction of tri-atomic oxygen, and other complex molecules and chemical factors that affect the atmosphere.

"Geological studies have proven conclusively that the Earth goes through cycles – has gone through cycles many times in the past – in which comparatively slight changes in atmospheric temperature have brought about periods of intense cold followed by periods of great heat. Temperature stabilization is a short-term phenomenon that may last for thousands of years, or that may last for millions of years. Fluctuations in sea level are caused by the state of water.

"During periods of intense cold, much of the terrestrial water is bound in the form of ice; sea level falls as a consequence. During periods of great heat, much of the water exists in the liquid state, and sea level rises. Earth was at the height of an Ice Age ten thousand years ago. Ever since then, the temperature has been rising, glaciers have been receding, polar ice caps have been melting, and sea level has been rising. This cyclical climatic change is an ongoing process, and continues irrespective of man's accidental tampering with the environment. I repeat, it has been established without a doubt that man's meddling is negligible.

"The culprit responsible for temperature variations is solar radiation. Not the amount of radiation that penetrates the Earth's atmosphere, but the amount of radiation that the sun emits. Uh, do you follow me so far?"

"I comprehend your words."

Prof dried his head and neck, and dabbed his scraggly beard. "The people of the surface world have found ways to counteract the adverse effect of increased solar radiation that is now affecting the Earth. While we cannot control the actions of the sun, we have discovered ways and means to create ozone, to absorb carbon dioxide, and to make other chemical changes in the atmosphere, all of which will help to stabilize, perhaps even to reverse, the increase in temperature.

"Most of the nations of the surface world are working together to build chemical factories that can accomplish this magnificent goal. We must cooperate if we expect mankind to survive. Already all our port cities are under water. New York – the largest city in the nation of which we are citizens – is submerged to a depth of many feet. The lower floors are flooded. The streets between buildings are waterways. Most of the city – and many others like it – has been evacuated. The few remaining inhabitants now refer to their home as New Venice.

"We have the technology to effect the salvation of the planet, but we are lacking in one regard: energy to operate the factories and manufacturing plants. Much of this energy exists under the land that is occupied by the bad hunters who detonated the nuclear bomb in your city. They control the flow of this energy. They are a selfish people. They want only to enrich themselves in the short term, regardless of the adverse affects that their stranglehold on energy production does in the long term. When their lands are flooded, they move their living quarters to higher ground and erect deep-water rigs to pump energy from more wells."

Prof paused to take some deep breaths.

Marzavan squinted his dark brown eyes. "Why do you look for energy in the sea and under the surface of the convex globe? Why do you not manage the energy from the sun?"

"The state of our technology in the collection of solar power and its conversion to electricity is unsatisfactory. That is why we constructed subaqueous cities and laboratories, in order to explore the seabed for alternative sources of energy.

Marzavan wiggled his fingers at Prof. He turned and held a lengthy conversation with his compatriots. Five minutes passed. Finally Marzavan turned back to the professor.

"The people of Parrallah believe that it is possible to provide aid to our brothers in distress while at the same time to provide aid to the people of Parrallah. There is no need to conduct barter." Marzavan took a long draft of blue liquid. "The people of Parrallah can make-by-hand the crystals that manage the fountain of energy from the sun, and can make-by-hand the electricity charge holders that store and transport the energy from the sun. The people of Parrallah can share knowledge with the good people of the convex globe, so that the good people of the convex globe can make-by-hand crystals to manage the fountain of energy from the sun, and can make-by-hand the electricity charge holders that store and transport the energy from the sun."

In the stunned silence that followed Marzavan's final remarks, Tod's voice sounded exceptionally loud. "Unless his words have been confused in translation, I think he just proposed a way to save the world."

Epilogue

Much finger wiggling and handshaking consummated the negotiations for alliance between the two civilizations.

The summit conference ended with Prof reading translations of the captured UPR communiques. It was learned that the UPR held great faith in the gold foil revelations. Already the UPR was planning a campaign to dispatch all the submarines at their disposal on a full-scale invasion of the Antarctic continent.

The transcribers worked hard to translate overlapping dialogue as thirteen people strived to talk at the same time. Everyone had something to say, and everyone wanted to hear every word that everyone else said. This impossible – or improbable – situation finally resolved itself when the "outside" lights dimmed in advance of darkness, or the night shift, depending upon point of view.

Quarters were assigned to Prof, Harker, Tod, and Lisa. The patriarchs and the pair of Benthocity elders departed with the promise to commence making plans for the salvation of the planet as soon as the ceiling lights started to brighten: either simulated dawn, or the start of a new shift.

Tod and Lisa were left with the transcribers.

Amina and Assad suggested that the Mallory's join them for an informal chat in the lounge. They settled comfortably into the blue foam cushions. Tod and Lisa sat close together so they could share a transcriber. Amina and Assad did the same so they could share the other transcriber. The two couples faced each other. Now that they were a mixed foursome, no one seemed to know quite how to open the conversation.

Tod admired the crystal optics that decorated the ceiling behind semitransparent shields. This led him to think about the vibratory state that must be necessary to generate microwave beams that could drill through rock and steel. His train of thought then pondered the presence of crossbows in a peaceful society. He asked for an explanation.

Amina said, "The people of Parrallah take relaxation from work by hunting in the city of Attallah. The city of Attallah is the ancient capitol of Parrallah. The city of Attallah was constructed in the jumbo caldera of an extinct volcano that bordered the ocean. The city of Attallah has been preserved the way the buildings stood before the Big Water. Plants and animals from distant lands on the convex globe were imported for food and sport. When the frozen water threatened to consume the city of Attallah, the people of Parrallah grew a roof of crystal over the city of Attallah, to protect it from the cold and from the frozen water. The people of Parrallah are skilled with the stick-shooter because they vie for ovation."

"Far out!" Lisa expostulated.

Amina and Assad exchanged looks of perplexity.

Amina said, "Distance is not a function. The skilled stick-shooter strives for accuracy of the heart."

"No, I didn't mean far out as in distance. It's just an expression of – of – " She turned to Tod. "Help me out, Hunk."

"You got yourself into it, Squirt."

Lisa was flustered. "Okay, uh, 'far out' is just an expression, an idiom. The phrase has a meaning of its own, one that is independent of the meaning of the individual words, or the way those words are connected."

Amina and Assad still looked perplexed.

"I guess their language doesn't have idioms," Tod suggested. "Or puns."

"What fun is that?"

Tod shrugged. "Do you hunt the mammals in Attallah?"

"The people of Parrallah hunt the Irish Elk and musk ox for sport and flesh. The people of Parrallah chase the aurochs not to perish, but to leap over bodies from horn to back, and to ride until dismounted.

The riders earn ovation for time-span of ride. For other sport, the people of Parrallah herd the aurochs with sticks, and throw loops of rope around their necks."

Lisa grimaced. "Poking and lassoing cattle sounds dangerous."

"No worse than bullfighting or bull running, like they used to do in Spain," Tod remarked to Lisa. "Sounds like a public competition." To Amina, "I was wondering about the giant birds in Attallah. Birds like that don't exist in the surface world, but there are legends that a giant bird called a roc was once revered by, uh, an old-time culture. Is the giant roc the national emblem of Parrallah?"

"I comprehend your words," said Amina. "The giant birds that you call rocs are called snake-birds by the people of Parrallah. The long feathered neck resembles a snake. The snake-birds are not revered. The snake-birds consume vermin such as rats, which consume the eggs of not-jumbo birds that nest on the ground. The people of Parrallah keep the snake-birds in maintenance to reduce the population of vermin. The people of Parrallah sometimes hunt the snake-birds because they are savory to consume. When I met Tod and Lisa in the Tabernacle of the Sun, my expedition was to hunt snake-birds. The snake-birds bed down at the approach of darkness. I command a fondness for their flesh."

"I'll bet they taste like chicken," Lisa said dryly.

In aside, "And I'll bet we already ate some, in the sandwiches that Amina gave us from the food dispenser in the cafeteria grotto." Tod pointed to the disruptor device and battery pack that Assad still wore around his waist. "Do you hunt with that, too?"

Assad glanced at the device but did not speak.

"The beam-shooter is not long in existence." Tears appeared suddenly in Amina's eyes. She choked out her next words in a halting fashion. The transcriber broadcast English equivalents without inflection. "The parents of Assad and Amina were perished when the bad hunters from the convex globe destroyed the city of

Kannallah with the jumbo explosive device. Assad and Amina inhabited the city of Kannallah, but Assad and Amina were not in the city of Kannallah when the city of Kannallah was destroyed. Assad . . . "

"They're orphans like us," Lisa breathed to Tod. To Amina and Assad, "The bad hunters from the surface world killed our folks, too. That is, we're almost certain they did. Their submarine disappeared with all hands during a routine voyage." Lisa cleared her throat several times but managed not to cry. "In their final transmission they issued a warning about an enemy sub in the area. That was the last we ever heard of them." Two tiny tears rolled down her cheeks. "The bastards."

Assad was stoic. "When the bad hunters from the convex globe emerged from the water at the edge of the city of Kannallah, they perished many people of the city of Kannallah with pellet-shooters and not-jumbo explosive devices. After the bad hunters from the convex globe destroyed the city of Kannallah, the bad hunters from the convex globe explored the passageways that connected the city of Kannallah to other cities. They perished more people of Parrallah. The people of Parrallah protected homes and children with stick-shooters, but the pellet-shooters of the bad hunters from the convex globe reached farther.

"In big anguish and anger I converted a digger to a transportable beam-shooter. With the beam-shooter I perished some of the bad hunters from the convex globe. I drove away the through-the-water machine of the bad hunters from the convex globe. I followed the bad hunters from the convex globe from city to city. Always I must shoot from cover and from farther reach. I could not always get to reach. I followed the bad hunters from the convex globe to the city of Cassorah. When Amina called Marzavan, I aided Amina.

"You did a good job, Assad," Tod said. "If you hadn't saved Denny Harker's life, we might still be fighting a losing battle with the bad hunters from the surface world."

Assad wiggled his fingers.

Tod wished that the transcriber could translate the finger wiggles. The gesture seemed to have multiple meanings.

By this time Amina's tears had dried. "Must you return to the good people from the convex globe? I will miss your presence."

Tod raised his eyebrows at Lisa. To Amina, "Well, I'd like to hang around for a while, if you don't mind. I like you – I mean, I like the people of Parrallah. I'd like to learn more about you. I mean, about the people of Parrallah, and, uh . . . "

"Why, Tod Mallory, I do believe you've got a crush on Amina."

Tod blushed so hard that a wave of intense heat coursed along his body, as if he had slipped into a bath of molten lead. Instantly he was drenched with sweat that his syntactic foam suit could not wick away.

"Don't feel bad. I'm kind of smitten over Assad."

Now it was the turn of the Parrallah pair to exchange looks. Both were more perplexed than ever. An embarrassing silence ensued.

Assad spoke next. "I also have great feeling for my companion in battle, but . . . "

After a while, Amina picked up the thread, "Do the people of the convex globe quit partners for change?"

"What – what do you mean by partners?" Lisa asked.

"Two people of opposite sex who try to make babies. Husband and wife."

Lisa gasped. "Why, Tod and I never – uh, I mean, we don't – uh, try to make babies. We're not married."

The expression on Tod's face was inscrutable. "Lisa's not my wife. She's my sister."

Eventually, comprehension dawned on Amina and Assad.

"That is good," Amina declared with a smile. "That is very good. Assad is my brother."

Lisa grinned wickedly at Tod. "Two matches made in heaven. I'll bet we can start a heck of a fire now."

Tod knew what to say but he was afraid to say it!